Widow's Walk

Widow's Walk

The Martha's Vineyard Murders

Raemi A. Ray

TULE

Widow's Walk
Copyright© 2024 Raemi A. Ray
Tule Publishing First Printing November 2024

The Tule Publishing, Inc.

ALL RIGHTS RESERVED

First Publication by Tule Publishing 2024

Cover design by eBookLaunch.com

No part of this book may be used or reproduced in any manner whatsoever without written permission except in the case of brief quotations embodied in critical articles and reviews.

This is a work of fiction. Names, characters, places, and incidents are products of the author's imagination or are used fictitiously. Any resemblance to actual events, locales, organizations, or persons, living or dead, is entirely coincidental.

AI was not used to create any part of this book and no part of this book may be used for generative training.

ISBN: 978-1-964703-61-9

Dedication

*For Mrs. Amanda, who hosts two murder-free Thanksgivings each year.
Miss & love you a million.*

Chapter One

THE HEAVY SHOPPING bags hit the foyer floor. The contents tumbled out. Kyra Gibson looked down at the mess she'd made with dismay. She let out a weary sigh and rubbed her forehead with the back of her mittened hand. The tiny grocery store serving her side of Martha's Vineyard had been utter bedlam. She should have known better than to go shopping the day before Thanksgiving. She'd been in life-or-death situations before, recently, but she'd experienced nothing as harrowing as fighting off other holiday procrastinators hunting down last-minute ingredients.

Kyra slipped her mitten off and rubbed the back of her hand, where a pale bruise was already forming. She'd nearly lost it, her hand and her patience, when a woman ripped the last tube of store brand crescent rolls from her grip. Her shoulder throbbed, and she rolled it back, wincing when the pain escalated to a sharp twinge. It wasn't yet a chronic condition, but it certainly was committed to becoming one.

A bang, followed by a muffled curse, came from the kitchen. Her aunt's voice was just discernable over the television blaring from the living room. Kyra grinned and bit down on her lip to keep from laughing.

"I'm back," she called loud enough to be heard over the

unusual racket.

"Kay!" Her uncle's head popped up from the couch.

His dark brown hair flopped over the rims of his tortoiseshell frames, making him look more disheveled and brainier than usual. He readjusted his glasses and squinted at her. His bright blue eyes crinkled at the corners when he grinned.

He pointed to the bags at her feet. "How was it?"

"Cam, can you call Kyra and tell her we need olives? Those lovely Spanish green ones like we get at Sainsbury's." Kyra's Aunt Ali walked into the living room, her eyes on her phone.

"I'm not going back out there."

Ali looked up, ready to protest.

"No, Ali." Kyra held up her hands. "It's straight madness out there. The Americans have all gone insane." Kyra wrestled out of her light blue parka and hung it in the coat closet.

It wasn't the right shade for her warm-toned complexion. The faux fur trim was atrocious, and it was puffy in all the wrong places. She felt like her arms stuck straight out when she wore it, but it had been on clearance, and more importantly, it was warm. So warm. Too impatient to wait on the island's sluggish postal service, Kyra had gone to the quirky general-slash-discount trading post to get it, along with fleece-lined boots, and other cold weather accessories that made her look ridiculous and left her hair staticky, but she wouldn't dare trade in her winter gear for anything more fashionable.

She'd unofficially, and presumably temporarily, moved

to Martha's Vineyard from London in July. She hadn't planned on staying so long, but August turned into September, and then October, and suddenly it was *cold*. Frigid. Winter in New England didn't come on gradually, easing the residents in. Oh no. It swept in without warning, like some spiteful arctic spirit. The heat and humidity of summer had been replaced with bone-chilling winds and rains that lashed horizontally. It felt like she'd gone from wearing shorts and T-shirts to anoraks and boots almost overnight.

Ali inventoried the groceries on the floor, her hands on her hips. Kyra's harried expression must have convinced her she wasn't going back out, because when Ali looked back up at her niece, she pressed her lips together, thinking, and said, "It's fine. We'll do with what we have. It'll be brilliant." She stuffed the escaped items back in the bags and hoisted up three. A soft grunt escaped her lips, and Kyra raised her eyebrow at her aunt. Grinning, Ali turned toward the kitchen.

"What time does everyone get here?" Kyra asked, heaving the remaining bags to her shoulder. She bit back a grimace when the pinching sensation intensified.

"Less than an hour. Cam," Ali called back over her shoulder. "Can you get Iggy up from his nap? And you'll both need to change."

Cam stood and stretched. He ran his hands down his rumpled button down.

"*Aye, m'eudail.*" He turned back to Kyra. "What does one wear to American Thanksgiving?"

Kyra was stumped. "I've no idea." Images of holiday movies from her childhood cycled through her mind. Men in matching flannel shirts, women in full skirts and aprons. Lots of trapper hats.

"Thanksgiving is tomorrow," Ali said. Then she stopped walking and turned around. "I think they call this a Friendsgiving? Fuck if I know." She retreated, back stepping into the kitchen, and raised her unburdened shoulder in a shrug.

"What does one wear to American Friendsgiving then?" Cam called after her.

"I've set your clothes out on the bed. And for Iggy, too."

Cam's eyebrows hitched up, as his expression morphed from indulgent to alarmed.

Kyra's eyes went wide, and she met her uncle's gaze. "She wouldn't." But Ali totally would. Her aunt lived for theme events. She loved any reason to get dressed up. The matchier the better. Cam wasn't as enthusiastic as his wife, over theme dressing. Kyra didn't bother hiding her amusement with her uncle's obvious dismay. Her grin turned sadistic, and she raised her shoulders in an exaggerated shrug. "Better you than me," she whispered. Kyra felt his glare burning into her back as she followed her aunt into the kitchen.

Ali dumped the bags on the wide granite island and clasped her hands together. She hopped from one foot to the other and let out her high-pitched Ali squeal. It sounded a bit like a small creature's death cry.

Kyra feigned a pained wince. "I know. You're excited. I know." She laughed.

Ali grabbed Kyra's forearm. "I remember Mum and Dad doing Thanksgiving when we were children. Mum cooked up this big dinner. We hosted kids from Dad's classes at the college who were unable to go home. And it was always horrible."

"I think that might just be the food," Kyra said, scanning the counters strewn with food-like things she couldn't identify. A lot of it looked pureed. *Did the pilgrims suffer from dental issues?* "What is all this?" She eyed something that was an unnatural orange color.

"Grace and Charlie gave me a list of the traditional Thanksgiving dishes." Kyra poked at it, and Ali swatted her hand away with a dishtowel. "I swear, Kay, the food is amazing. Well, it is, if it's done properly." Ali's mouth dipped in an uncertain frown as she assessed the orange dish.

Kyra schooled her features so she wouldn't make a face. She doubted that the gloppy messes before her were done properly. But she wouldn't know. Kyra couldn't remember if she'd ever had a traditional Thanksgiving dinner. When she was a little girl, she and her mother would fly to meet her father in some far-off place, and then after her mother died, she was sent to live with Ali, her mother's much younger sister, in London.

"You're going to love it. I promise. We've got it all. The stuffing, the potatoes, sweet potatoes," Ali said, pointing to each dish of foodstuff. "And Gully's bringing pie. You know, America could solve all its geo-political issues if it started with pie." Ali went to the stove and fiddled with a pot threatening to bubble over.

"Ali, again, I'm so sorry that our plans were waylaid, and we're not doing a proper Thanksgiving tomorrow, like you wanted."

Kyra's aunt and uncle had flown in with their infant son the weekend before to spend the holiday with Kyra on the island. Originally, they had planned to spend tonight at the *Wraith & Bone*, Kyra's favorite local pub, and host Thanksgiving dinner for Kyra's island friends tomorrow, but they'd had to change their plans when Kyra received the gala invitation.

Loriann Oma, the chairwoman and majority shareholder of one of England's premier media companies, Omega Media, and Kyra's biggest client, was coming to Martha's Vineyard. For the past four months, Kyra had been entrenched in an M&A deal between Omega, and a US-based company, Global Media, and they were finally winding down the negotiations and preparing the documents for signatures. There were only a few tiny details left, but everyone, including her managing partner and boss Assaf Maloof, was optimistic the papers would be signed any day now.

And in true Loriann fashion, she wanted to memorialize the momentous event. She'd reserved an estate on Chappaquiddick, the smaller companion island to Martha's Vineyard, for the week to iron out the last wrinkles, and begin the *integration process* with a *festive autumnal gala*. From what Assaf had told Kyra, Loriann had invited at least a hundred people. People eager to give up their holiday evening with their families to wine and dine with other self-important suits.

Frankly, it sounded terrible, but when Kyra had tried to decline, explaining she was hosting dinner for her own family who'd traveled all the way from England, Loriann simply invited them, too.

"We're all going to be one big family, Kyra!" she'd exclaimed, or rather, her assistant Aysha had, but with much less enthusiasm.

"Can I, *we* get out of this?" Kyra had asked, first to her boss, who'd snorted, "Don't be daft, Gibs." Then to Aysha who had said, with much more empathy, "Afraid not, Kyra. Even Asher couldn't talk her out of it."

And it was a done deal.

If Asher Owen, Loriann's righthand, and the CEO of Omega, had been unable to dissuade her that a party or his presence was necessary, there was no way Kyra would, and so she'd reluctantly agreed that she and her family would attend.

When she'd told Ali and Cam the bad news on their next video call, Ali's eyes had gone wide as dinner plates.

"Verinder House!" Ali's voice reached an epic pitch. Even Cam flinched. "It's legendary, Kyra! It's like the Breakers or the Elms. But it was abandoned decades ago. Left to rot. I'd heard someone bought it and it was only recently renovated and turned into an event space. I would die to see it."

"But what about Thanksgiving dinner?" Kyra had wheedled, choosing the lesser of the two available evils.

"We'll just do it Wednesday. It'll be perfect." And at her aunt's wholesome grin, the one that lit up her entire face, and made her dark blue eyes, ones she and Kyra shared, sparkle, Kyra had folded.

Ali had taken Kyra in when she was barely more than a girl herself, cared for and loved her when Kyra had no one else. If this would make her aunt happy, Kyra could bite her tongue and endure a few hours of inane conversation and fake smiles over champagne and canapes.

Ali stopped rifling through one of the kitchen drawers and turned around. "Don't be ridiculous, Kay. Wednesday, Thursday, Friendsgiving, Thanksgiving. What difference does it make? The day is about us being together." Ali put her arm around Kyra's shoulders and gave her an enthusiastic squeeze. Kyra bit back a wince. "And also, it's about the food. Lots and lots of food. And drinks. Lots of those, too. I think we've got those things covered, don't you?"

"I suppose we do," Kyra said, trying not to sound glum. She cuffed back the sleeves of her sweater. "What else needs to be done?"

She looked around her kitchen. It was in a state of barely contained chaos, and she felt a flutter of apprehension. Kyra had never hosted or co-hosted a holiday party or even a dinner party before. She couldn't in good conscience call her meager food preparation skills *cooking*. She could toast things with varying degrees of unburnt success. That was about it. But Ali had insisted, and she'd promised she'd take care of everything.

Taking care of everything, it turned out, meant Kyra was dragged grocery shopping, table linens shopping, clothes shopping, more grocery shopping, and then sent out on last-minute errands to gather forgotten items. And she'd do it a thousand times over. Perhaps not the grocery shopping on the Wednesday before Thanksgiving. That was a onetime misjudgment.

"Give us a hand?" Ali asked, nodding to the backdoor.

Kyra followed her aunt out onto the patio. She froze.

"Ali," she gasped.

The patio table was covered in more trays of food, all prepared and ready to be cooked off. Her aunt had made herbed fingerling potatoes, carrots with the green tops, a colander full of fresh green beans sat in a bowl, ready to be sautéed with butter and thyme. She must have been cooking for hours.

"You did all this?"

"Are you kidding?" Ali scoffed, but her eyes shone with pride and love.

She pushed a platinum tendril behind her ear. She'd grown her hair out over the last several months and had taken to wearing it in Veronica Lake style waves. On anyone else, it would look like she was trying too hard. On Ali, it looked effortless. And beautiful.

"Impressed?"

"Very." Kyra bit her cheek hard, a little overwhelmed. "Thank you."

Ali bumped her hip against hers. "Help me bring these in."

Kyra set a large bowl on the counter and returned outside to retrieve more dishes. Her aunt glided in; platters balanced across her arms like a Cirque du Soleil performer. Kyra raised an eyebrow, and Ali grinned.

"Nandos."

Kyra stuck her tongue out. She knew for a fact that Ali's teen waitressing career had lasted for all of twenty-five minutes. The woman just had excellent balance.

"What else?" Kyra asked.

"That was it." Ali wiped her hands on her apron.

The ovens were on, heating to temperature. Kyra peered

inside. They were empty.

"Shouldn't there be a turkey in there? Doesn't it take a long time to cook?" She pointed to the stack of double ovens that she'd not once used in the past four months.

"Chase is bringing it. He said we're deep frying it? Apparently, it only takes an hour?"

"Deep fry a turkey? A whole one?"

Ali's mouth twitched in an *Americans. Who knows?* Look. "Cam is thrilled. He's been researching how to do it all morning." She was opening and closing drawers, looking for something, and pulled out a roll of aluminum foil. "They'll be here soon. You should get dressed."

Kyra gave her aunt a look, and it was returned with one of feigned innocence. "I'm not theme dressing, Ali."

"No, of course not. You'd never. You have no sense of fun." Kyra turned to leave, but Ali stopped her. "But, Kay, you could wear the Princess Di outfit." At Kyra's confused expression, Ali grinned, and said, "You know, with the boots."

Kyra huffed an agreeable laugh. That she could do.

Chapter Two

KYRA STEPPED BACK from the full-length mirror she'd had installed in her walk-in closet. She took in her outfit, the one her aunt suggested she wear. Tailored, blue oxford, her favorite jeans, and caramel-colored suede boots that inched just past her knees. She'd bought the boots in a boutique in Edgartown on her visit last spring. Kyra frowned. Something was missing. She grabbed the cream Aran-style cashmere sweater from the shelf and pulled it on over her head. She fixed her collar and unclipped her hair so it fell down her back. With her dark hair and olive complexion, one would need to be blind to compare Kyra to Princess Diana, but even so, she thought she looked nice.

Her phone buzzed from the bedside table, and she stumbled over her discarded clothes, rushing to answer it.

"Hello?" The call clicked through, just before it was sent to voicemail.

"Hey," Tarek Collins's deep, melodic voice greeted her.

She heard his smile and couldn't help her own. "Where are you?"

"Woods Hole. The wind has kicked up and they're canceling ferries. I think this one is going, but it's delayed." Kyra moved closer to the wall of windows that overlooked her backyard and Crackatuxet Cove. It was overcast, and the tall grass surrounding the cove snapped an awkward dance in the breeze.

"Is there a storm?"

"No, I don't think so. It's just windy. Probably remnants from a hurricane or nor'easter that's blown out into the Atlantic." Kyra heard rustling on the line, then Tarek came back. "We're being allowed to board. I'll see you in about an hour."

Before she could respond, he hung up.

Kyra went into the bathroom. She took a little extra care on her makeup, adding a winged liner that made her made her eyes appear bigger. She was being silly, but she was a little nervous.

They hadn't seen each other in nearly six weeks. Tarek had been consulting on a case in St. Louis. It was the longest they'd been apart since he'd kind of unofficially moved in during the summer.

It still surprised her sometimes, probably because it'd happened so gradually. After rescuing her and Chase from the sea caves, Tarek had driven her home... And stayed. She'd hardly noticed when his clothes took up space in the closet and he returned to his friend Gully's house or his apartment in Worcester less and less frequently.

One day, it'd dawned on her that they were living together. Whatever it was between them had grown into something more, and she was happy sharing her days, her nights, her life with him.

And then he'd had to leave.

Shortly after the incident with the *Keres*, he'd accepted a position as a profiler with a private consulting firm specializing in complex investigatory support. He would be called away with little notice, sometimes for days, often for a week or more, to support local and national law enforcement teams, and consult on mostly violent crimes.

When he was on an assignment, he could be distant, shielding her from whatever terrible things he was investigating. All she ever knew about his cases was what was reported in the news, and often that was horrific. But once the investigation closed, he'd return and slip back into their routine as if he'd never left.

He was assigned his most recent case in October. He'd flown out to St. Louis. It was supposed to have been a short stint, a week at most, and he'd have returned long before Cam and Ali's visit. But a lucky break that then turned into a lengthy evidentiary review had kept him onsite much longer.

"We're here!" a voice boomed from downstairs.

Kyra grinned. *Chase.* She swiped on some lip gloss and hurried downstairs. She was still two steps from the bottom when she was yanked into the air and wrapped in a warm hug.

"Down," she squeaked.

Chase set her on the floor and stepped back, his hands still on her arms. His blue-green eyes shone with mischievous merriment.

"We're here," he said, softer this time.

"I can see that." Another man stepped out from behind Chase. He was a few inches shorter, a few years older, and nearly as handsome. "Hey, Gerry, how are you?"

"Couldn't be better." Gerry stooped down to press his

perfectly groomed, stubbled cheek to hers. "Happy Thanksgiving."

"Are we saying that? It's not actually Thanksgiving." Chase frowned.

"What would you have us say?" Gerry asked, his dark eyes sparkled. Chase's frown deepened.

"Did you bring the frying mechanism?" Cam appeared from the kitchen.

Kyra's jaw dropped open, and she gaped at her uncle. "What are you wearing?"

He'd changed into jeans and a plaid flannel shirt. He was wearing an apron with a cartoon turkey brandishing a baster like a weapon while presenting a platter of a cooked turkey, complete with paper frills.

"Isn't it amazing?" Ali appeared from behind him in matching flannel and apron. Her smile was a thousand watts.

Kyra had other adjectives in mind. *Absurd, appalling, cannibalistic.*

"I found these at one of those shops on Circuit Avenue. They even had a baby size for Iggy." She turned her son on her hip.

Kyra's eyes widened in horror at her little cousin, dressed to match his parents. Sans apron. Thank god.

"What have you done, Ali? Isn't this when he creates core memories? He'll remember you torturing him like this." Iggy looked like a tiny, pudgy lumberjack. It didn't seem to bother him. He made a sloppy noise and tried to stick his fist into his mouth.

"*Pfft.*" Ali waved her hand. "Core memories, shmore memories. He looks adorable."

Cam grinned. "I like it. Reminds me of home." He ran his hand along the green and blue plaid. His forehead creased. "It's the wrong colors, though."

"Where do you want us to set it up?" Gerry asked and threw a warning look at Chase, who was slowly unbuttoning his navy-blue coat, to reveal … a red plaid flannel shirt.

Kyra blinked. *Seriously?* "You, too? You hate theme parties."

"Yeah, but Ali asked, and I look good. Red's my color." Chase looked down at his shirt, and grinned, much too pleased with himself.

Gerry, at least, was dressed like a normal person, his shirt a single, solid color.

"No embroidered turkeys?" she asked him, referencing the festive clothes he and his sister wore during the summer months.

"No, not this time." He chuckled and shook his head. "Maybe I'll find some for next year. Get us all matching ones."

"Absolutely not," Kyra protested at the same time Ali exclaimed, "Yes!" And everyone laughed.

"I think we're supposed to be some meters from the house," Cam interrupted, all business. He was staring out the large glass windows that made up the back wall of the house. "Should we set up in the back courtyard?"

"Sounds good. It's in my trunk. We can bring it around back. Ger?"

"Coming." Gerry handed Kyra a bottle of wine, and he and Cam followed Chase back outside.

Ali took the bottle from Kyra's hands. "Wine?"

"Desperately." Kyra followed her aunt back into the kitchen.

Ali put Iggy in one of those moveable baby-containment contraptions along with a few noise-making toys. Cronkite, Kyra's long-haired white cat, slunk into the kitchen and leaped into Iggy's playpen. The little boy made a high-pitched baby giggle while Cronk turned a few times before plopping over, his feather duster tail flicking in lazy swipes.

Cronk had claimed the tiny human as his own. He'd been suspiciously absent from his regular place in Kyra's bed since the Babcock family's arrival. The little beast also took a sadistic pleasure in rubbing against her uncle, setting off his allergies. She narrowed her eyes at her house demon. Cronk just blinked his emerald-green ones at her and yawned.

Ali placed a glass in front of Kyra. "Cheers." She raised hers in salute and took a sip. "You look lovely, by the way." Her aunt was always quick to compliment, but she did so sincerely.

"You told me to wear this, but thank you." Kyra glanced down and pulled at the bottom of her sweater. When she looked back up, her aunt was watching her with her trademark smug, know-it-all smile. "What?" Kyra didn't really want to know.

"When does he arrive?"

"Soon." Kyra groaned. "Please don't make a big thing of it."

Ali scoffed. "I raised you. Of course I'm making a big deal of it. My little baby girl is all grown up and has a live-in *boyfriend*." Ali stage whispered the last word.

Kyra made a face. Ali's smug smile turned into a manic

grin, all feral at the edges. Kyra attempted to glare at her aunt.

"Raised, really?" Ali had been barely twenty-two when Kyra was sent to live with her. She'd been twelve. "It's not like I've never brought anyone home before."

"True, but not anyone you actually cared about." Ali grinned. "You're blushing," she said with unsuppressed glee.

"Just try not to embarrass me. Please?" Kyra touched her warm cheeks and grimaced.

"No promises."

"Ding, dong!" a voice sang from the foyer. Grace Chambers shuffled into the kitchen carrying a heavy-looking Mander Lane Farm tote bag. "Happy Thanksgiving, dear!"

Her wife, Charlie, followed a step behind, struggling with her own grocery bag. Kyra reached out to help, but Charlie waved her off and set it on the counter with a *thunk*.

"I'm so sorry we're late. Julia took a catering job and only told us about it at the last minute. We've been entirely on our own since Sunday. She was supposed to put a basket together for you, but it must have slipped her mind."

Kyra glanced at Charlie, who rolled her eyes. Kyra highly doubted Julia had forgotten. In her experience, Julia's memory was a steel trap, all the better for holding grudges. The Chamberses' chef was not Kyra's biggest fan.

"I tried to put something together, although I suspect it's lacking. Char picked up bread from Café Joy this morning, and we brought wine." Grace placed the bottles on the counter, her sculpted eyebrows curved in apology. "I know it's not the same."

"Please. Don't apologize. You needn't have brought anything. We have more than enough," Kyra said, smiling. "But thank you."

Julia's homemade bread and butter was some sort of witchcraft, like the Turkish Delight in Narnia. It was life altering. Kyra had been talking it up to Ali for days. But she was only a smidge disappointed. They may not be getting Julia's sorcery, but the sourdough from Café Joy was Kyra's second favorite on the island. She pulled the thick loaf from the bag and inhaled the tangy, yeasty scent and sighed.

"I told you not to worry, Grace." Charlie rolled her eyes. "Happy Thanksgiving." She gave Kyra and Ali hugs. Charlie pushed her wild curls off her forehead and slumped against the island. "I hadn't realized how much we'd come to depend on Julia. It's been terrible this past week. On Monday, Grace had a meeting with the council. *I* had to cook dinner."

"It really wasn't that bad, love."

Charlie rolled her eyes again, and mouthed to Kyra, *It was worse*. She shook her shoulders in a mock shudder.

"You must be hungry then. Good thing Ali made enough food for..." Kyra waved to the kitchen surfaces covered in dishes. "The whole island, I'd say."

"Starved." Charlie sighed. "For days. It looks delicious, Ali. Kyra never said you cooked."

"It's new," Ali said proudly. "But I've never done Thanksgiving before."

Grace pulled off her Canada Goose parka and draped it across the back of one of the barstools. Kyra noted, with a touch of dismay, that Grace's coat did not make her look like a swollen marshmallow peep.

Ali pulled down more wine glasses and poured one for Grace. She raised the bottle to Charlie, who stood there, her big brown eyes on her wife. She bounced on her toes.

"Oh, just go, Char." Grace waved her hand.

Charlie grinned and pulled a six-pack of beer from the bag. She practically ran for the backyard.

"We walked up just as the boys were unloading the frier." Grace sighed and shook her head.

"At least she's not wearing flannel," Kyra muttered and shot a pointed look at her aunt.

"Oh no, dear, she is. And a utility vest."

A raucous cheer went up when Charlie joined the men on the patio. A propane frier setup sat in pieces around them. They were hunched over Cam's phone.

Grace smoothed her perfect blonde bob and took a seat at the island. She took a long sip of her wine. Kyra watched the older woman's shoulders drop as if she was finally letting herself relax. Kyra reached out and rubbed her shoulder, earning a grateful smile.

Grace patted her hand and turned to Ali. "Tell me, dear. How has your visit been?"

Kyra hadn't seen Grace or Charlie in nearly a week. They'd all spent an evening together when Ali and Cam had first arrived, but they'd been busy since, and Kyra had missed her friends.

Charlie's real estate management business was preparing her clients' properties for the off season, arranging for upkeep and repairs. Grace had been working on the Martha's Vineyard Community Council's activities, the national election, and the fallout from Senator Hawthorn's abrupt announcement that he would not be seeking reelection late last month. Chase still refused to discuss his father's legal troubles, but Kyra knew he wasn't taking any of it well.

"It's been fab." Ali came around to the other side of the island and clinked her glass against Kyra's. "I showed Kay our old house on Lake Tashmoo. We had breakfast at the airport, shopped in Edgartown. It's been a trip down memory lane." Ali dropped her head to Kyra's shoulder. "I'm glad we were able to share this with her."

Kyra and Ali had spent hours on Monday going through old family photo albums. They'd drank too much, and stayed up half the night laughing, then crying, then doing some strange combination of the two.

"It has been special," Kyra conceded, and wrapped her arm around her aunt's waist.

"Are you looking forward to visiting Verinder House tomorrow?" Grace asked.

"I am so excited. Even if Kay isn't." Ali shot Kyra a sympathetic smile and stepped away to add the finishing touches to the charcuterie and cheese platter she'd been assembling.

Kyra shrugged. She wasn't looking forward to the gala, the forced social niceties, or whatever spectacle Loriann had planned, but even she had to admit the house sounded incredible.

"Oh, that's right, Kyra said you design restorations for historic buildings."

"*Mmhhmm*, that's my specialty, but my architecture firm handles all sorts of projects. When Kay told me about the estate Omega had rented, I spent the flight researching it. It looks magnificent." Ali told Grace about the building's history, the famous architect who'd built it in the 1800s, and the recent renovations. "Are you familiar with it?"

"Char grew up on the island, so she probably knows more about it than I do, but I'm vaguely familiar. Julia worked there years ago, and I believe her husband was their groundskeeper for a while, until he started his construction business. Back then, it was still a private residence."

"Is that where she learned to cook?" Kyra asked.

"Oh, no, dear. And don't let her hear you say so. Julia was already a very accomplished chef when she came to the States. She doesn't talk about her time at Verinder House much. I think she and her husband left long before the family sold the property."

"It's too bad you and Charlie aren't able to come to the party tomorrow," Ali said.

"I know." Grace sighed. "But Char hates formal events, and we've committed to a few already this season." Grace left the rest of it unsaid, but Kyra knew the real reason they'd declined the invitation was Charlie's refusal to step foot on one of the small ferries that served as access and transportation to and from Chappaquiddick. Charlie's boat phobia was a growing point of contention for the couple.

"I'll take this into the living room." Kyra picked up a platter of appetizers.

She set it on the coffee table and straightened the napkins, the coasters. Her nervous energy had her fussing. She fluffed the pillows and straightened a throw blanket. She turned on the gas fireplace, adjusting it so the flames were just so. Kyra ran her palms down her thighs. This would be the first time Tarek would meet her aunt in person, and although she knew her aunt was teasing, she really wanted Ali to like Tarek and for him to like her.

The trees shook as a gust of wind blew. Leaves flew across the yard. It didn't seem to bother her uncle or the others. They were standing in a semi-circle around the turkey frier that appeared to be somewhat assembled. Charlie's hands were moving as she told some presumably ridiculous story, and Chase was bent over with laughter. Kyra's phone buzzed, and she turned away, smiling and perhaps a bit jealous. Charlie was a wonderful storyteller. She fished it from her back pocket, expecting it to be Tarek. It was Asher, Omega's CEO. From his personal account.

"When you've a chance, ring me."

Kyra frowned. If it was related to the merger or Omega, he'd have texted her from his work account and if it was urgent, he'd have called. Kyra tried to remember. She thought he'd said his flight arrived yesterday. He was likely stuck inside with Loriann, bored stiff, and was looking for entertainment. She wasn't going to let him weasel an invite to her aunt's party tonight, which would be such an Asher thing to do. He could be such a charming bastard. She swiped her thumb across the call back icon.

The front door swung open, and with a blast of icy air, Tarek stepped into their foyer. Kyra ended the call before it could connect and pocketed her phone. She'd call Asher back tomorrow. Tarek's eyes found hers and his mouth quirked up in that half smile she loved. He dropped his bag on the floor and met her halfway. She paused, looking into his dark green eyes, for a half a second before he pulled her into his arms.

The cold clung to his jacket and seeped through her sweater. She shivered as his cool cheek pressed against her neck.

"I missed you." His whisper sounded like a sigh.

"Me, too."

"Ahem." Ali announced her presence by faking a strange high-pitched cough.

Kyra let Tarek go and turned narrowed eyes on her aunt. Ali wasn't bothering to hide her giant shit-eating grin.

"Oh, Detective," Grace hummed, her eyes sparkling with the same meddlesome energy. "Lovely to see you."

"Just Tarek, Grace. It's nice to see you, too. Happy Thanksgiving." Tarek pressed his lips together like he was trying not to laugh. He laced his fingers with Kyra's, pulling her close.

Kyra shifted on her feet. She gestured between Tarek and her aunt with her free hand. "Ali, this is Tarek. Tarek, Ali."

"A pleasure to finally meet you in person," Tarek said, letting Kyra go and offering Ali his hand.

Ali pushed his hand aside and flung herself at him, hard enough he stumbled back. His eyebrows shot up and he gave Kyra a wide-eyed look. Kyra huffed out a long, apologetic breath. Ali was going to be Ali.

Her aunt stepped back, looking up at him, her whole body vibrating with excitement.

"I'm so glad you're real!" she screeched.

Kyra squeezed her eyes shut, gathering her patience.

"I was sure Kyra made you up so I wouldn't worry about her dying alone and being eaten by her cats."

"You've literally talked to him on video chat a dozen

times. And it's just the one cat. That you made me keep," Kyra grumbled.

"There are amazing things you can do with Photoshop these days." Ali's grin somehow widened, and Kyra groaned inwardly. Ali was loving this.

"Tar, you made it." Chase strode into the room, followed by Charlie, Cam, and Gerry. "We're about to put the turkey in," he said, thumping Tarek on the back.

Kyra introduced her uncle. Ali disappeared and came back into the living room with Iggy. Tarek held the little boy, bouncing him on his hip, while he listened to Cam's theories on turkey frying. Tarek handed Iggy back to his mother and excused himself to freshen up after a long day of travel. Chase and Cam promised to wait for him for the *big descent*.

"I like him," Cam whispered in Kyra's ear right before Charlie dragged her uncle back outside.

Kyra let loose a long breath. It had gone as well as she could have hoped. She was only mildly embarrassed by Ali, and Tarek had taken it all in stride. Actually, she thought he might have been amused. The anxious band that lived around her chest, just underneath her ribcage, relaxed.

Tarek returned, and Kyra snorted in surprise, swallowing her wine just in time. It burned her nose and down the back of her throat, making her cough. Apparently, he'd received Ali's dress code memo. He was wearing a plaid shirt identical to Cam's. She must have bought him one too, when they were in town. When or how she'd gotten it to him, Kyra had no clue, but she had to admire her aunt's commitment.

Before she could ask, Tarek gave her a wink and slipped

outside. A few minutes later, another boisterous clamoring came from the patio as the turkey was lowered into a boiling vat of peanut oil.

Ali and Grace settled into seats beside Kyra, and they chatted about the island, Grace's involvement with the community council, other events. Kyra half listened and half-watched the turkey-frying activities through the windows. Every so often, one or more of the folks outside would pop back into the kitchen for more beer, snacks, and eventually, bottles of small batch bourbon to sample.

"Gerry, you're responsible. Please don't let them burn down my house," she begged when he and Chase came inside for more ice.

"You are insured, right?" he deadpanned, and laughed at Kyra's frown.

Kyra poured another glass of wine.

"He's an ER doctor, not a firefighter, Kay." Chase emerged from the kitchen with a tray of finger foods Ali must have had ready.

Kyra took one of the little bacon-wrapped figs he offered to her.

He ran his eyes over Gerry and smirked. "But a firefighter would be hot."

Gerry made a dismissive sound, but he looked more intrigued than anything.

"I'm sure I can get my hands on a uniform at the next fundraising committee meeting. What's your size, again, dear?" Grace offered.

Gerry turned a mottled pink, and they all burst out laughing.

Just as the sun was dipping behind the trees, the turkey was pulled from the fryer, the side dishes from the ovens, and someone with sense assembled a salad made of fresh produce that Chase confirmed was sent by his farm manager. Kyra's house didn't have a dining room, something that she'd never missed before.

"What will we do?" she asked, her hands on her hips surveying the mountain of food.

"We'll set up everything on the counter here and eat in front of the fire in the living room. They'll love it." Ali patted her on the shoulder. "Here, make yourself useful." She handed Kyra a basket with the bread the Chamberses brought and shooed her into the living room.

Kyra placed it on the coffee table and stood back, watching her aunt distribute plates and cutlery to their guests and arrange a queue. Her friends and family jostled for seats on the sectional or the floor, their plates piled high.

She swallowed back a tight feeling at the base of her throat. She'd never had this experience. Holidays, those she had celebrated with Ali, had always been small, casual affairs. It was just of the two of them, and then later, Cam, who avoided his family as much as possible, made three. They would order Indian takeaway, or heat something Ali bought at Waitrose and watch movies or play board games. It was ... quiet. She rubbed her chest with the heel of her palm.

"Kay?" Chase said, his voice soft.

She startled. She hadn't realized he was right beside her. His eyes, the color of a mountain lake, glimmered, and she saw in his face that strange warm feeling she felt buzzing behind her lungs. She smiled up at him, realizing what it was. She was happy.

"I know," he murmured and stooped to press his lips to the top of her head and she leaned into him.

Kyra and Chase had grown close after she solved the murder of his then boyfriend. They'd supported each other through shared trauma, nightmares, and a terrifying trek through a hidden cave system. He was over the top brilliant, beautiful, kind, and utterly ridiculous. She loved him to bits.

Chase's head snapped up. His voice rose over the crowd. "Don't you fucking dare, Collins! One of those legs is mine!"

Kyra wandered into the kitchen. Ali was the only one left. She was mashing already mushy sweet potatoes into a pulp for Iggy.

"Ali?"

Her aunt turned around, wiping her hands on her barbaric apron. "Sweetheart, what is it?" she asked, and Kyra looked up at her aunt, barely an inch taller, and threw her arms around her.

"Thank you." Kyra sniffled.

"Aw, babes. No, thank you." Ali stroked Kyra's back. "We're so happy to be here with you." Ali pulled back and wiped a tear off Kyra's cheek and made a *tsking* sound. "None of that. You don't want to ruin your eye makeup for your fit detective."

"He's not a policeman anymore."

"No, but consultant, or whatever he is, sounds so corporate." Ali scrunched her nose up, and then her eyes went wide. "You made him keep the uniform though, yeah?"

"Ali!" Kyra tried to push her away, but Ali held her close and gave her another squeeze before releasing her.

"Alright, enough. We'll talk more about that later, and you can show me the pictures."

Kyra would be doing no such thing.

Ali picked up the bowl. "I'd better feed Iggy before this gets too cold. Make yourself a plate and come on out."

When Kyra came back with her own plate, everyone was comfortably stuffed in the too small room. Someone, Tarek, she assumed, had set up a chair for Cronk. He sat, a king on his throne, a little plate of turkey skin in front of him. Tarek had held her a spot next to him on the floor in front of the fire. When she sat, he gave her a warm smile and stroked her knee with his thumb.

Once everyone was settled, and Iggy was happily gumming his baby spoon, Cam cleared his throat. "It may not be American tradition," he said, his Scottish brogue more pronounced after a few drinks. "But in my village in Scotland, we say a blessing whenever good fortune brings loved ones together." He held his glass aloft and repeated a prayer Kyra had never heard him say before, his Gaelic lyrical and beautiful. He raised his glass. "*Sláinte.*"

They clamored back a response, loud and jubilant.

Tarek wrapped his arm around her shoulders and murmured, his breath hot on her ear, "Happy Thanksgiving."

Chapter Three

Kyra and Tarek had moved to the couch. They'd discarded their shoes and were lounging on the chaise, under an old afghan, while Grace and Gerry loaded the dishwasher. Chase was in the wine cellar with Cam hunting through Kyra's late father's expansive scotch collection. She was tempted to run, or waddle, upstairs and change into lounge pants. The waistband of her jeans felt uncomfortably snug and her head comfortably fuzzy.

There was a knock at the door, and Tarek untucked himself to answer it.

"Tar!" a voice boomed.

Kyra turned around to see a giant of a man, wearing a bright orange vest over his puffer coat, taking up the whole of the doorway. His reddish-brown beard was somehow more unruly than the last time she'd seen him.

He raised a massive mitt in greeting and his beard split, showing a flash of white. "London!"

"Is that Gully?" Chase bounded up the stairs, his arms laden with bottles. Cam was right behind him, with more. "Hey, Gully. Just in time. We're doing a tasting. Cam is explaining whisky." Chase halted. "What the fuck are you wearing?"

"Visibility vest." Gully started unbuttoning it. "I found three hunters on my property last week. They're culling the deer population, but someone is bound to get shot if they're not careful." He patted the neon orange nylon. "Me being careful."

"They hunt deer here?" Kyra asked.

Martha's Vineyard wasn't a large island at about ninety-five square miles. She was surprised it could sustain a deer population at all.

"Oh yes, dear," Grace hummed. "With no natural predators, they become quite the nuisance. Just last week, Julia made a delicious venison stew from the buck they brought home."

Kyra caught Tarek's slight frown as he retook his seat beside her.

"As requested, I brought the pies," Gully announced and stooped to set two pie plates on the coffee table. "Apple and blueberry. Traditional."

"You made these?" Kyra asked, taking in the intricate latticework made of golden crust. Gully's eyebrows flattened out in a look that said she should know better than to ask such a stupid question. "They look professional, Gully."

His eyebrows went flatter.

Gully Gould was Tarek's best friend. They'd grown up together in Worcester, a small city in central Massachusetts. He owned and ran Kyra's favorite pub on the island, the *Wraith & Bone*, which everyone referred to simply as Gully's. During the summer, they'd bonded over researching a famous sunken pirate ship, and talking about Tarek like he wasn't in the room.

"I am a professional," he said with an air of indignation that had Tarek laughing.

"I didn't know you made desserts, too."

"I don't, but it's not because I can't."

Kyra and Grace distributed hot cups of coffee and tea while Charlie cut thick slices of pie.

"Do we have ice cream? Pie non-à la mode just isn't the same."

"Char!" Grace admonished.

"We have some. I put it in the freezer." Gerry went to the kitchen and returned carrying four pints of ice cream from a local chain and a metal scoop that he also must have brought with him. "Which kind?" he asked as he pulled the tops off the containers.

Charlie pointed to the caramel, and he dolloped a scoop atop Charlie's triangle of apple pie.

"You are a prince." She took an enormous bite. Her eyes fluttered closed with a moan. "Julia never makes pie. Grace, why doesn't Julia make *pie*?"

"Cam, which goes best with blueberry?" Chase pointed to the bottles in front of him.

"A speyside, I think." Cam stuck his tongue in his cheek while he turned the bottles, studying the labels.

"Gully, how did the excavation go? Any surprises?" Tarek asked.

He'd left for St. Louis shortly after the salvage efforts began. It had taken three weeks to raise the wreck of the eighteenth-century pirate ship, *Keres*, from a ravine in the Vineyard Sound.

"Depends who you ask." Gully rubbed his beard. "You

may have heard. It'd been cleaned out. Sunk with her hold empty. Funny thing was the damage it sustained. Looked like the hull had been blown out from the inside, not like it'd run aground. The keel was in good condition, all considering."

"What does that mean?" Kyra asked at the same time Chase said, "It was scuttled?"

Gully licked the back of his spoon. "*Mmhhmm.* That's Terry and I's theory, right now. The Wraith must have emptied the ship and sank it. I'm researching if he or Helena show up in any public records after that hurricane." Gully's massive shoulders lifted in a shrug. "But even without the treasure, the ship is a remarkable find. The council wants the museum. They're thinking Aquinnah."

"And did you hear back from that producer?" Tarek asked.

The strip of skin above Gully's beard turned pink. "I did." He nodded, and at everyone's questioning faces, he cleared his throat. "I've been asked to do an interview for a special on one of those streaming services."

"That's brilliant news, Gully," Kyra said.

"I should be thanking you." At Kyra's surprised expression, he explained, "The production green lit the docuseries' feature on the Wraith because of that article you wrote for the *Island Times*. One of them has a house in Wellfleet, and he read about the wreck."

"Oh, it was nothing," Kyra waved it off self-consciously.

The editor-in-chief of the small local paper, and apparently a friend of her father's, had contacted her after the incident in the sea caves and asked if she'd like to write a guest column about the wrecked pirate ship and the salvage efforts. It'd garnered enough attention it'd been reprinted in a few national news outlets, and now she had a standing offer to submit articles as a featured columnist. She hadn't been surprised that people were interested in the story. The public was fascinated by pirates. What had surprised her was how much she'd enjoyed writing the article. She hadn't felt that much satisfaction in her legal work in, well, never, actually. Since the article published, Kyra had been toying with the idea of submitting more.

"You're going to be on TV?" Chase leaned forward. "Is it about us, too? And that bird psycho who chased us into the caves?"

Gully shook his head. "I don't think so, but I can ask."

"Oh no, I don't want to be on TV ever again." Chase shook his head.

Kyra had little desire to be on the show either. She wasn't keen to relive the claustrophobia of being trapped in a cave system.

Gully cleared his throat again. "Kyra?" She sat up straighter, surprised he'd used her name. "Would you mind reviewing the contract for me? They're sending it next week? If you have time."

"Of course. Happy to help." Kyra grinned.

"Anyone want more pie?" Chase asked, knife in hand.

"No, Char." Grace sent a warning look at her wife and Charlie slumped back with an exaggerated frown.

"Here, you can have the rest of mine." Gerry handed his half-eaten pie to Chase. "Is anyone else doing the turkey trot tomorrow?"

"What's a turkey trot?" Cam asked, pouring whisky into a glass and giving it a long sniff. He poured four more and distributed them around the table.

"It's a road race, dear. We host it every year. It's very popular."

Charlie rolled her eyes. "Some of the more insane islanders wake up at six a.m. on Thanksgiving Day and run for three miles around Oak Bluffs before gorging themselves." Charlie's deep frown revealed how she felt about early morning exercise.

Or perhaps any exercise, Kyra thought, remembering Charlie's vocal complaints about her tennis lessons.

"Anyone can sign up?" Kyra asked Gerry.

"*Mmhhmm.* Normally, I volunteer at the first-aid tent, but they wouldn't appreciate me being hungover, and with tomorrow promising to be another long night, I thought I'd get in some early morning cardio."

"Char and I work the signup tables. We'll be there."

Kyra chanced a glance at Charlie. She did not appear pleased with the prospect.

"Me, too," Gully added. "I have a coffee and donut stand for the runners."

"We should do it," Cam said, slapping his thigh. "Kay, wanna run with your old uncle?"

Kyra rolled her lips, thinking it over. Cam did marathons. For fun. It was his least likable quality. "I suppose I can," she said with little enthusiasm. "Anyone else?"

Cam and Gerry chatted through the logistics with Grace and Gully. They made plans to meet in Oak Bluffs. Then Chase asked her uncle about some distiller's process and the conversation moved back to Scotch. Smiling, she watched her guests from under heavy eyelids. Kyra sank back into the sofa's soft cushions. She struggled to keep her eyes open, snuggled beneath Tarek's arm.

"It's okay. I'll wake you," he whispered against her hair, and Kyra let herself drift.

Chapter Four

A HOWLING WHINE startled Kyra awake. She sat up, her hand falling to the mattress, still warm from where Tarek had slept. Cronkite was curled up on his pillow. A gust of wind hit the wall of windows, rattling the glass in their panes. Kyra flinched and even Cronkite stirred, his ears rotating, whiskers twitching.

"It's just wind," she murmured and reached out to stroke his back. One bottle green eye shone through the barest slit, before he nestled further into Tarek's pillow. Kyra slid out of bed and crept toward the window. The sky was clear and the sun, still low in the sky, cast long shadows across the lawn. Crackatuxet Cove's normally calm waters churned. She could almost see the wind sweeping over the surface as the water rippled and swirled. She shivered and wrapped her arms around herself.

"I brought you coffee." Kyra spun around as the door clicked closed. Tarek held two mugs. He'd pulled on a pair of thin joggers and his worn Boston University sweatshirt.

"Is everyone awake?"

"No, just Cam. He's downstairs with Iggy. He said he's letting Ali sleep."

"Probably smart," Kyra said, and turned back to the

window. "She was in rare Ali-form last night."

When Kyra had finally stumbled to bed, Ali and Chase were battling over a game of Scrabble that had gotten heated over American versus British spellings.

She heard the soft *tink* of ceramic on wood and felt Tarek's hand around her wrist. He pulled her away from the window and down onto the couch, wrapping his arms around her.

"Mmmm." He hummed against her shoulder. "You're warm."

"Did I agree to run a road race this morning?" She asked and reached for her cup.

The coffee was hot. Soft swirls of steam danced above the rim. She took a long sip, savoring the taste. It was always better when he made it.

"You did. Cam wanted me to remind you. For the record, I wasn't going to."

Kyra groaned. Knowing Cam, he'd want to run it twice. Another gust of wind hit the house, causing the siding to creak. Kyra grimaced. A run sounded awful.

"There's a hurricane, well, a tropical depression now, that's blown out to sea, but we're getting some of the winds. I bet there's a surf warning." Tarek's arms tightened around her waist as he looked outside. "We may want to get to Chappaquiddick earlier, rather than later."

"Won't it be too dangerous to go?" she asked, sounding hopeful even to her ears.

It was tempting to blame nature and cancel the trip. Stay here in this room with Tarek all day. She pulled away to look up at him and she could tell by the soft gleam in his eyes he'd thought the same.

"No, but there may be a long wait at the ferry station. Bad weather is part of life on the islands, but the islanders don't let it affect them. I've seen the Chappy ferries run even when Edgartown was underwater. With the holiday and the road race, they'll go back-and-forth right up until close."

Kyra sighed, a little disappointed. *Fine.* She felt his soft laugh against her back.

"When will the ferries close?" she asked for what she knew was the hundredth time, hoping for a better answer.

Because of the holiday, the little boats stopped running earlier than usual, right when Loriann wanted to serve dinner, but instead of scheduling dinner earlier like a rational person, Loriann insisted all the guests, who couldn't get home, stay the night. As if a formal event full of work colleagues and strangers wasn't awkward enough, she also had to sit through a breakfast. Kyra was not looking forward to it. At all.

"Don't answer. I remember. What time do we need to leave for the race?" Kyra asked, standing and stretching.

Tarek reclined with a long breath. "About now."

Chapter Five

KYRA BLEW INTO her hands and bounced on her toes. She'd had to pull Ali from her bed, and they'd arrived at the race site with mere minutes to spare before sign-ups closed.

She'd seen Chase walking through the crowd near Gully's booth. Even if he didn't stand a head taller than most people, it wouldn't have been hard to spot him. The crowd seemed to separate for him, like he was Moses parting the Red Sea. People would stop him, shake his hand, clasp him on the shoulder. He would answer every inquiry with polite aloofness and flash a charming smile. The attention drained him, and she was glad he'd be able to hide in the back of Gully's tent if he needed to disappear.

Tarek was already with Gully, setting out coffee, hot chocolate, and cider along with trays of fresh apple cider doughnuts. She could smell the cinnamon from the starting line half a block away.

"You ready?" Cam asked, stretching one arm across his chest, then the other. He did a few deep knee bends.

"No." Hot sugared drinks sounded much better than running against the wind. Just as she thought it, another blast struck them, and the crowd of runners collectively recoiled. "Shit!" she hissed. The sun had given up, and gray clouds covered the sky. The temperature hovered just below chilly, dipping down to frigid with each brutal gust of wind.

"Suck it up. You'll be fine. We've had worse. Remember the run we did in Edinburgh?" Cam slapped her on the back. How he was functioning this morning, she didn't know. She gave him a wary look. He looked back over his shoulder and raised a hand. Kyra followed his line of sight to see Ali pushing a stroller, with Iggy bundled like a caterpillar in the chrysalis stage standing next to Gerry. Gerry grinned, waved, and pulled a knit cap over his head. Like civilized people, they were queued up with the twelve-minute milers. She and Cam? The sevens.

"Maybe we should queue up with Ali and Gerry," she started, but then broke off, frowning.

A beautiful woman was on the sidewalk, on the other side of the rope barrier. Her dark hair was covered by a beret. She threw back her head, laughing at whatever the man standing beside her was saying. He leaned in close to the woman cutting her off from Kyra's view, but something about her was familiar. *Aysha?*

"What's that? Go where?"

She shook her head. "Oh, no, never mind." She scanned the crowd again, but the woman was gone. Cam craned his neck. "Sorry, I thought I saw Aysha." At Cam's *Who?* expression, Kyra explained, "Loriann's assistant. But I'm mistaken. She would be with Loriann." But Kyra could have sworn… Aysha was distinctive looking. Model distinctive. But Kyra didn't have time to reconsider, because the starting bell rang, and they were off.

Twenty-four horrible minutes later, she and Cam crossed the finish line. It wasn't her best time. It was probably one of his worst, but running into the wind—wind that kicked up saltwater spray and sand—had been grueling. Her fingers, cheeks, and nose stung with salt and cold, but her core felt feverish and sticky from the exertion. Kyra pushed strands of wet hair that had come free from her ponytail behind her ears.

"Gully's tent is over there." She pointed, and they made their way through the crowd.

Gully waved a giant paw when he spotted them. "London! How'd you do?"

"Not terrible. Gully, you remember my uncle."

"How could I forget? How you doing?" Gully shook Cam's hand and handed them two water bottles from the table. "Tar and Chase are in the back."

Kyra pushed through the plastic drape separating the booth from the preparation space inside the tent. Inside, Tarek and Chase were sitting in folding chairs. Chase was wheezing, doubled over in laughter. Charlie stood, her back to Kyra and Cam. Her hands and black curls flew through the air as she mimed something that could have been an explosion.

"What are you telling them?"

Charlie whirled around. Her eyes sparkled, and her grin was infectious. "Hiya. About the time the Ferris wheel broke the day before the ag fair, and Grace went nuclear. It was fantastic. Hot drink?" She pointed to the tables lining the sides of the tent holding large carafes and trays of doughnuts. "How was the run?"

"I survived. Barely." Kyra poured a cup of coffee and held it between her frozen fingers. She glared at Chase for abandoning her. "I thought you were going to run."

"I think I made the right choice." He leaned back in his chair and crossed his ankles.

"Have you lot just been sitting here the whole time? Not helping?"

"We tried to help," Tarek said. "Gully sent us back here. He called Chase a nuisance and said I scared the customers. Charlie came by because she's cold."

"Hey, we're helping," Chase protested. "We're back-of-the-house support. We fill the carafes and trays he sends back."

Charlie pointed to the space heater. "And it's heated in here."

It was cozy. Kyra frowned into her cup, annoyed that they were all together, warm and dry, while she froze her ass off, running through a gale.

Charlie handed Cam a hot cider. "Here, and try a donut."

"Thanks," he said and turned to Charlie. "And thank you, again, for watching Iggy tonight. Ali is looking forward to it. We haven't had a child-free night in a while."

Charlie shook her head. "Pleasure is ours." Her expression changed, pleased, and something more Kyra couldn't quite decipher. Perhaps a little sad? "I love kids and we don't see my nephews often." At Kyra's questioning look, Charlie shrugged. "My brother and his family live in Dumbo."

Brooklyn? Kyra had ventured there once when she was at Columbia. The trek had been sufficiently inconvenient.

Once had been more than enough.

"Tar, we need more doughnuts." Gully's gruff voice came from the front. "The last of the runners are in." Tarek grabbed a tray.

"I'd better go meet Ali and Iggy," Cam said with a stretch. "We still need to pack and get him situated. We'll bring him to your place around noon, if that works, Charlie?"

Chase stood and rolled his shoulders. "Yeah, I need to get going, too. And I gotta find Ger. We'll get packed and come to your place." Chase bent down to kiss Kyra's cheek but stopped a few inches away. He gave an exaggerated sniff and grimaced. "Better not." He grinned when she showed him her favorite finger.

Chapter Six

KYRA ADDED A fleece pullover to her already stuffed overnight bag. She rubbed at her arms, trying to get warm. Even after a scalding hot shower, she still felt a bone-deep chill. She told herself she hadn't warmed up since the run, that this wasn't her body manifesting her apprehension of her Martha's Vineyard and London worlds combining.

Ali and Cam had met Assaf and Asher before. They'd been fillers at her firm's charity dinner tables too many times to count. She worried about Tarek and Chase, though. They only knew her on holiday, had never seen her as a lawyer. They hadn't witnessed the undermining, the jabs, and the backstabbing she experienced every day. She wasn't the nicest person in that world. She couldn't be and survive. It wasn't personal. It was just business, and it required her to separate and lock down her emotions. Kyra worried that if they saw how she let herself be treated, they'd feel compelled to stand up for her, or worse, think she was a doormat and lose respect for her. She sighed. There would be at least a hundred people at the gala. She'd just have to steer clear of Assaf and Loriann as much as possible, not give them any opportunity to embarrass her. Kyra rubbed her forehead. It wasn't a great plan.

The bathroom door opened, and she turned when she heard his feet on the floorboards.

"Still cold?" Tarek asked as he came to stand beside her, a towel wrapped around his waist. "Shouldn't you be used to this weather?" he asked, nodding to the windows where outside it'd begun to mist. "Doesn't it remind you of dreary London?"

"I think I've permanently acclimated to the heat. I'll never get used to the cold again. And London isn't windy, at least, not like this."

"This is nothing. It gets much worse. Windier, colder. Then it starts snowing. February in New England is unbearable." Kyra's gaze traveled back out to the cove. Would she still be here in February?

She had planned to return to London in September, but with the Omega–Global Media merger and negotiations with the Americans, Kyra was working US hours and Assaf and Asher were flying to New York every few weeks. It made sense for her to stay on the island and travel to the city when necessary. She hadn't really thought through what her next move would be after the merger signed. She would no longer have a good argument to stay on the island. Work would want her back in the London office. She wasn't sure she wanted to go back to her old, lonely life, though. Nor was she sure what she'd do if she stayed on Martha's Vineyard. It was a big, life-changing decision. One she'd been avoiding, but she'd have to face it soon.

"Hey." Tarek must have noticed her contemplative silence, because his hand landed on her hip, turning her toward him. "Don't worry. We can spend the coldest months somewhere else. Many islanders do. I won't let you freeze to death." He'd misunderstood.

Tarek seemed content taking it day-by-day. He didn't pressure her, giving her space to make her own decisions. He didn't ask about her long-term plans or ask her to stay. Some days, she wished he would. Kyra forced a smile, not ready to share the thoughts that plagued the back of her mind.

"We're islanders now?" She kept her tone light, teasing, matching his.

"It depends who you ask. To anyone who lives on the mainland? Yes. To the people who grew up here? No. Never." Another gust of wind hit the house, and the panes shivered. The ragged scrub pines lining her yard shivered and bowed. Tarek's grip tightened before he released her, his expression serious. "The wind is getting worse. We should probably hurry."

Kyra turned back to her packing. She reevaluated the outfits she'd chosen, double-checking she hadn't forgotten anything. Her dress and Tarek's suit were already in the garment bag hanging on the door. Loriann loved a formal event. Tonight's dress code was black-tie, but the island's culture was a casual, laid back one, and Kyra hoped that *black-tie* was up to some interpretation. She snapped her fingers. *Heels.* She walked into the closet and froze.

"What are you doing?"

Tarek was sliding a black holster into the shoe compartment of his bag.

"I can't leave it here," he said, and zipped the clip into a separate pocket.

Kyra knew little about guns other than she loathed them.

Being held at gunpoint twice gave one a healthy respect and a visceral hatred for the vile things.

"Why not? Can't you leave it in the office?" They'd had this discussion already. The first time he'd brought one into the house, she'd lost it and with more patience than he exhibited now, he'd explained why he was issued a firearm, and why he was required to carry it.

One night while Tarek was away on an assignment, over drinks on the Chamberses' patio, Kyra had complained about how uncomfortable she was with a gun in the house. Charlie, in rare seriousness, suggested Kyra may consider having a gun safe installed in Ed's office.

"He uses the study when he's on the island, doesn't he?"

Tarek kept all his things in a tidy pile at the side of the desk, as much out of the way as possible. He wouldn't dare change a thing in her late father's office or anywhere in the house. When she'd told them about his sad little pile, Kyra realized Tarek may still feel like a guest in their home.

The very next day, she'd made a few calls, and someone came out to install the safe. She spent two days cleaning out the office, redistributing the curios from Ed's world travels throughout the house, and to the island's second-hand shop. He'd been touched when she'd surprised him with a space he could call his own upon his return. Since then, she'd often found him and Cronk there, reading in her dad's ratty old clubman chair.

"I'm required to keep one with me. You know that." Tarek ran his hand through his dark hair and his features sharpened in annoyance.

Kyra bit back a ready retort. After all, it was his job. She averted her gaze, grabbed her favorite suede heels, and stuffed them into her bag.

The front door banged open, and Kyra jumped.

"*Ho-ney*, I'm *ho-ome*!" Chase hollered from the foyer.

A *thud*. A baby started crying. *For the love of god.* Kyra closed her eyes and counted down from ten. She did it again. She ran a final mental check and zipped up her bag.

This won't be that bad. It felt like a lie.

Chapter Seven

Downstairs, Chase was perched on the couch arm, watching Gerry play with Iggy and Cronk on the floor. His expression was a combination of fascination and bafflement. Kyra's mini-yeti blinked his poison apple eyes and rolled on his back, baring his soft belly in nature's most effective trap.

"It's a baby. He can't hurt you," she whispered to Chase. "Unless you're worried about the floof-goblin. He can, and he will hurt you." Yowling his disdain for being outed, Cronkite bolted from the room.

Ali stumbled down the stairs laden with bags overflowing with what Kyra assumed were baby things. Gerry and Chase scrambled to help.

"I think I packed everything Iggy will need. Are you sure Grace and Charlie aren't just being nice by offering to babysit?"

"They'd have given you the name of a babysitter if they didn't want to do it. And I think Charlie said her friend Lisa is coming, too. She was a teacher. I'm sure she knows tons about babies." That may have been a bit of a stretch. Lisa had taught middle school before quitting to take over her late husband's business. "But if you're not comfortable, we don't have to go…"

"No! I'm dying to see that house," Ali insisted. "And have a night off," she said more softly.

"He'll be fine," Cam said from the stairs, carrying down more bags and dropping them at the front of the door. "He'll play, eat, and go to sleep. Knowing the two of you, we'll be home in the morning before he even wakes up." Ali nodded, but Kyra could tell her aunt was still nervous.

"I'm not really worried about him," she said as she stuffed her son's arms into his coat. "I'm worried your friends will hate you." She opened the closet. "I'm taking your coat, Kay. Cam, do we need anything else?"

Cam shook his head. "No, we can walk him over now, if you're ready."

The door closed behind them, banging shut from the wind, and Chase turned to Kyra. "Grace didn't want to come to your boss's fancy party?" he asked. "This seems like something she'd kill to be invited to."

"They were invited, but Charlie won't get on one of the little ferries," Kyra said. "She's only just started taking the big ones to the mainland." Kyra didn't tell them Charlie still suffered from panic attacks. "I'm still surprised you agreed."

"Actually, I didn't. Old-people prom isn't really my scene." Chase grinned at her, but it didn't quite reach his eyes. Despite his clubbing and bar hopping public persona, his scene was on his farm or sailing around the island. "The invitation was to the Hawthorn family, so, you know, Phil and Margot. Mom RSVP'd me and a guest to go in their place." Chase's lip curled. "I'd planned on ignoring it, but then you said you were going." He shrugged. "I figured the six of us could probably have some fun, even if everyone else sucks."

Chase hated society events almost as much as he hated Margot's interferences. Kyra was glad he was coming, though. "Thank you."

Chase stood and gave her a warm hug. "Shut up." He dropped a kiss on the crown of her head.

"Who else will be there, do you know?" Gerry asked.

"Well, Assaf Maloof, one of the managing partners at my firm, and my boss. Loriann, who owns the company, her PA, and executive team, probably. Definitely the CEO, Asher Owen. Probably the same from the Global Media side. Grace said the council leadership had been invited, so them, I suppose. And I imagine some other investors and important people in east coast media businesses who'd benefit from the merger?" Kyra wasn't sure. "I didn't ask, but back home, her parties are very exclusive, in the worst way."

Gerry's expression turned thoughtful. "You mean like royal exclusive?"

Kyra leveled him with a look. "The NDAs I've signed prohibit me from confirming or denying that."

Gerry grinned.

"I bet," Chase scoffed. "Come on, let's get this shit in the cars."

Chapter Eight

KYRA LOOKED OUT the window of her Range Rover. Tarek was in the driver's seat chatting with the ferryman, dressed in head-to-toe yellow rain gear. Another ferryman navigated the tiny three-car boat, the *On Time II*, across the 527-foot expanse between Edgartown and Chappaquiddick. The current swirled, and the wind buffeted the car and the boat. Kyra clutched the grab handle as they rocked. Whether it was just the car on its wheels, or the entire boat, she didn't want to know. She shivered and pulled her leather jacket tighter around her shoulders. It wasn't warm enough, but Ali had kept her parka.

Her aunt, along with Cam, Chase, and Gerry, were already on the other side. She could see Chase's freshly cleaned Bronco pulled off to the side of the road, waiting for them. Kyra rubbed the space between her eyes, and Tarek's hand found her thigh. He gave it a gentle squeeze and reached over to turn on her seat warmer.

"Happy Thanksgiving, folks. You know that we're shutting down early today, right?" the ferryman said in a thick Boston accent.

"Yes, thank you," Kyra said, accepting their return trip pass.

The man sucked in his cheeks and let it go with a smack. "Weather looks like it's gonna get worse. Tide's coming in and with this wind we'll get some swells. I heard they shut down the big boats a few hours ago." He shook his head. "Good thing you folks got into the queue when you did."

Yeah, good thing. Kyra bit down on her lip lest she say something sarcastic out loud.

The man pointed to a sign with an AM radio station. "Keep an ear out for updates." He adjusted the brim of his baseball cap under his hood. "Detective, ma'am." Kyra made a face when he turned away.

Tarek was smiling, failing to contain his chuckle. "You know, whenever anyone calls you ma'am, you shoot them a death glare."

"I do not." She did. "Ma'am makes me sound old. He called you detective."

"Because I was one, and he knows me. He plays softball with Gully."

A wave, bigger than the rest, hit the port side, sending a spray of water up over the railing through Tarek's open window. The ferry shuddered.

"Dammit," Tarek hissed and rolled it up.

Kyra laughed at the water dripping from his nose. She arched an eyebrow, imitating him. He feigned a glare at her, then broke into a laugh, wiping away the saltwater.

The ferry slid into the docking station at Chappaquiddick. After a few *clanks* and *cranks*, the ferryman drew back the safety gate, and waved them through. Tarek put the car in gear and drove down the ramp. Chase's arm popped out of his window. He waved them forward and pulled out behind them.

"Do you know where we're going?" Kyra consulted her phone. "Oh, for fuck's sake."

"What?"

"No service." She held it up to the windshield.

Tarek huffed. "Oh, yeah, and you thought the cell service on the big island was bad."

"Aysha's text says, make a right at the last private road off of Road to the Gut. Last driveway." Kyra frowned. "Road to the Gut?"

"It's way on the other side. Near the lighthouse. On Cape Poge."

Kyra slid her useless phone into her purse and watched out the window as Tarek drove down the main street. This was her first time visiting Chappy. She knew little about it, other than its infamous political history. They drove past a tiny convenience store boasting essentials, beach supplies, and fresh sandwiches. According to Tarek, it was the only one on the island. Everything else had to be brought in from Edgartown.

Houses were fewer and farther between, each one hidden deep in the woods away from the road. The only evidence that the island was inhabited was the swirls of smoke rising through the trees, and the scent of wood-fire in the air.

The radio turned fuzzy, and Kyra changed the station. Tarek shook his head and turned it off. "There isn't a radio tower here, either." He gestured outside. "When it's overcast like this, we won't get anything on the FM stations."

In the cushioned silence of the car, the landscape became eerie. The wind moved the sand and dried leaves across the asphalt in swirls. Kyra swallowed back an uneasy feeling as they drove further and further away from civilization.

"No murder podcast?" she teased him, trying to distract herself.

Last summer she'd learned that Tarek's guilty pleasure was true crime podcasts, particularly those with rabid female fanbases.

Tarek glanced at her from the corner of his eye. "In the last episode, Marjorie and Kelsey said they were exploring a new cold case. They're on hiatus."

"What's that?" Kyra leaned forward, her hands hitting the dashboard.

Through the mist, a dilapidated wooden single lane bridge appeared ... and disappeared into the fog beyond. To the side, a few cars were parked, or abandoned, half in a ditch.

"Dike Bridge. It connects us to Tom's Neck." Tarek's tone changed, went serious. He rolled down the window. "You have to be careful driving over it, especially at night." Tarek reduced their speed to a crawl. "People have gone over."

The tires made a *thumping* sound as they rolled over the wooden slats, and the bridge creaked and groaned.

"Is it safe?" she asked, but Tarek didn't answer.

He was steering with one hand, his other arm slung out the window. His eyes flicked back and forth between the road in front of them, and where his tires were hitting the bridge below. Kyra looked back. Chase was waiting for their car to clear the bridge before proceeding. His Bronco slowly disappeared from view as they drove deeper into the fog. The

Range Rover bumped as the tires exited the bridge and hit the dirt road. Tarek pulled over to the side and got out.

"Can it not hold the weight?" she asked through the window.

"It probably can. It was rebuilt not that long ago, but better safe than sorry. Stay here. I'm going to signal to him we're over."

Tarek jogged back up the bridge and into the mist. She heard him holler, but it was dull and muted, making him sound faraway. When he returned, his hair was windswept. He slid back into the seat and held his hands in front of the vent, rubbing them together.

"It's cold out there." He shivered.

Kyra heard the thumping of a car and Chase flashed his lights. He pulled up behind them and got out, followed by Gerry and Cam.

Kyra met Ali's eyes through the rear window. She was leaning forward between the two front seats. Her shoulders raised and dropped in an exaggerated shrug. Then Ali lifted a flask in a cheers motion and took a swig. Kyra made a face at her aunt, who smiled a self-satisfied grin. *That's why she insisted on riding with them.* But she was glad Ali was already relaxing and having fun.

"We have to take air out of tires," Tarek said, opening the door. At her confused expression, he pointed to the sandy road. "The road isn't paved." She glanced back and saw both Chase and Gerry squatting down by each front tire.

"I can help."

Tarek leaned over, pressed his lips against the corner of her mouth. "Nah, Cam and I've got it. Stay warm." And he was gone. The car's electronics hummed as it recalibrated. When he got back inside, he flicked through the system and selected the sand mode. *There's a sand mode?* He put his arm out the window and motioned to Chase to pass them. The Bronco moved forward. She bit her bottom lip and ran her hands down her thighs.

"He knows where we're going?"

"He's more familiar with these roads and if we get stuck, he can pull us out."

"And if he gets stuck?"

Tarek's pause lasted a second too long. "Let's hope that doesn't happen." Kyra's eyes went wide.

The cars moved slowly, jostling over the uneven terrain. The road, little more than a trail of packed down sand with deep tracks, ran alongside the waterway connecting Pocha Pond to Cape Poge.

Without taking his hands from the steering wheel, Tarek pointed up and to the right at the tall sand dunes, higher even than their car. "They build them up in the winter to protect the road. On the other side, is East Beach. On very clear days, you can see Muskeget Island. It's part of Nantucket."

As they drove further out, the road became increasingly more treacherous. In some places, the tracks were so deep the undercarriage of the car scraped against the sandy mound between the divots. The road narrowed when the waterway widened and opened to Cape Poge. Wind blasted the car from the left. Sand peppered the windows and doors, and Tarek grimaced.

"This is one of the many reasons people don't have nice

cars here," he said.

Chase banked sharply to the right, driving up the dune. In front of them, the road had entirely washed away. Tarek cursed under his breath and followed. The tires slid on the loose sand and Tarek eased off the gas until the all-wheel drive found purchase and the car surged forward. Kyra felt a sense of reluctant relief that they were staying the night. Even if the ferries were running, driving back in the dark would be suicidal.

"Many of the year-round residents on Cape Poge have their own boats and helicopters," Tarek said as he guided their car back onto the path. Kyra wasn't entirely surprised. She'd heard that the tiny island was popular with the ultra-wealthy. That Loriann had even agreed to host her party there suggested it catered to the upper echelons of elite society.

They continued on the road as it narrowed and twisted. Tarek's forehead creased in concentration and his grip on the steering wheel paled his knuckles. After what felt like forever, the top of the lighthouse came into view and the road forked, The Road to the Gut leading left toward the water.

"The last road on the right?" Tarek asked, and Kyra nodded, leaning forward, her hands on the dashboard. The road was barely a road at all now, just a cleared stretch of sand, with muddy offshoots that disappeared into the brush. Tarek followed Chase as he made a sharp right and turned off the road onto a crude muddy path barely wide enough for their cars.

"This can't be it," Kyra murmured, a feeling of dread pooling in her stomach. If they couldn't find this place, and they ended up sleeping in their cars, Chase and Ali would kill her.

"Do you see any driveways?" Tarek squinted.

The red brake lights of Chase's Bronco flashed, casting a bloody glow on the ground. Then the white reverse lights came on. Tarek stopped. Chase's head popped out the window, and he pointed. Kyra followed the line of his finger to a barely visible break in the foliage.

"Is Loriann mad?" she mumbled. "It can't be through there." Something tapped on her window, and she jumped with a yelp. "Jesus, shit!"

Gerry grinned and made a "roll it down" motion. Tarek pressed the button.

"We think this is the driveway. I'm going to run down and make sure. Sit tight." He jogged off, disappearing through the trees.

Two minutes.

Three.

Kyra was beginning to think he fell into the ocean when he emerged and motioned them in. Tarek put the car in gear and turned onto the narrow trail. Gerry held back one of the longer branches and the car went through, mostly unscathed.

Beyond the brush barrier, the driveway changed from soft sand to hard packed gravel and curved around a copse of scraggly birches. Sitting forward, Kyra's eyes widened as the manicured lawn, with neat flower beds and English-inspired gardens came into view. As they rounded the turn, the house appeared.

"Wow." She hadn't meant to say it out loud.

House didn't really do the structure justice. Neither did

mansion. In France it'd be called a chateau, in England, a manor, but in America this was one of the *cottages*.

Verinder House.

A summer house for the Gilded Age's uber-wealthy.

Keeping with its neo-Georgian style, Verinder House was imposing and very symmetrical. From the vertically aligned windows, Kyra counted three floors. Tall windows framed the wide front entrance. Chimneys dotted the north and south sides of the roof, and she could just make out railings. It could have been a widow's walk facing the sea.

She turned in her seat, looking for Chase's car. If she hadn't passed out from the excitement, Ali was definitely telling them the entire history of the house's design, in excruciating detail. Perhaps Kyra felt the tiniest bit bad for Chase and Gerry. She felt Tarek's hand warm on her thigh.

"It's not so bad, is it?" he asked, his eyes sparkling.

No. No, it's not.

Chapter Nine

TAREK PULLED UNDER the porte cochere. A man dressed in khakis and a lavender fleece embroidered with the Verinder House logo appeared as if out of nowhere, and Tarek rolled down his window.

"Happy Thanksgiving."

"Happy Turkey Day and welcome to Verinder House."

Turkey Day? Kyra made a conscious effort not to cringe. She leaned forward to speak around Tarek. "Hi, I'm Kyra Gibson. This is Tarek Collins. We're guests of Omega Media."

"Ah yes, the Gibson party of four." He glanced in the back seat and gave her a questioning look.

"My aunt and uncle are in the other car with Chase Hawthorn."

"And the Hawthorn party of two." His smile was wide and warm. "We've been expecting you. Ms. Oma was telling me how pleased she was that you were still able to attend. It's too bad, you know? But island weather, what can you do?"

Kyra opened her mouth to ask what the man was talking about, but he stepped back and gave the top of the car a pat. "Go on and unload here, and you can pull the cars around to the side. You'll see the signs for the guest parking area. If you hit the pool, you've gone too far." The man guffawed like he'd told the world's funniest joke.

Car doors opened and closed, and Kyra saw Cam and Gerry unloading their bags in the side-view mirror.

"What the hell did he mean by that?"

"The pool? I don't want to know." Tarek shook his head and got out to unload their bags. He handed them to Gerry. "I'll meet you inside," he said, getting back in the car.

The lavender man ushered them in, holding the heavy doors open. The sound of the SUVs crunching on the drive was silenced when the doors shut with a loud *bang* that reverberated through the foyer. Kyra flinched. And then her eyes widened as she took in the space.

The first thing Kyra noticed was the scent, a heady mixture of jasmine, orange blossom, and something she couldn't name. Ali sneezed.

"Let me get the lights on for you. I didn't realize how dark it'd gotten." A crystal chandelier sputtered on, casting scattershot light on the floor. Dim wall sconces illuminated the edges of the room in a soft glow. The lighting was clearly designed to draw the eye to the foyer's central visual feature, the grand double staircase. Each side curved up to the second-floor balcony landing and disappeared into the separate wings of the house. It reminded her of an introductory scene of some period drama, where the female main character attended a ball or met the rich, handsome love interest dressed in formal wear. Ali grabbed Kyra's forearm. Kyra winced.

"Ow!"

"Sorry!" Ali's eyes shone like stars, and her smile grew

wondrous. "Look at the period detail, Kay. The tiles." She pointed to the gleaming checkerboard floor, and to the intricate border where the floor met the molding. "I bet it's natural stone."

"Good eye. It is." The lavender man tapped his toe on the tile. "The white ones, well technically, it's a dove gray, came from a quarry in New Hampshire, and the dark gray stones came from a quarry outside of Boston. All original. Both quarries have long since gone out of business, so we had to restore the tiles as best we could, but I think our mason did a good job, don't you?" The man's smile was inviting and indulgent, like he'd had the same conversation countless times, but didn't mind.

"And the mosaic border?" Ali asked.

"Ah," he said and took a step closer to the wall.

Directly under the sconce, Kyra had a better view of him. He was average height, and trim, with light brown hair that he swooped over his forehead, making him look younger than he probably was, but Kyra would have guessed he was in his early thirties, not much younger than she.

"Unfortunately, those are not original."

Ali nodded. "To accommodate piping and electrical, right?"

"Yes," he said, his eyebrows raised.

Ali bumped her shoulder against Kyra's and grinned. Kyra suppressed the urge to roll her eyes.

"We had to go to a French artist to replicate the original design." He took a step back, looking up at the chandelier. "We don't have too many historic mansions like this on the Cape. It's more of a Rhode Island thing. Verinder House is unique. Its original occupants, the Verinder family, were true innovators, ahead of their time, and the house has many modernist idiosyncrasies."

Kyra had no idea what he was on about, but from the gleeful vibrations humming off her, Ali did.

"I read it was built in 1880?" Ali moved closer to the lavender man.

Cam sighed behind Kyra, and they shared a conspiratorial, self-sacrificing look.

"That's right." He unzipped the pockets of his fleece and slid his hands inside. "By Malcolm Verinder. He made his fortune during the Civil War importing goods in from Europe."

"What kind of goods?" Kyra asked.

"Materials for munitions, mostly." The lavender man shrugged. "He bought the property to create a family getaway. He wanted a hunting cabin, inspired by those he saw during his travels to Bavaria. But without much to hunt on Chappy, Verinder House became more of a summer home. The family continued to use it until about twenty years ago, when they abandoned it for their other more fashionable properties. It was allowed to fall into ruin. Six years ago, Cape Hospitality bought it. We renovated it and now it's used primarily for private events, like the one Ms. Oma had planned, you know, charity galas, corporate retreats, and the like, and of course, weddings."

Kyra glanced around the ornate room. She could picture a wedding here. *It must be beautiful in the summer.*

"Fascinating. Oh, I'm Ali Babcock. I'm actually an architect. I specialize in historical renos."

"Ben." The lavender man shook her hand. "Ben Hastings. I'm the property manager here. I should have guessed. Not many of our guests know about hiding the utilities around the perimeters. If you're interested in the updates, I'd be happy to give you a tour before your scheduled events this evening."

The front door opened, and the guys hurried inside. Wind blew through the room, sending leaves swirling across the floor. The chandelier swung from the ceiling, and the light from the swinging crystals splintered and fractaled around the room. Tarek barely made it through before the door slammed shut with a crushing *boom*.

"That wind is fucking insane," Chase hissed and tried to smooth down his long hair.

"You're making it worse," Gerry said, rolling his lips and earning a half-hearted glare.

"It gets wicked windy up here, but I've never seen it as bad as tonight without a storm. We get it off both sides, but we get some mighty gusts off Cape Poge," Ben said, while he consulted his phone and typed out something before shutting off the screen and giving them his attention. "So now for the official welcome." He smiled. "Light refreshments have been set up in the library. It's through there. Ms. Oma requested cocktail hour at five thirty, in the Garden Room, and dinner will be served at seven in the dining room." He glanced up at Ali. "If you, or anyone else, are interested in a tour, I can meet you in the library in an hour. It won't take long. You'll have plenty of time after the tour to rest and dress for dinner."

"Oh, that sounds brilliant. We'd love a tour." Ali clasped

her hands together. "Cam?"

Cam blinked back resignation and said, "Sounds enthralling."

Ali narrowed her eyes at him.

"This is the coatroom." Ben opened a closet door concealed in the fluted paneled wall. "You can store your coats and even your luggage here. There isn't much closet space in the guestrooms, unfortunately. This is one of the modern updates." He winked at Ali and hung up her coat. "Ah, Camilla, there you are." A woman, probably in her mid-twenties with thick, dark hair, and wearing head-to-toe black, appeared as if out of nowhere. "Camilla is our manager of guest services. If you need anything, she's the one to ask. Camilla, would you mind showing our guests their rooms?" Ben back stepped to the left. "Your rooms are all in the north wing." He pointed to the staircase curving up to the right. "I will see you shortly, in the library. Enjoy your stay at Verinder House." Ben disappeared down a darkened hall.

"Please, follow me." Camilla motioned for them to follow her up the grand staircase. "You can leave your bags here. I'll have someone bring them to your rooms."

"I've got ours, not a problem," Tarek said, picking up his and Kyra's overnight bags. She took their garment bag from his shoulder.

"The two wings are on separate sides of the house. They're connected by this bridgeway." Camilla pointed to the landing that connected the two staircases. "Your party has the entire north wing to itself, so you'll have some privacy."

Where are the other guests staying? Kyra was going to ask, but Ali spoke first. "Is there anything unique about the wings?"

"No, they're pretty much identical, except for the rooms. Each guest suite has been decorated in its own theme and they have different layouts." Camilla paused on the bridgeway, her hand resting on the thick railing. "Did Ben offer to give you the tour?"

"Yes," Ali said.

"You'll enjoy it. He knows everything to know about Verinder House and its history." Camilla said it with no enthusiasm, and Kyra caught Chase trying not to laugh.

Kyra wondered how many times the poor woman had suffered through the tour.

They followed Camilla up to a wide, dark hall.

She turned right to the front-most room and consulted her phone. "Mr. and Mrs. Babcock?"

Ali and Cam had the first room, Chase and Gerry took one a few doors down, near the center of the hall. "And Ms. Gibson and Dr. Collins?" Tarek stiffened and Kyra smirked. He was still so uncomfortable with the honorific.

"Just Kyra, please. And Tarek."

"Of course. Your room is this way." They followed her to the end of the long hall, far away from the staircase and from any natural light. The sconces flickered and Kyra's pulse quickened. She couldn't determine whether the electrical was spotty, or the sconces were intended to mimic candlelight.

Camilla stood to the side and gestured to the last door. "This is your room." She unlocked it and ushered them inside. She set two key cards on the small desk. "The bathroom is back there, and those doors open onto a terrace. Although tonight it'll be too cold. Wi-Fi connection details are in this binder. If you need anything, dial seven on the house phone." She pointed to an old-fashioned phone on the antique desk. "The fireplace is electric, and the switch is to the right of the mantel. Can I get you anything else?"

"No, thank you," Kyra said, looking around the room.

Tarek handed Camilla some bills and thanked her.

Once the door clicked closed, Kyra dropped her bags on the bed and inspected their suite. It was roomy, with a king-size, four-poster bed that was so high she'd have to hop to get onto it. There was a cozy sitting area in front of the fireplace. The bathroom was one of those contemporary wet rooms, where nothing separated the shower from the rest of the space, and a large soaking tub sat under a window overlooking a garden below.

Kyra came back into the bedroom as Tarek was looking out the windows. "There's a balcony out here."

"You thought she lied?"

"No, but it's bigger than I thought it'd be."

"Let me see." She peeked beside him.

The balcony ran the length of the main living space, with a wrought-iron railing. A small table and two chairs were set off to the side. Beyond the railing, Kyra saw the grounds that swept down to the beach and Cape Poge. In nicer weather, it'd be the perfect place to sit, watching the sea, or perhaps having a morning coffee.

Kyra picked the garment bag up from the bed and pulled out her dress and Tarek's suit. She hung their clothes in the armoire that served as the room's closet.

"It's really quite beautiful."

"Hmm?" Tarek said, looking up from his own bag.

"Verinder House. The room." She gestured to the opulent space, tastefully decorated in muted shades of rose and cream, to the bed stacked with pillows. "It's just not what I expected." Kyra pressed her finger to her lips. "I guess I thought it'd be more Capey. More, beachy." She toed the thick oriental rug.

Tarek zipped his bag closed and dropped it on the floor of the armoire. He crouched down to open the small safe. He set the code and placed his gun and the magazine inside before closing the door.

"I know what you mean." He stood up and turned in a semi-circle. "It's very…" His voice drifted off as he glanced around the space. "Industrial tycoon?"

Kyra laughed. *Exactly.* He stepped around her and stopped at the desk. He flipped through the guest-services binder, then checked his watch.

"We have some time before the cocktail hour. Did you want to see what's in the library, get something to eat? And there's the tour."

Kyra ignored the comment about the tour. She was hungry. She hadn't eaten anything all day. "Does it make sense to eat now before we eat again in a few hours, though?"

Tarek's smile widened. "That's the whole spirit of Thanksgiving."

Chapter Ten

CHASE AND GERRY were already in the library when they arrived. Tarek and Kyra had run into Ali and Cam in the hall, also on their way to the library. Ali claimed she knew—generally speaking—where it should be. As it turned out, Ali did not know where the library was, and they'd wandered past many dark rooms before finally finding it.

When they did, Kyra couldn't believe how they'd missed it. It was enormous, with high ceilings and bookshelves lining the walls. Two large windows overlooking the garden flanked either side of the ornate stone hearth. A roaring fire had been set, and the room was just nearly too warm.

Intimate sitting areas were spread around the space, inviting guests to engage in soft conversation. Gerry was lounging on a chaise, his ankles crossed, scrolling through his phone. Chase was flipping through a book he'd pulled from the shelves.

"Ohmagod! Kay!" Ali grabbed Kyra's arm. "They've got one of those library ladders." *So cool.* Anyone who denied having dreams of a library with a ladder was a liar. "Do you think they have a fantasy romance section?"

Kyra gave her aunt a deadpan look. "Oh, I'm sure. Probably next to the collection of pro-labor monographs."

"You're a brat." Ali made a face and gave her a playful shove.

A soft pop came from the side of the room.

"Champagne?" Chase asked, holding the bottle. He was standing next to a sideboard table, laden with trays of light snacks and drinks.

"I'll take a coffee if they have one," Tarek said.

"Coming right up."

"This place is very wedding, isn't it?" Kyra said as she wandered around the grand space.

"It is." Chase replied. "Can you put this away for me?" He handed her the book and poured himself a glass of champagne. He took a sip. "It must cost a fortune to host one here."

She took the book, glanced at the title—*The Complete Shakespeare Vol II, The Tragedies*—and slipped it back into its slot. "I bet," she said, not caring to guess.

It was sure to be a staggering sum. As was probably the cost of this event.

Ali accepted the glass Chase handed her and walked around the room. "It's actually pretty accurate with the period's architectural and interior designs." She stopped at the fireplace and ran her fingers along the stone mantel. She pointed to the crown molding at the ceiling. "I'd bet that's all original. Look, Cam." Idly, Kyra scanned the titles on the library shelves, only half listening to Ali explain material sourcing in post-Civil War America.

The door opened and a striking woman in her twenties stood framed in the doorway.

"Ah, Kyra. Ben said you'd arrived." Aysha Skye's syllables

were elongated by her French-Moroccan accent. She catwalked into the room on impossibly high heels and bent at the knees to press her cheeks to Kyra's in a *la bise*. Kyra took in Aysha's tailored pantsuit and perfectly styled dark curls. As usual, the former model looked runway-ready, and Kyra tried not to think about her own windswept appearance.

"I'm so glad you and your friends were able to attend tonight. I wouldn't have survived another stuffy dinner with just Loriann and Asher for company."

"What do you mean?" Kyra asked, stepping back.

Aysha waved her hand, brandishing her long acrylic nails like weapons. "You know how they can be, Kyra." She shook her head, and her gaze fell to Kyra's jeans and sand-caked sneakers. "And you know Loriann is still insisting on formal attire tonight, right? Asher wasn't able to change her mind, even now." Aysha's dark brown eyes rose to the ceiling and then arced to the side where they snagged on Chase.

He was leaning against the back of Gerry's sofa, talking over his shoulder. Aysha blinked like she couldn't believe what she was seeing.

"Aysha?"

"He came?"

Kyra leaned forward to hear her better. "What?"

Aysha flashed her teeth in a polite smile, but her gaze remained locked on Chase. "I'm sure you have everything you need. And your friends, are they settled?" Aysha's gaze flickered around the room before returning to Kyra with an expectant upturn of her mouth. A request. Kyra heaved an internal sigh.

"Let me introduce you." Kyra stepped to Aysha's side.

"Aysha, you remember my aunt, Ali." Ali waved from across the room, where she was still studying the fireplace. "And her husband, Cam." Cam shook her hand and returned to filling his plate with cheese cubes. "That's Tarek Collins, my..." Kyra stumbled, unsure how to describe Tarek. Boyfriend felt juvenile and perhaps insufficient, but Aysha wasn't listening. Her gaze flickered to Chase and back impatiently. Kyra forced a brittle smile, and said, "And this is Chase Hawthorn, and doctor..." But Aysha walked away, moved closer to Chase and Gerry.

Chase looked up; his brows raised in surprise. Gerry turned around.

"It's so nice to see you again, Mr. Hawthorn." Aysha's voice had gone silky and sweet. "When we received Mrs. Hawthorn's RSVP for Mr. Hawthorn and his guest, I'd assumed she meant your father."

Chase stared at Aysha for half a beat. Kyra watched as he gathered himself back into himself and transformed into his playboy public persona. He pasted on his trademark smarmy smirk.

"No, the family is celebrating the holidays in DC. I'm afraid you're stuck with me tonight."

"I can't say I'm sorry to hear that." Aysha let out a dainty laugh. "How have you been?"

"Fucking fantastic. And you? Since..." His voice trailed off.

"The Oscars?" Aysha's eyebrows hitched together as much as her Botox would allow. Chase stared at her. "Remember? Three years ago?"

"Right. Good times that," he said dully. He picked up

the empty champagne bottle and shook it out over his glass. "Damn. Can we get more?" He thrust the bottle at her.

"Oh, I'll alert the kitchen right away. Do you and your guests need anything else?" Aysha grasped the bottle.

"Nope. Thanks." Chase gave her an exaggerated wink and slid away.

Still clutching the bottle to her chest, Aysha left the library.

When the door shut behind her, Chase turned to Kyra. "Who was that? Should I know her?"

"Aysha Skye? The model," Gerry said. He tilted his head to the side with a smirk. "She seems to know you."

Chase's eyes went wide. "I don't think I know her, but maybe?"

"You've been to the Academy Awards?" Ali was staring at Chase with wonder. "The real ones?"

"No." He shook his head, then his mouth hitched up like he was remembering something deliciously sinful. "Just the after parties." He turned his focus to Gerry. "How do you know who she is?"

That had Kyra's attention, too.

"She was the spokesperson for one of those designer perfumes? You know the commercial. A woman on a yacht off Capris or Greece, or one of those Mediterranean islands and the man in a suit. It was everywhere." At Chase's arched eyebrow, Gerry's expression turned resigned. "The nurses control the TV in the breakroom. We watch a lot of Bravo." Gerry sounded so forlorn about it; Kyra couldn't help but laugh.

"Does that happen to him all the time?" Ali whispered,

nodding toward Chase.

"People thinking they know him? Yeah. You get used to it."

"And will he?"

"No, probably not," Kyra said softly with a sad shake of her head.

Kyra suspected he didn't realize how beautiful or magnetic he was. Even when he was playing his part as a spoiled rich kid, he was irresistible. Everyone wanted to be close to him. It had made him cynical and insecure. He didn't trust the motivations of people vying for his attention—whether they wanted him for the tabloid darling he played, his family connections, or the sensitive, kind person he hid from the public.

Over the past few months, though, she'd seen him resort to his alternate ego less and less often. On the island, on the farm, around her and their friends, day by day, he seemed happier, more himself.

"You don't know her?" Gerry asked, all teasing gone from his voice.

"I don't think so." Chase ran his hand through his hair, then shook his head. "She must have been at one of those parties. I don't remember much from that night, to be honest. You said she's a model?"

"Was," Kyra said. "Now she's Loriann's personal assistant."

Chase moved to the sideboard. "Do you think there will be more people like that? People I'm supposed to know?"

"I'm afraid so," Kyra said with a sympathetic smile.

"Ugh." His head fell forward. "There's an excellent

chance I'm just going to drink through the whole night." Chase ducked down and popped back up with two more bottles. "Anyone else need a top up?"

"Where'd those come from?" Cam asked.

"There's a whole case back here."

"I do." Ali raised her glass.

Kyra watched them pop open another bottle and swallowed her sigh. She could handle a drunk Ali or a drunk Chase, but together? Verinder House might not survive. Her gaze slid to Tarek.

His mouth stretched down in a quizzical smile, as if to say, *What's bothering you?*

"Where do you think the other guests are?" she asked him under her breath.

But before he could answer, the library doors swung open, hitting the walls, making Kyra jump. Kyra spun around, her heart banging against her ribs. *Fuck's sake!*

"Gibs!" Kyra's boss, Assaf Maloof, strode in like the lord of the manor. *Crap.*

Chase mouthed, *Gibs?* and Kyra just shrugged. How could she explain without words that her boss could be an insufferable asshat?

Assaf was dressed in his cool-lawyer uniform—bespoke navy suit, open collar, and blindingly white Prada trainers. In Kyra's opinion, he always looked like he was trying too hard.

"You made it!" He clasped his hands together. "This venue is tops, don't you think?" He turned to Ali. "Mrs. Babcock, a pleasure as always." He took Ali's hand, and in an overt show, raised it to his lips.

Ali ate it up. Her eyes sparkled with utter delight. Kyra

shut hers to keep from rolling them.

"We only just got here, but yes, from what I've seen so far, very impressive. Let me introduce you to my friends."

Kyra doled out quick introductions.

Assaf wandered toward the sideboard, and Kyra followed behind him. "Have you met the representatives from Global Media yet?" she asked.

"Yes. Mr. Elmer and his wife, Elise. They arrived this morning."

Chase's lazy smile faltered, but he recovered so quickly, Kyra thought she may have imagined it. She mouthed, *What?* at him, but he just shook his head, downed his drink, and poured another.

"Pour me one?" Assaf pointed to the crystal flute in Chase's hand. Chase obliged. Assaf raised his glass in thanks. "Cheers."

"Who are the Elmers?" Tarek asked.

"The Elmer family is the majority shareholder of Global Media," Assaf explained. "Well, at least for now. That's going to change any day, won't it?" He nudged Kyra with his elbow. Assaf plopped down on a loveseat and crossed his ankle over his knee. His pant leg hitched up, showing off his Fendi logo socks.

While she'd spent most of the last few months working on the merger, all of Kyra's interactions with Global Media had been with their lawyers. "I haven't spoken to the owners. What are they like?" she asked Assaf.

Assaf took a long sip of champagne and smacked his lips. "That's nice." He held up the glass, examining the bubbles. "Very nice. I only met them briefly when they arrived.

Loriann and Asher took a private tea with them earlier. It'd have been nice if you'd been here." Kyra ignored Assaf's passive aggressive reproach. She had no doubt it was just the first of many to come.

He'd wanted her with him for the duration of his trip, and she'd declined. Apparently, he was still ticked off about it. Her presence wouldn't have changed anything, unless it'd been Asher who had been the one to kick Assaf out.

Asher detested Assaf almost as much as Assaf loathed him. Too many times she'd had to mediate between the two. At least with a crowded gala, they would have little reason to interact. Small blessings.

"When do the other guests arrive?" she asked. Assaf cocked his head to the side and frowned. "For the gala," she prompted and waved her hand, gesturing to the mansion around them. "Loriann's big do tonight?"

"Aysha didn't tell you?" Kyra looked around at her friends and family and saw only blank faces mirroring her own.

"Tell me what?"

"Strange. Plans changed, unfortunately."

"Chrissakes, don't be a cryptic asshole, Maloof." Asher Owen's deep baritone announced his entrance into the room. "Kyra, love. Sorry to be the bearer of bad news, but the gala's been canceled."

Kyra's mouth fell open, and she stared at Asher. "Excuse me, what?"

"Afraid so. It was called off yesterday. Most of the guests were coming from out of town. London, New York, a few from DC. All the flights to Martha's Vineyard Airport were canceled, and then we received word that the boats would likely shutdown. When the flights from Heathrow were canceled, well, that was that, I suppose." He raised his hand, then let it fall to his side. "Can't say I'm disappointed."

"Of course not," Assaf scoffed.

"So, there are no other guests? Just us and ... and who?" Kyra heard the pitch of her voice rise.

"Keep up, Gibs. Loriann's team, me, the Elmers, and your lot."

"It's just us?" she repeated.

Kyra's mind was spinning. The only thing worse than a party for a hundred people would be a party for twelve.

"Yes, well, I do apologize that no one from Omega was in touch with you." Asher adjusted his shirt cuffs and gave Kyra a pointed look.

Realization struck her and her stomach hollowed out. *His text yesterday. Shit. Shit. Shit.* He'd tried to tell her, and she'd forgotten to call him back. It had slipped her mind, what with Friendsgiving dinner, then the race, packing, and driving over to Chappy.

"Nonsense, Owen. Loriann wanted her here."

"Indeed."

And that was why Asher had used his personal line. He hadn't wanted Loriann to know he'd contacted her.

While Omega Media was technically her client, she worked closest with Asher. They'd met when she first returned to London from New York. He'd been her very first client meeting in her new role. Asher was a brilliant economic strategist. He was all sophistication and charm, but hidden beneath his witty remarks and slow smiles, lurked something minacious and predatory. She once told him he was a real-life Bond villain, which he took as the utmost compliment.

Asher slid his hands into his pockets, and his mouth stretched into a cold smile. "Kyra, love, since we're all here, might as well introduce me to the friends who've kept you so busy."

Another jab, one she deserved.

"Oh, yes, of course." But she didn't get any further because Aysha pushed open the library doors. She was closely followed by Camilla, pushing a cart laden with more champagne. She wore a lavender apron tied over her black pants. With a nod to Asher, she pushed the cart to the sideboard and began replenishing their refreshments. She rounded the room, refilling their glasses one by one. Kyra declined, murmuring her thanks. She needed to keep her wits about her, at least until she determined her next move.

Assaf held his glass out for Camilla to fill, and then set it on a side table and brushed a nonexistent something from his thigh. "So, Owen," he said, his voice too casual. "How was your tea with Mr. and Mrs. Elmer?"

"It was tea. It was hot and herbal."

Assaf frowned, displeased with Asher's non-answer.

"Loriann messaged me a moment ago," Aysha interrupted, and held her phone up. "She and the Elmers are on their way down. She wants to meet her guests."

"Loriann is coming now?" Asher asked, his gaze skating around the room. Aysha lifted a single shoulder in an elegant shrug. "Kyra, I really do have an urgent matter to discuss with you. Preferably in private."

"I say, Owen." Assaf made a grumbling noise, but before

he could continue, Loriann entered.

Loriann Oma was the great, great granddaughter of some long forgotten English aristocrat, one that had been far removed from the monarchy. But based on the way she carried herself, one would think Loriann was the queen herself.

She was followed close behind by a couple. A heavyset man Kyra estimated to be in his late sixties, and a much older woman. She was easily in her eighties, frail and stooped. In one gnarled fist, she clutched a cane, and the other gripped her husband's sleeve.

Loriann clasped her hands together. Her diamond rings glinted in the flickering light.

"You're all here. Lovely. Just lovely."

Asher muttered a curse and slumped into one of the high-backed chairs.

"Ah, Kyra." Loriann's mouth stretched into a thin smile.

Her smiles were never prompt or casual enough to convince you of her sincerity, but she could never be accused of being impolite, either. Loriann was fastidious in her adherence to proper manners.

"You had no trouble finding us, I presume. Verinder House is a bit off the high street. Aysha sent instructions."

"Mrs. Elmer, let me help you." Camilla reached for Mrs. Elmer's elbow.

"Back off!" Her voice came out like a high-pitched rasp, and she jerked her arm back.

"Oh, I'm sorry." Camilla recoiled and clutched her apron.

No one spoke. The only sound in the room was the soft

thud of her cane hitting the floor over and over as Elise Elmer made her way to a chintz armchair. She was still struggling to lower herself into her chair when Mr. Elmer, with a grunt, flopped into the seat next to his wife's.

The Elmers were a strange couple, and not just because of the age difference. In just a few brief moments, Kyra got the impression that Mr. Elmer barely tolerated his wife's company. He watched Elise with a scowl, his mouth twisted in resentment or disgust.

Loriann made a noise like a cough requesting Kyra's attention. Out of the corner of Kyra eye, she saw Asher cross the room to speak to Camilla, probably apologizing for Elise's impertinence.

Kyra swallowed. "Yes, Loriann, Aysha's instructions were vital. Thank you."

"Excellent. I'm glad to hear it. Losing one's way is such an inconvenience, don't you think?"

"Umm, yes, very," Kyra said, uncertain what Loriann was getting at.

Loriann stepped around Kyra and spoke to the room, "Ah, now that we're all here, we must all get acquainted. We'll be having a lovely evening tonight, and then if all goes well, we'll be one big happy family, won't we, Hedge?"

Mr. Elmer made another sound, this one more like a noncommittal *harrumph*. Elise perked up and opened her mouth as if to say something, but Hedge shushed her, then barked, "The happiest."

Loriann swiveled her head, pretending to look around the room. "Where's the girl? Ah, you there, what activities can I offer my guests before we reconvene for cocktails?"

Camilla stepped away from Asher and smoothed her apron. "I can recommend…" But before Camilla could list off the amenities, the door swung open and Aysha reentered, carrying a glass of water. Kyra hadn't even noticed she'd left.

"Loriann." Aysha handed her the glass and slipped something into her hand.

"Already?" Loriann made an exaggerated grimace. "Very well." She swallowed back the pills and her mouth hitched. "Anything to stay young." She chortled and handed the glass back. "If you're done mothering me, Aysha, I'd love to meet the rest of my guests. Kyra?"

Kyra introduced her aunt and uncle, Tarek, and Gerry to Loriann and the Elmers.

"And this is my good friend from the island…"

"That there is Chase Hawthorn," Mrs. Elmer interrupted. She banged her cane against the floor. Kyra shut her mouth, stunned. "When Loriann's assistant said the Hawthorns were invited, I thought she meant Margot and Phil." Mrs. Elmer's mouth twisted.

"Elise, Hedge. Pleasure as always." Chase raised his glass in a salute. "How is Mazie?"

Elise glared at Chase. Her teeth scraped her bottom lip, leaving a pale trail in her frosty pink lipstick.

"Oh, still not speaking to you? Imagine that."

Elise's glare sharpened into something venomous.

"You seriously cannot still blame me for that." He scoffed.

"You're acquainted?" Loriann asked, her gaze pinged between them.

Kyra bit down on her lip. Now she knew why the

Elmers' name had been familiar. Mazie Elmer had been a friend of Chase's until he took the blame for sinking her grandfather's yacht. Hedge's yacht, apparently.

"You could say that." Hedge's jaw shifted. "Mr. Hawthorn attended Milton Academy with our granddaughter. Until they kicked him out." He set his glass on the table next to him. "Where are your parents?" He directed the question at Loriann.

"Unfortunately, they had a prior engagement they were unable to reschedule. The Department of Justice can be so unaccommodating. Mother asked me to attend in their place. How could I refuse?" Chase flashed that too bright smile.

Loriann's gaze pinged between Hedge and Chase, her expression troubled.

"Excuse me, Ms. Oma," Camilla interrupted. "I'm needed back in the kitchen. Will you and your guests be needing anything else?"

"Oh, fine. Go on." Loriann waved her out.

The door closed with a soft *click*, and Kyra felt like the room had shrunk down three sizes. Mrs. Elmer was staring daggers at Chase, and he kept shooting her vicious smiles, even as Gerry pulled him to the other side of the room to join Ali and Cam.

"Aysha, what have you planned for us this afternoon?" Loriann asked.

"Let me see." Aysha pulled out her phone and began reading options out loud. "There's the pool, tennis courts..."

Kyra stopped listening and her gaze traveled over the guests. Asher was standing against the wall, his arms crossed over his waistcoat. When he caught her watching him, he tilted his chin toward the door. A sign to meet him outside.

"What's that about?" Tarek asked.

She wasn't sure whether he was referring to Chase and the Elmers or the silent exchange between her and Asher.

Kyra rubbed her arms, chilled, but it had nothing to do with the temperature. She wished she could melt into the floor, or better yet, go back in time to yesterday and call fucking Asher back.

She glanced across the room at Chase, who was surrounded by her aunt, uncle, and Gerry. "I'm not sure, yet."

Chapter Eleven

"So then, Loriann, Hedge, do tell." Assaf feigned a casual tone, but his eyes glinted with a hungry look Kyra knew too well. "How did our discussions progress? Are the documents signed? Are we unofficially official?" He raised his glass like he expected someone to fill it. When no one moved, he got up and filled it himself.

"Assaf," Loriann tsked and the side of her mouth stretched down. "Please don't."

"Come now, I assume it's all good news, or we wouldn't be celebrating and my associate, sorry *colleague*, and I would be holed up in a conference room finishing the deal." He tossed Kyra a sly grin.

Asher caught Kyra's eye and rolled his. He might have been the only one who noticed the slight. Assaf was making a statement, notifying the Elmers that Kyra had no authority, and that Assaf was the dealmaker here. She waited for the insult to sting, but she only felt mild irritation. It should have infuriated her, that it didn't, that she didn't care much at all, was much more concerning. Kyra stepped into Tarek's space. His arm wrapped around her waist, holding her against him.

"Assaf," Loriann warned. "I told you tonight is a social

event. A holiday, and in the American tradition, we're not discussing business but uniting our two families."

"Of course, of course." Assaf rolled his wrist, flashing his Cartier watch. "But come now, the party's been canceled. And for people like us, business is pleasure. Right, Owen?" He chuckled.

Loriann turned steely eyes on her outside counsel, her thin lips set in a line.

"Excuse me, am I interrupting?" A head popped around the door and Ben Hastings flashed a friendly grin.

"Ah, Benjamin, perfect timing. My guests are growing restless. Can we offer them some recreative activities?"

"It's Bennett, but Ben is fine," he said in a tone that suggested he'd had this conversation with Loriann before, but his smile remained easy and gracious. "The Billiards Room is open where we have many indoor activities and game tables. The gym is in the south wing and is state-of-the-art. Of course, you can help yourself to any of the books and board games here. On the grounds, we have the gardens, tennis courts, and one of the state's oldest shooting ranges." Ben frowned and gestured to the window. "Unfortunately, the weather isn't cooperating today. I would recommend staying indoors or, if you must go out, remain on the grounds. Winds like this often mean strong riptides and tide surges."

Kyra couldn't imagine anyone venturing into the ocean on a day like today.

"And my offer to give a tour of the property still stands, if anyone is interested?"

"A tour?" Loriann exclaimed. "Wonderful idea. Who'd like to attend?"

The Elmers declined at the same time Ali enthusiastically accepted the invitation. "Unless you'd rather we go home?" she whispered, and Cam nodded his agreement.

They'd leave if Kyra wanted to go. Kyra snuck a glance at the rapidly receding daylight. Traversing that dangerous road at twilight was only fractionally more unappealing than Loriann's intimate dinner party.

Kyra shook her head. "No, we should stay. When else will we get a chance to stay here?" The dinner may not be the gala they were expecting, but in Kyra's experience, Loriann's events, regardless of size, always included copious amounts of the most delicious food. And, she figured, at most, it would only be a few hours she'd have to share with the Omega / Global people. She gave her aunt a smile. "Seriously, we'll stay. It'll be fun."

Ali beamed, and Kyra found herself smiling back. "It will be! Thank you." With her hand firmly wrapped around Cam's, Ali dragged him across the room to Ben. "I am so excited for this tour," Ali whispered to her husband, and Kyra hid her smile behind her hand. *Poor Cam.*

"Seriously, Loriann." Assaf rose to his feet and glared at his client. "You want to spend the afternoon on a tour of an old house? We've hundreds of them in England. Nicer ones. You bloody well live in one." He strode for the door. "Some of us have actual work to do." He turned around and his gaze fell on Kyra. She stiffened, waiting for him to summon her to take on some probably unnecessary tasks to make up for the billable hours he was losing. Instead, he shook his head, and he stormed out of the room.

"Not a fan of history, that one," Asher murmured. Kyra

smirked. "Will you and your, ah, Mr. Collins be going on the tour?"

"No." Kyra shook her head, and Tarek quirked an eyebrow. "Trust me." She lowered her voice. "You do not want to go on an architecture tour with my aunt. I'm saving you both."

Ali's head whipped around, and she stuck out her tongue at them.

"Oh, Asher, do come on the tour." Loriann waved for him to join them. "Aysha has been saying it's very informative."

Asher heaved an annoyed sigh and pasted on a dutiful smile. "I'd be delighted, Loriann." He offered her his arm, and with a rueful smile to Kyra followed Ali and Cam out into the hall.

"Remember, that cocktails will be served in the Garden Room *promptly* at five thirty," Aysha called over her shoulder, but she didn't follow behind the tour group, instead she turned to the right and disappeared.

"Ma'am, do you need assistance?" Tarek's soft voice pulled Kyra's attention away from whatever Aysha was doing. He was holding his hand out to Mrs. Elmer, who was struggling to get to her feet.

"No." She flapped her hands at him, and he stepped back. "I'd like to go to my room. Hedge?"

"I think I will go on that tour," Hedge said, standing up. He gave his wife a sour look.

The old woman watched her husband disappear through the doors and her knuckles turned white around the head of her cane. She pushed herself up. Her breathing became labored with the effort, but eventually, she stood.

They watched Mrs. Elmer shuffle out the door, her cane *thwumping* with each stilted step. It was difficult to sympathize with her, but Kyra wasn't heartless. It was obvious Elise Elmer was in a fair amount of pain.

Chase flopped down on the chaise Gerry had been occupying before Loriann had interrupted them. He stretched out, his feet dangling well off the end. He looked absurd.

"You're too tall."

Chase gave her a shrug as if to say, *So goes my life.*

"What was that? With the Elmers?" Tarek asked.

"You didn't say your client was in merger discussions with Global Media." Chase's stunning eyes searched hers.

"It was confidential. I couldn't tell anyone. I'm sorry."

His head dropped back, and he pushed his long hair off his forehead. "I went to boarding school with their granddaughter, Mazie. They have a house near Menemsha where Elise spends some of the summer. Margot and Elise are..." Chase's eyes slid closed, and his eyebrows hitched together. "My mother doesn't really have friends, just people she can use. Let's say acquaintances." His eyes popped open, and they sparkled. "And then there was that whole thing with Hedge's boat and it sinking a few years ago."

"You didn't sink that boat."

Chase's grin was all teeth. "That's not the public story." Kyra frowned. His voice went soft when he said, "And it's easier for everyone if they think I did."

"If you want to leave, I'd understand. I can make an excuse for you and Gerry."

"No. They're not my biggest fans." His smile gentled,

turned real. "But I'd still rather be here with you. And who knows? It may turn out entertaining."

"We can hope." But Kyra was less and less optimistic with each passing minute.

Chapter Twelve

KYRA SLIPPED HER feet into her black suede pointed-toe heels. They pinched, but were still her favorite pair, bought in a secondhand shop in Chiswick. She balanced on the thin stilettos and studied herself in the mirror. Her strapless black cocktail dress was too casual for a typical Loriann function, but it was all she had with her on the Vineyard. She gathered her thick hair at the base of her neck and yanked out some face-framing pieces. The result was more haggard scullery maid than she'd been going for. With a frustrated huff, she dropped her hands and her hair fell around her shoulders. *It'll be fine down.*

"Are you going to tell me what's bothering you?" Tarek asked as he came out of their en suite bath, buttoning up his dress shirt. "You've been quiet since we left everyone downstairs."

"It's nothing."

"Kyra?"

That the party had been canceled, and she hadn't been told, was bothering her. Loriann's actions, or lack thereof, felt duplicitous. She was also angry with herself for not returning Asher's call. "I'm just annoyed. With Loriann and Asher, and myself. Mostly myself. It's put me in a foul mood, I suppose."

"You think?"

Kyra's smile was rueful. She was in a terrible mood. "Asher tried to warn me that the party had been canceled. Yesterday he texted me to call him back, but I forgot. If I hadn't, we would be home and not forced to endure this awkward evening. We could be doing something fun with Grace and Charlie and Gully. Chase wouldn't be floundering. I feel like this night has gone entirely to shit, and it's my fault."

"It's not your fault. I wonder why they didn't tell you."

"Right? Loriann didn't want us to cancel. But I think there must be something more to it. Asher said he still needed to talk to me about something in private."

Tarek cocked his head to the side. "Asher would go behind Loriann's back? Isn't that a conflict of interest for you?"

"It would be, but Asher is unwavering in his loyalty to Loriann. And Loriann would accept nothing less." Kyra shook her head. "I can't imagine what he wants to say to me. I'm being paranoid. It's probably something stupid, like Asher wanting to complain about Assaf." Kyra reached behind her, cocking her elbow out to pull up the zipper at her back. "And Loriann does love formal events. She will use any excuse to dress for dinner. You'd think she grew up in the Gilded Age."

"Explains why she chose Verinder House." Tarek shrugged on his suit jacket. "Here, let me help."

Kyra pulled her hair over her shoulder so Tarek could pull the zipper up along her spine. His hands wrapped around the tops of her arms, and he pressed his lips against her bare shoulder. "I remember this dress," he murmured against her skin.

Kyra smiled over her shoulder, surprised. "You do?"

"How could I not?" He quirked his eyebrow.

She'd worn it on a chilly night in April, to a cocktail party held in honor of a now disgraced senator. It was the first night she and Tarek had worked together. She hadn't realized he'd noticed. Kyra turned around and wrapped her arms around his neck. His hands were warm through the fabric of her dress. She pressed herself against his body, letting him hold her.

The gala would have been annoying, but at least she could have hidden amongst the crowd. Without the shelter of a hundred other guests, Kyra and her little crew would be under scrutiny. And Loriann could be critical.

"You're okay with this, then? A small dinner with my work colleagues?" She pulled back to look up at him. "It's not what we signed up for."

"I want to spend tonight with you. I really don't care about the hundred or however many other people are here." His kiss was soft, and he was smiling when he pulled back. "We'll make the most of it. Or at least Ali and Chase will."

Kyra laughed. Ali and Chase wouldn't let the lack of a grand party interfere with their fun. She pushed her anxious thoughts from her mind, determined to make the best of her night. Her hands dropped to his chest, smoothed his lapels. His dark gray suit skimmed his body, highlighting his swimmer's build.

"You look nice." It was a gross understatement.

Tarek smiled as he held her gaze. He placed his hands

over hers. She could feel his steady heartbeat under her palms.

After a long moment, Tarek let go of her hands, and he stepped back, letting loose a long breath. "We should probably go downstairs if we're going to meet up with Chase and Gerry."

"I just need a few more minutes," Kyra replied, stepping into the bathroom to check her makeup.

Chapter Thirteen

"Do you know where the Billiards Room is?" Kyra asked. Her left hand rested on the railing, and her other was tucked into Tarek's elbow, as they descended the grand staircase. With the wind howling, and the lights flickering, she felt like a heroine from a gothic novel.

"All the directory said was that it's on the first floor. Not helpful."

No, she had to agree. The first floor was massive. The entire house was.

Earlier, before leaving the library, she and Tarek had agreed to meet up with Gerry and Chase in the Billiards Room to watch the last half of the afternoon football game. American football on Thanksgiving Day was a time-honored tradition, or so Kyra was told.

Tarek and Kyra wandered down the north hall, peaking inside the open doors. They found a parlor decorated in colors of sage and cream at the front of the house, where a bar and large cooler of ice had been set up. They found the library now empty. The tables of refreshments had been cleared away; the fire extinguished. Kyra rolled her shoulders against the chill that had settled over the darkened room.

Tarek laced his fingers with hers as they meandered. Kyra

pushed open an interior door, revealing another dark sitting room. Tarek tilted his head, and they continued down the hall.

When he first moved in, Tarek's reticence had unnerved Kyra. She wasn't used to living with a quiet person, her aunt and uncle being irredeemable prattlers. Tarek could go for hours without speaking. He never felt compelled to fill silences with wasted words.

After getting to know him, she realized he was quietly taking things in, observing, and filing the details away to recall or analyze later. His brain was always in information gathering mode. In this way, they were alike. Kyra's brain was always whirring, processing a dozen random things at once, and sometimes she didn't have the bandwidth to allocate to idle chitchat, and other times she had full-on conversations with the cat.

"Will she be disappointed?" Kyra blurted.

"What's that?" Tarek asked, unfazed.

"Your mother? Don't you normally spend Thanksgiving with her? Will she be upset that you're at this ridiculous dinner and not with her?" It'd been needling her since she'd accepted Loriann's invitation. Tarek was close to his mother. Weekly phone calls close.

Tarek blinked, then he smiled. "No. She isn't particular about holidays."

"She's not?" Kyra found that hard to believe.

"No, not really. She moved here from East Africa for nursing school when she was nineteen. She didn't grow up with American traditions, and the hospital pays time and a half on all holidays, so she'd volunteer to work. But she'd celebrate with me and Gully when she had a night off. It's never about the date, so much as time set aside to be together."

Kyra smiled to herself. She liked that. It mirrored what Ali had said yesterday. Tarek's unconventional childhood wasn't that different from her own. Both their families bucked the formality of tradition to embrace the sentiment.

"But…" And he sounded a tinge apprehensive. His walk slowed even further until he came to a stop. "She may have asked if we would like to visit her. She wants to meet you. Maybe sometime after Ali and Cam leave, if that's something—"

Kyra didn't let him finish his sentence. She pressed her lips to his.

Pulling back, she said, "I'd love to. I want to meet her, too." It earned her one of his rare full smiles.

They continued walking toward the far end of the house, closest to the ocean. A single sconce cast a semi-circle of dim light on the carpet. At the end, the hall split into two doorways, one opposite the other. The door to the left was propped open, giving them a view of a narrow vestibule. Tarek, gripping her hand, stepped inside.

It was another corridor. It continued straight into the heart of Verinder House, disappearing into the gloom. And to the right was a spiral staircase. It climbed up in a sharp curve, the treads of each stair narrowing from the outside to a point on the inside. Kyra craned her neck, looking up, but the stairs disappeared into the darkness.

"This must be the old servants' staircase," Tarek said. "They probably use it as a service-way now. Many of these old houses have different accesses so the servants could move around without being seen."

"Hmmm," Kyra hummed. Thanks to Ali, she knew of hidden servants' corridors but had never been in one before.

Tarek turned his phone's flashlight app on and shined it up the stairwell. "I bet it goes all the way up. Want to check it out?"

Kyra eyed the staircase warily, but her curiosity won out. "Yes, please."

Tarek started up, and she followed. There was no railing, and Kyra flattened her palm on the wood-paneled wall for balance. The stairs spiraled up in a dizzying curve. Sconces cloudy with dust cast dim light, lengthening the shadows, making it near impossible to see. She cursed her favorite stilettos. She could only place the tips of her toes on the risers. Her heels hung in midair. Her calves pinched with each step, and she breathed a sigh of relief when the stairs finally opened up onto another narrow landing.

Tarek peeked out of the doorway and into the hall. "Oh, that's our room. I didn't even notice this door, did you?" He stepped out into the hallway, careful not to let the door close.

"No." She followed him into the hall for a better look at the door.

It was no wonder they hadn't noticed it. It was concealed, decorated to blend in with the wall. Its bottom was painted in a dark oxblood that was almost black, and above the chair rail was the same botanical wallpaper. A flat plastic panel was set into the wall just to the left of the door, just like the one next to their guestroom.

"Look, Tar. A keycard panel. I don't think we're supposed to be in here."

Tarek pulled his keycard from his pocket and pressed it against the lock panel. A red light glowed and dimmed. "No, probably not." He stepped back into the service hall and looked up. "Do you want to keep going?"

"I do," she said, feeling a little spark of excitement.

Kyra went first this time. Her hand pressed against the wall as they climbed. Tarek placed a steadying hand on her hip, and she was glad for the extra stability.

The stairs opened onto another landing, nearly identical to the ones below, except it L-turned one more time, to a narrower, iron staircase that rose straight up, and at the top was a door with a decorative iron grate.

"Do you think that's the widow's walk?" Her voice came out in a whisper, and her heart thumped in her chest in anticipation.

Tarek may not have heard her. He was already in the third-floor hallway. "Looks like there are more rooms up here. It must be where the staff stay. Come on." Kyra threw a glance at the small metal door before following him.

They walked down the hall. The carpet here was the utilitarian kind that saw lots of foot traffic. Kyra felt her heel tips snag in the cheap fabric. The second door on the right was open and Tarek stepped inside. He turned on the light. It was a sort of breakroom. On one side, there was a kitchenette with a full-sized refrigerator, a stove, a table with six mismatched chairs. On the other was a couch facing a television, and a worn coffee table with a laundry basket full of lavender-colored cloth. The room smelled like stale coffee mixed with the caustic scent of cleaning supplies.

Kyra backed out of the room feeling like she was trespassing. "We are definitively not supposed to be up here."

"No. You're right."

They retraced their steps back to the staircase. In the vestibule, Kyra paused.

"Do you think it's open?" she asked, pointing to the metal door, and when Tarek frowned, she climbed the stairs and gave the knob a twist.

If it was the widow's walk, she wanted to see it. The knob turned, but the door didn't budge. She pushed harder, leaning into it. Her toes slipped on the metal tread. Kyra lost her balance and pitched forward. She gasped.

"Whoa, careful." Tarek caught her before she face-planted into the door. The intricate detail of the cast iron would have left a nasty mark.

"Thanks," she said, her voice breathy.

"Let me try. Hold on." Tarek braced his feet and used his shoulder to push against the door.

It cracked open. The wind howled on the other side. He opened it inch-by-inch, then suddenly the wind caught it, and it flew open with a *crash*. Tarek stumbled, catching himself on the doorjamb.

He reached for Kyra's hand and helped her through the doorway. It was low enough they had to stoop.

Outside, the wind hit Kyra's bare skin like shards of glass. She shivered. The widow's walk ran the entire length of the house's roof line, ending at either end in a *T* to access the chimneys anchoring each side of the house. On one side was the slate roof, pitching up to the roof's ridge, on the other a low rusty railing.

The decking beneath her stilettos creaked, and she shifted her weight on the slippery boards. The platform was in bad condition. It sagged and slanted in places. Kyra took a tentative step forward.

"Wow." Again, she didn't mean to utter it aloud.

From their vantage point, they could see the entire back grounds of Verinder House and beyond to Cape Poge. She imagined that during the day, she would be able to see all the way to State Beach across the sound, but in the last dregs of twilight, the sky and water merged in the murky darkness.

Eolian moans sent chills down Kyra's spine. The water churned, crashing onto the beach below. If she'd been a gothic heroine inside the house, here she was a specter, mourning her lost sailor for all eternity. She ventured further out, pulled by some phantom string. She stepped closer to the railing that barely reached her knees. Her heel caught between the slats, and she stumbled forward, just as a powerful gust of wind slammed into her, throwing her further off balance. The ground tilted up. The wind ripped the scream from Kyra's lungs.

Then, hands were on her waist, yanking her back. She fell against Tarek's chest.

"Jesus, shit," she hissed through her teeth.

"Fucking hell," he mumbled at the same time.

Her heart banged against her sternum. Or maybe it was his.

I could have gone over.

If she'd fallen... There was nothing below but the stone patio. She turned as if to look, but Tarek's arms tightened around her.

"Inside. Now." He didn't give her any choice, pulling her through the door. She stumbled down the stairs. Tarek struggled against the wind to pull the door closed. It slammed shut with a *bang* that shook the walls.

He ran his hands through his hair. His eyes were a little wild, and his breathing erratic. He set his hands on his knees and sucked in a deep breath.

"Do not go back out there."

Kyra stiffened at the command, but given that she could have died, and that her heart was still hammering against her ribs, she didn't argue. She had no intention of going out there again. Kyra willed her body to calm down. Her gaze traveled up the stairs, lingered on the door. The intricate metalwork, in the shape of a swan under an arbor, felt like a warning now. She shivered.

"Were you hurt?" Kyra shook her head, still not trusting her voice. "You're okay? You're sure?"

"I'm sure." She sounded croaky. "Just a little shaken. You?"

"I'm fine," he said, but she could tell he was lying. He was just as freaked out as she was, maybe more. "Come on, let's go find Chase."

Kyra followed Tarek down the servants' stairs. The descent was even worse than the ascent. She was still shaky from her near fall, her knees and ankles spongy and weak. Her feet didn't fit on the treads, no matter how close to the wall she pressed herself. She had to crab walk down, crossing one leg in front of the other. It was made more difficult by the slim cut and boning of her dress. The stairwell, its closeness, the heavy weight of the darkness, felt smothering, constricting, too much like being trapped in the caves last summer. A cold sweat broke out down her back.

After five or six steps, Tarek stopped. He turned around. "Take them off. You're going to kill yourself." Using him for balance, Kyra slid her heels off, and Tarek took them from her. "Stay close."

She walked down, one hand on the wall, the other gripping his shoulder. They didn't stop at the second floor but continued the spiral down. Kyra blinked against the threat of dizziness.

"This is making me nauseous," Tarek grumbled. "There's no way this is up to code."

We could ask Ali. But Kyra didn't say her joke out loud. She was too focused on not falling to her death.

They reached the ground floor, and Tarek helped her down the last few stairs. He handed Kyra her shoes and held her steady as she slipped them back on. Kyra took a slow, deep inhale. One, two, three … exhale, three, two, one.

The door to the hallway was now closed, and it revealed another door. Beside it, on the wall, was another one of the keycard panels.

Tarek cocked his head and tapped the panel next to the door that would open into the north hall with his finger. "We are definitely not supposed to be in here." He shot her a conspiratorial grin and she couldn't help but laugh. It was a giddy, breathy sound.

"What if we're locked in here?" she asked.

His shoulder raised in a noncommittal shrug as his gaze roamed over her body. His smile, more of a smirk, really, was all mischief. "I'm sure we'd find a way to pass the time." She failed at an indignant glare that made his smile widen into a grin.

Tarek pulled on the handle, and the door swung open. He held it for her, and closed it behind him, taking care not to let it latch.

His phone buzzed.

"It's Chase. They scored on a kickoff." He sounded ... disappointed.

"But that's good, isn't it?" Kyra didn't know, but "score" sounded like a good thing.

"Yeah, but I missed it." He frowned, and Kyra laughed.

"Let's go. You can probably catch the rest of the match."

"Game. Football *game*."

"Whatever. Maybe it's that one?" She asked, pointing to the open door across the hall. The only one on the north side they hadn't tried yet.

"Maybe." Tarek didn't sound hopeful. "This house is a maze."

Kyra didn't blame his lack of enthusiasm. She'd begun to wonder whether the Billiards Room was even real.

She crossed the hall and stepped inside the room. It was another parlor. French doors were ajar, revealing the dark patio beyond. The heavy drapes twisted in the wind. A man in a thick coat and a trapper hat was crouched in front of the fireplace, stacking wood. He turned when he heard them.

Kyra did a double take. *What?*

Wes Silva's mouth twisted, and he rose to his feet.

Tarek took a protective step in front of her. Silva squared his shoulders. He was taller and broader than Tarek. His size alone was intimidating, but accompanied by his cruel grimace, Wes Silva looked dangerous. Kyra swallowed.

"What are you doing here?" Tarek demanded.

Wes didn't answer. Slowly, one finger at a time, he pulled his work gloves from his hands, never taking his eyes off Tarek. He stuffed them into his pocket.

"What does it look like I'm doing?" he said.

His tone was bored, but his watery eyes narrowed to slits.

"Tar," Kyra warned and placed her hand on his biceps.

His muscles were rigid beneath her fingertips.

Last spring, Silva had broken into her house. He'd threatened her, tried to frighten her into leaving the island. Instead, she'd exposed his Ponzi scheme and ruined his business. The Silvas blamed her for their financial trouble and, by the way he was glaring at them now, she suspected Wes's opinion of her had only worsened.

His eyes flicked to her over Tarek's shoulder, and his sneer deepened, turned menacing. Her heart rate sped up, but Kyra lifted her chin and stared right back. She refused to let him see her fear.

Wes made a disgusted noise in the back of this throat. "Fuck this. Tell the old woman to light her own damned fire." He kicked a piece of wood into the hearth and stormed outside, yanking the doors closed behind him.

They didn't catch and sprung back open, blasting Kyra and Tarek with icy air. Tarek forced them closed, flipped the latch, and drew the curtains over the door. When he turned around, a muscle in his cheek jumped, and he crossed his arms over his chest.

The interaction had left Kyra feeling discomfited. She'd

spent the last few months carefully avoiding Wes Silva. On a normal day, Wes was unpleasant and surly, but Tarek's presence seemed to antagonize the other man to no end. She supposed it was more of the islander versus off islander nonsense that she couldn't really comprehend.

He squatted down by the fireplace and began re-stacking the wood. The logs *thunked* together with more force than necessary, and Kyra winced. He shredded a newspaper and stuffed it under the logs.

"Did you know he was going to be here?" Tarek's green eyes flashed.

"No."

Tarek grabbed the matches from the mantel. He swiped one across the striker paper, breaking it. He cursed, threw it into the fireplace, and tried another. This one burst into flame with a soft *fizz*. He held it to the newspaper. Smoke swirled above the pile as it fought to ignite the kindling. Tarek stood and wiped his hands on his trousers. In the flicker from the fledgling flames, Kyra noticed the hard set of his jaw.

Kyra smoothed her dress. She felt like she'd done something wrong, but she wasn't sure what. Maybe she should have anticipated something like this. Martha's Vineyard was a small community, especially in the off season. The residents relied on seasonal summer work, but they wouldn't turn down extra opportunities when they arose over the winter. Verinder House was supposed to have hosted a hundred or more people tonight. It would have needed staff.

"What is it?" Tarek's brow creased as he took in her troubled expression.

"About two months ago, Aysha phoned me. She wanted recommendations for Loriann's gala. The venue, staff, catering, drivers. I gave her Grace's contact information."

"Grace would have recommended Silva after last spring?" Tarek frowned. "The guy's a con artist. He's dangerous."

Kyra shrugged helplessly. After she'd given Aysha Grace's name and phone number, she'd pretty much forgotten about it.

"I don't know what Grace told her."

Tarek tossed two more logs onto the fire, causing sparks to fly up and dance in the updraft. "I don't like it—that he's here." He ran his hand through his hair.

"What would you have me do?" Kyra said, gesturing to the fireplace. "It's not like we can demand he leave. We'll just stay out of his way, Tar. He'll likely do the same. I doubt he'd have taken the job if he'd known we were going to be here."

Tarek stared out the French doors before finally shaking his head. "I know. You're right. I'm sorry. This isn't your fault. I just don't like the guy or trust him."

"If it helps, I don't either."

"Miss Gibson? Dr. Collins?" A woman's voice.

Kyra turned around.

Camilla was in the doorway, her hands full of crisp white linens. "Ms. Oma requested coffee and dessert service in here after dinner. I was about to set up. Is there something you needed?"

"No, sorry. We got a bit turned around looking for Chase and Gerry," Kyra responded. "But, Camilla, I was curious. Is Verinder House open year-round? Do you work here all year?"

If she thought the question a strange one, she didn't let it show. Camilla smiled and stepped inside the room.

Setting the linens on a chair, she said, her tone conversational, "We are technically open, but we don't have very many events in the off season. Unless there's an event, it's just Ben and I. We're the only full-time, year-round staff members. Everyone else is seasonal, but I assure you the staff here are all very qualified." Camilla glanced at the hearth, where the fire was roaring. "Why did something happen?"

"No, nothing like that. I was just wondering if Wes Silva worked here."

"Oh." She dropped the napkin she was folding and ran her hands down her lavender apron. "My brother warned me you may have a problem with it."

"Your brother?"

"Rene. Rene Ramos. He mentioned he met you last summer. And that you're not a fan of our cousin."

Kyra remembered the awkward interview with Rene Ramos. Kyra and Tarek had questioned him about his boat charter business. Wes had been there at the time, and while he hadn't done anything more than gripe and glower at them from a dark corner, he had made his disdain for Kyra and Tarek crystal clear.

Camilla's friendliness melted away, and she regarded them with an air of suspicion. "Ben engaged Wesley for the duration of Ms. Oma's stay and to help with tonight's event." Camilla folded her hands in front of her and leveled a look at Kyra, like she was daring her to complain about Wes's presence.

"Oh, that's nice," Kyra said lamely. She glanced at Tarek.

"Thanks, Camilla," he said with a disarming smile that didn't appear to work. "We were looking for the Billiards Room. Can you point us to it?"

Camilla's eyes narrowed, like she wasn't sure she believed they would let it go. "It's in the south hall. Go to the front foyer, and past the stairs. It's the second set of double doors on the right." Kyra nodded her thanks, and they turned to leave. "But, Dr. Collins," Camilla called out, halting them at the door. "I saw Mr. Hawthorn and Dr. James on my way here. They were heading to the Garden Room. Everyone is gathering there for Ms. Oma's cocktail hour. That room is in this wing. Go down this hall and it's the last door on your left."

"Thank you. We'll go straight there."

They retraced their steps back up the hallway. Kyra couldn't help but regret how the interaction with Camilla had played out. She felt like she'd made an enemy of the woman without meaning to. She'd only just begun not to feel like an outsider on the island, but she clearly hadn't been accepted by everyone. Kyra didn't think she'd ever fully understand the island's complex social dynamics. It was like navigating a minefield.

"This is it," Tarek said, stopping in front of the last room. It was one they'd found earlier, but now the door was closed. Low voices came from inside.

"Ready?" Tarek asked, his hand on the knob.

Kyra swallowed back her unease. She'd figure out a way to smooth things over with Camilla before she left. She nodded, and Tarek pushed the door open.

Chapter Fourteen

"Kay, Tarek!" Ali beamed and her eyes sparkled. She and Cam were standing close to the fireplace, looking like a still from an old film. Ali was dressed in a floor length, red satin gown with a high halter neckline. The long ties hung down her back between her bare shoulder blades. With her platinum waves pulled over her shoulder and striking blue eyes, she looked like old Hollywood glamor come to life.

"You missed the most amazing tour." Her matching red heels clicked on the parquet floors as she crossed the room. She grabbed Kyra's wrist and Kyra bit back a wince. Her aunt was stronger than she looked. "Ben took us through the servants' halls. Normally in renovations of homes from this period, to maximize space, they demo them and open up the rooms, you know."

Kyra gave her aunt a bland look, which Ali ignored.

"Ben was saying they kept some of them to preserve the historical integrity and for service access and extra storage. They're like these creepy haunted house secret passages, but with built-in cupboards. Such an ingenious way to make use of dead space. I can't wait to use those ideas in my own designs. Fascinating, don't you think?"

"Fascinating," Kyra deadpanned, but she couldn't help smiling at her aunt's enthusiasm. Ali was practically glowing, and it made Kyra glad they'd decided to stay. "You look beautiful, Ali. I love your dress," she whispered.

Ali smoothed the satin over her hips. She dropped her voice low so only Kyra could hear, "I bought it at Harrods. I told Cam I got it at Primark. Do not tell him."

"I'd never."

Ali gave her a sharp look.

"I won't. Promise." She meant it.

The dress was worth many times whatever Ali'd spent on it. It looked like it was made for her, and by the way Cam was watching his wife, he agreed.

"Good, because who knows when I'll get to dress so posh next? Someone refuses to get married." Kyra began to protest, but Ali's sharp laugh cut her off. Her smile turned smug. "Funny how you thought I was talking about you. So, you've thought about it?"

"Ali, no."

Her aunt hummed a self-satisfied sound and glanced around the room. She gestured to the bar set up in the corner. "Do you think that's a good idea?"

Tarek was waiting while the bartender made his drink. Asher was leaning against it. He was saying something to Tarek, and from his expression Tarek wasn't impressed.

"I don't think Tarek will punch him." Kyra eyed Asher and frowned. "Probably." Ali snickered.

"Kay!" Chase appeared beside her. "Someone cleans up nice." He dropped a kiss on the crown of her head.

"Thank you."

"I meant Ali." Chase avoided Kyra's halfhearted swat. "What happened to you? I thought you were going to meet us in the game room."

"We got lost. Then ran into Wes Silva."

"Silva's here?"

"Apparently, he works here," Kyra said.

Chase's mouth pressed in a straight line, and he shot a glance at Tarek. "Hmmmm."

"Who?" Ali asked.

Kyra bit into her bottom lip. If she told her aunt that the man who'd broken into her home and threatened her was here, at Verinder House, Ali would completely lose the plot. Kyra had zero doubts Ali would punch Wes.

"Just someone we know from the island. It's not important." Ali gave her a look that said she knew Kyra was lying. "Really. It's nothing."

"Would you like a fresh drink, Mrs. Babcock?" Chase asked with faux formality, and offered his elbow to Ali, who lit up.

"I would indeed, Master Hawthorn." Ali threw Kyra a delighted look before taking his arm and letting him lead her to the bar.

Kyra hid a smile behind her hand. She'd have to thank Chase later for distracting her, but he may have bitten off more than he could handle with Ali. She was as shameless a flirt as he.

Kyra took advantage of a brief moment alone to observe the others. Cam was talking to Gerry. Loriann and Elise were pinned to chairs while Assaf spoke down to them, his hands moving wildly, clutching his phone. Aysha was behind the bar, speaking with the bartender. *Where's Hedge Elmer?* He was the only guest missing, and as the event was held in his honor, his absence was noticeable.

"Tiresome, isn't it?" a gravelly voice asked, and Kyra looked up over her shoulder.

Asher. His smile held no humor. She took in his trademark three-piece suit, this time in a charcoal gray, the burgundy and gold—Omega Media colors—tie, and she tipped her chin in appraisal. Asher was the only person she knew who could casually wear a waistcoat without looking like an extra from a mobster film.

"Didn't feel like adhering to the dress code?" she asked, but with a glance around the room, she noticed that none of the men had donned tuxedos. Knowing Loriann, Aysha would probably get an earful for it, too.

"I put as much effort into this charade as it warranted." He leaned in close. "If it wasn't clear, it warranted none." He straightened.

"I thought you supported the merger?" Asher had been working tirelessly night after night, trying to close the deal. She knew because often she was on late-night calls with him.

"I do. But it's a business deal. I don't support this pageantry." His hand clasping his whisky glass moved in a semicircle around the room. "This is utter bollocks. She should have canceled it."

"You know how she is." But Kyra shared Asher's irritation. Loriann's *business is family* mantra was about as convincing in its democratic idealism as the English empirical monarchy. At the end of the day, hers were the only interests that mattered. Loriann was the irrefutable sovereign of her dominion.

"I do. I don't have to like it."

Kyra gave him an odd look, surprised by his admission. In their years of working together, Asher had always been devoted to Loriann. Even when he disagreed with her, he had her best interests in mind.

"How was the tour?" she asked, steering the conversation to something that felt safer.

Asher cocked his head to the side as if carefully selecting his words. "Informative? Your aunt is very knowledgeable about structural beams. And masonry." He gestured to the ceiling.

"I tried to save you. Ali's passionate." Kyra imagined everyone but Ali suffered a little on that tour.

"I'd say." But Asher's smile was genuine, and Kyra relaxed. Of course, her aunt would have charmed him.

"Did you see the widow's walk?" she asked. Asher was tall, nearly as tall as Chase. She couldn't imagine he'd have felt safe out there with the short railing.

"No, Alicia asked. It's decorative only now. Ben said that the company decided against renovating it when they learned that to bring it up to code would have obstructed the visual symmetry of the classical architecture." Asher spoke like he was repeating words he'd heard but didn't really know, or care to understand, their meaning. "Apparently, it's not safe." He went quiet, and his gaze shifted over the room. He stepped closer to her and when he spoke, his voice was low, just loud enough so she could hear. "Kyra, I still need to speak with you. Before dinner. It really is quite urgent."

"What is it? Should I get Assaf?"

"No," he said too quickly. His eyes darted around the room, and he stepped closer still. He leaned down and spoke low in her ear. "We can't speak here. Can you slip out to meet me?" He paused, rolling his lips. "Meet me in the library. I'll wait for you for ten minutes. Don't let anyone see you." He glanced in Loriann's direction and back.

Before she could object, Asher slipped behind the bar. He spoke with the bartender, who nodded and opened a concealed pocket door. Like the service door across from her suite, it matched the wallpaper and wainscotting. But once you knew where to look, it was obviously visible. Kyra smiled to herself. Ali would be thrilled. She loved pocket doors. Asher caught her eye. He pointed to his watch before disappearing through the doorway.

Kyra watched the door slide closed. Was she really going to steal away to meet her client in a darkened library? Normally, she wouldn't consider it. But it was Asher, and he'd asked her three times, now. Whatever it was, it must be important.

Tarek was chatting with her aunt and Chase by the fireplace. Kyra debated telling them she was stepping out for a few minutes, but with Wes Silva lurking somewhere in the house, Tarek would want to go with her. If she said she needed the ladies' room, her aunt would insist on coming. No, she decided. She needed to get in and out of the Garden Room unnoticed.

Kyra back stepped to the door. Ignoring the churning apprehension in her stomach, she double-checked that no one was paying attention and slipped out into the north hall.

Kyra pulled the door closed. She clenched her teeth

when the latch caught with a *click*. The sound reverberated in the dark, empty space. She strained her ears listening, but the soft din of conversation coming from the Garden Room carried on uninterrupted, and she let loose a breath. They hadn't noticed she'd left. With a final glance at the door, Kyra made her way to the library.

Chapter Fifteen

FROM HER EXPLORATIONS earlier, Kyra gleaned that Verinder House was designed so that many of the grander entertaining spaces and guestrooms were set along the perimeter of the house. Its intricate system of hallways, corridors, and smaller rooms snaked through the interior, where there was little to no natural light. These spaces were lit only by antique fixtures and the odd desk or floor lamp.

With all the doors shut, the north hall was dark and cold. Kyra didn't have her phone to light her way. With nowhere to keep it on her formfitting dress, she'd left it upstairs in her suite.

"Dammit," she muttered.

She didn't know which of the many doors along the corridor was the one to the library. Everything looked the same and, admittedly, she'd paid little attention earlier in the afternoon. When she and Tarek had found it earlier, the doors had been open.

Kyra hastened down the hall. Her heels sank into the thick carpet, something probably period-specific, and absurdly expensive. But she was thankful for it. The likelihood of slipping and falling on her face was lower as she hurriedly searched for the library. Asher would be true to his word. He wouldn't wait a second over ten minutes. She tried each door: the first was locked, the second room, another drawing room, was dark and empty.

The third door she tried was unlocked. It swung open on well-oiled hinges. Light fell across Kyra's shoes.

A man whirled around.

"What do you want?" Hedge Elmer demanded, scowling. His bowtie, embroidered with tiny mermaids, hung askew. His tuxedo jacket was undone, the right side of his shirt untucked. Camilla Ramos was behind him. Her apron, the lavender one, was crooked on her hips. She wrapped her arms around herself and swayed. Her face was ashen. Her brown eyes, wide and glassy.

"Oh, I'm..." The apology died on Kyra's lips as her brain processed what she'd interrupted.

It was clear that Camilla was neither a willing nor receptive participant in whatever was happening. *The actual fuck?*

Kyra pushed down her fury. She schooled her features and pasted on a haughty smile. One she hoped was reminiscent of Loriann's. "There you are, Camilla. I have a problem with my room. Do you have a moment?"

Camilla just stared at Kyra with wide, vacant eyes.

"Now, actually." Kyra's impatient tone seemed to jolt Camilla out of her trance.

"Yes." Her voice came out high pitched and shaky. "Excuse me, sir. Cocktails are being served in the Garden Room. Last door on the left." Camilla walked around Hedge, giving him a wide berth.

She stepped through the door Kyra held open for her.

Kyra yanked the door shut behind them. "Are you

okay?" she whispered.

Camilla straightened her apron with shaky hands. "How can I help you with your room?"

"Camilla." Kyra grabbed the other woman's elbow and pulled her down the hall, out of sight from the door and Hedge Elmer.

Camilla let herself be led, but her footsteps were slow and heavy. Kyra hoped she'd interrupted them in time and that Hedge Elmer hadn't hurt her. She steered Camilla to the back parlor, the one where she and Tarek had run into Wes.

The room was warm and cozy. Someone had been tending the fire.

"Camilla? Are you okay?" Kyra asked again, searching Camilla's face. "Did he touch you? Are you hurt?"

Camilla shook her head, her expression wary. "Ms. Gibson..."

"Kyra." Kyra took a step back, giving the other woman space. She held her hands up, palms out. "Please, I don't work for the Elmers. If he did something inappropriate, if he hurt you, I'll report it. Asher and Loriann would want to know. And Tarek, er, Dr. Collins is part of law enforcement." Not quite a lie. "Please, just tell me. Are you okay?"

Camilla clawed her hair away from her face. Her bottom lip quivered, and her eyes slid closed. She shook her head slowly.

"Camilla," Kyra warned.

"No, really. He grabbed me, but I ... nothing happened."

Kyra clenched her teeth hard enough to cause a pinch in her jaw. The implication was clear. If Kyra hadn't stumbled upon them, something would have happened. Her stomach roiled at the thought.

"We should still report him." Kyra patted her hips, her bum feeling for her phone. She needed to text Asher. *This fucking dress.*

"No, Kyra, please." Kyra stilled. "I swear. He didn't hurt me. I'm just shaken. I'll be fine. Please, don't say anything."

Kyra eyed Camilla, uncomfortable with her refusal. "Is it Ben? Would he not believe you? Us?"

"No, if Ben knew, he'd throw Mr. Elmer out. But the Elmers are important people in the Martha's Vineyard community. The owners of Verinder House won't care about me or what really happened. They'd fire me just to avoid the bad press or having to deal with the Elmers. And I need this job. Please. He's leaving tomorrow. I'll just stay out of his way." Camilla smoothed her apron, her shirt, her hair. She was putting herself back together.

Kyra let out a long sigh. "I won't say anything, if that's what you want." She agreed, but she didn't like it.

"Thank you." Camilla glanced at the door. "I've got to get back. I need to finish setting up in here and help my aunt prep dinner. Do you know your way back to the Garden Room?"

"Yeah, last door on the left, right?" she said with a weak smile. Kyra followed Camilla out into the hall.

"Yes, that way."

Camilla fished a keycard on a lanyard out of her pocket and pressed it against the panel in the wall. A doorway to one of the service corridors opened. The same one Kyra and Tarek had found themselves in earlier.

"Kyra?" Camilla said, her voice soft and still a bit shaky. Kyra paused. "Thank you."

Kyra made her way back up the hall. She checked each room, knowing it was fruitless. When she finally found the library, the lights were on. And it was empty. Asher was long gone, and there was no way her absence hadn't been noticed by now.

Kyra stood outside the Garden Room door. She smoothed the front of her dress and sucked in a long breath. Kyra pushed open the door.

Chapter Sixteen

CHASE TURNED TO face the door just as Kyra stepped inside. His hand went to Tarek's shoulder. He nodded in her direction, and Tarek turned around. He scanned her, and even from across the room Kyra felt the clinical assessment of his gaze, but he only dipped his chin in a curt nod and turned back to his conversation.

Her relief faded too quickly. Eventually, she'd have to explain where she'd been, and what she'd witnessed, but she intended to avoid that conversation, at least until she'd wrapped her own head around it. Hedge Elmer was lounging in a chair beside his wife's, like nothing had happened. Kyra made her way to the bar.

"What can I get you?" the woman asked, placing a napkin down.

Like the rest of the staff, she was dressed in black, with the signature Verinder House lavender apron tied around her waist. Something about the woman's face struck Kyra as vaguely familiar.

"She'll take a glass of the Bordeaux, Tali." Asher set an empty lowball glass down with a soft *thud*. He leaned back against the bar, elbows propped up. "I'll have another, as well."

Tali stepped away to pour their drinks, and Asher stared down his nose at Kyra. His eyebrow hitched up, waiting for her excuse.

"I..." Kyra's voice trailed off.

She had no good answer, or not one she could reveal. The irony was that if she told him, Asher would understand, and he'd take action, but she promised Camilla she wouldn't say anything, and she wouldn't, at least not yet.

"I'm sorry. Something came up."

"Something?" Asher's eyebrow rose the slightest bit and Kyra looked away, unable to meet his eye. "I see."

"Asher," Loriann called from where she was still sitting. "Bring me another boulevardier and a chardonnay for Elise? And do come have a chat with us."

"Right away." Asher accepted his drinks from Tali with a thanks and bent down so his lips were close to Kyra's ear.

He said, his voice harsh and annoyed, unconcerned about being overheard, "When it all goes to shit, just remember, I tried."

Kyra's skin broke out in goosebumps. She watched as Asher took a seat next to Loriann. He tapped his glass to hers with an indulgent smile. There was no mistaking the bad feeling that crept over Kyra, and she knew in her heart she'd come to regret not hearing whatever Asher had wanted to tell her.

Kyra took her wine and made her way over to Tarek and Chase. Chase glanced between them.

He shook his half empty glass. "Oh, look at that. My drink is low," he murmured and walked away.

Kyra stared after him. *Traitor.* She waited for Tarek to

say something, but he only held out a small plate filled with fancy-looking hors d'oeuvres—structured, bite-size things that were hard to identify.

"Hungry?" he asked.

She recognized it for what it was, a peace offering, and took one that looked the least offensive. She bit into it, and tasted something briny and salmony, creamy and herby all at the same time. It was delicious.

She made a small noise that had his mouth moving into her favorite half smile. "Good?"

"God, yes."

"I'll get us more." He handed her the plate.

Chase returned to her side, drink still half empty. "So, where did you slip off to?"

Kyra's eyes traveled to where Asher was sitting next to Loriann and Elise. Hedge Elmer was still in the chair next to his wife. When his gaze met hers, he scowled.

Chase pressed his lips together. "If I wasn't personally acquainted with the full-blown assholery of Hedge Elmer, I'd wonder what you'd done." Then his eyes went round in alarm. "Did something happen?"

"Not to me, no." But before Chase could ask any more questions, Kyra shook her head. "It's handled. For now."

Chase cocked his head to the side and his hair slipped forward. He pushed it back, his fingers entwined in the strands, while he studied her. "Are you sure?" Kyra nodded and his hand dropped to his side. Chase's gaze flickered to Hedge and back, and he looked troubled for a moment. "And you'll tell me later?"

Kyra nodded again.

"Then I suppose I should save him." Chase tilted his chin to the corner of the room. Gerry was standing against the wall, empty glass in hand, cornered by Aysha. "She's held him hostage for at least as long as you were gone."

"What could she possibly be talking to him about?"

"The island, mostly. She wanted to know what we thought of the Nest and where to eat in OB." Chase shrugged.

How Aysha knew about the tiny dive bar in Edgartown, the Raven's Nest, Kyra couldn't begin to guess. It wasn't the sort of place that Loriann would patron.

"Alright," Chase said, as much to himself as to her. "Going in." He moved across the room and threw his arm around Aysha with a too loud laugh.

Kyra set her still full wineglass on a table. She glanced at Asher, hoping to get his attention. Maybe he could tell her what he needed now, while everyone was preoccupied, but he was engrossed in whatever Loriann was talking about. She became aware of her aunt's presence at her shoulder when she inhaled the familiar scent of her freesia perfume.

"Are you enjoying the party, Ali?"

"*Mmhhmm*," she hummed. "Where did you escape to?" Ali asked and took a sip of her champagne. "Don't say the loo." When Kyra raised an eyebrow, Ali shrugged. "He noticed within two minutes of you disappearing."

Meaning Ali saw Kyra leave. Kyra hadn't been as stealthy as she thought.

Kyra glanced in Chase's direction. Now he was standing beside Gerry, his smile too big. He winked at her over Aysha's shoulder. Then schooled his features back into polite interest, refocusing on Aysha, nodding at whatever she was saying.

"I was only gone a few minutes for a work thing."

"So why was he worried?" With zero subtlety, Ali glanced at Tarek and back.

"I'm sure he wasn't. There's nothing to worry about."

Ali peered into her empty glass. "If you say so. I'm going to get a refill." Ali flashed a soft smile over her shoulder as she sauntered to the bar, the hem of her dress gliding on the floor.

Kyra sighed and rubbed her forehead.

"Gibs."

Kyra dropped her hand and looked up at her boss, forcing a polite smile. "Assaf. Are you having a nice time?"

Assaf bit his cheek. He shook his whisky glass, the ice *tinkling* inside. "Tell me, have you gotten any information from Loriann or Asher yet?"

And that's a no.

"No."

"But Asher was speaking to you. What did he say? Did he say anything about the new executive team? Did he tell you about the status of the contract?"

"No, Assaf. He was just complaining about tonight. You know he hates Loriann's events."

Assaf grumbled something that sounded like "ungrateful pillock." Assaf did not hate Loriann's events. He loved them. Large or small, business or social, he always weaseled an invitation.

"I don't like that they're keeping us out of the loop. Do you think they've hired another firm?"

Kyra considered it for a moment. If Omega Media was at all unhappy with her or Assaf, Loriann would have no qualms seeking alternative representation, but then why would she insist upon this dinner?

"No, I don't think so. I haven't heard any complaints about our work and I've been on the phone or conference calls with Asher daily. The deal is mostly done. There are only a few details left, and Loriann is handling those personally."

"The new executive team and workforce assets diligence?"

Kyra nodded. While it wasn't unusual for Loriann to see to some details herself, Kyra found it odd she was taking such an interest in the people aspect of the merger.

"And there's nothing else outstanding?"

"Nothing big. I sent the last set of drafts to Global's counsel earlier this week."

Assaf sucked in his bottom lip, displeased.

"Assaf," Kyra tried to sound placating. "You know if Loriann needs anything from us, she won't hesitate to provide an instruction."

"I know. I know." His frown deepened.

"Hey, the salmon ones must have been popular," Tarek said and set down a plate on the nearby side table. "There were only two left, so I chose some other ones." He gave Assaf a polite smile and held out his hand. "We haven't officially met. I'm Tarek Collins."

"Assaf Maloof. Pleasure." He shook Tarek's hand, then smoothed the lapels of his raisin-colored dinner jacket.

"Assaf's my managing partner. At the firm."

Tarek nodded. "The name sounded familiar." An uncomfortable silence descended on them.

Kyra could tell Assaf wanted to talk more about Loriann and the merger, but he wouldn't, not with Tarek standing there. Really, it didn't matter. She had no more information for Assaf.

"Tarek is a forensic profiler."

Assaf's frown disappeared, replaced by curiosity. "Really? What kind of cases do you work on?"

Kyra almost felt bad for delivering Tarek up to her boss. Assaf loved gritty crime dramas, especially ones filmed on location. She'd been an unenthusiastic guest at many of his and his wife's finale watch parties. He'd be fascinated by Tarek's job.

She half listened as Tarek explained in nondescript terms that he hunted murderers and rapists. That he was exposed to so much violence made her heart ache for him, but he patiently answered Assaf's questions about procedure and interrogations, and whatever else Tarek did when he wasn't on the island.

The service door behind the bar slid open, and Camilla entered the room. Her color had come back to her cheeks, but the way she stiffened when her gaze alighted on Hedge Elmer made Kyra think she was still shaken up by what'd happened in the library. Camilla smoothed her apron and made a beeline for Loriann.

Loriann nodded, and she held her hand out to Asher. He helped her to her feet. She made a polite coughing sound, a request for the room's attention. Conversation stalled, except for a feminine giggle coming from the corner.

"Dinner is being served. If you will please accompany me to the dining room."

Chapter Seventeen

LORIANN LED A procession out of the Garden Room and after a minute or two of activity, Kyra found herself alone.

Between disappointing Asher, Assaf's paranoia, Hedge Elmer's predation, and keeping an eye out for Wes Silva, Kyra felt like she was being pulled in a million different directions. She needed a minute to mentally prepare herself for the spectacle Loriann's dinner promised to be.

Kyra gripped the edge of the bar. She stared at the bottles neatly displayed behind it. She picked one and examined the familiar-looking label. A rare single malt she recognized as Asher's favorite. Loriann, or more likely Aysha, at Loriann's request, must have specially requested it. Loriann could be thoughtful, almost kind, when it came to her grandnephew.

Aside from Assaf, Kyra was the only other person affiliated with Omega Media who knew Loriann was Asher's great aunt, the result of his biological father's *teenage indiscretion*, as Asher put it. When he'd been a young boy, Loriann hunted him down in Wales, rescued him from his neglectful mother and a long line of men who were either uninterested or too interested in her child. Loriann had put him through the best schools, and hired him, promoting him through the ranks all in an effort to unseat her eldest brother—Asher's grandfather—and put someone loyal to her in charge of the day-to-day operations of her company. Asher owed everything to Loriann.

Kyra replaced the bottle. With the room empty, the keening of the wind was noticeable, a continuous low-pitched whine at just the right frequency to be uncomfortable and unsettling. The fire danced, snapping and sputtering under the onslaught. She moved closer to the window, one that looked out onto the front of the property. The trees and shrubbery swayed and bowed, casting trembling shadows across the lawn. Even if it hadn't been a holiday and the little ferries were not on a limited schedule, she suspected they'd have been canceled. Kyra felt an overwhelming sense of being trapped. She tried to suck in a slow, calming breath, but the bodice of her dress pinched her ribs and they came in sharp, shallow inhales, instead.

"Kyra?" She whirled around, her hand to her heart. Tarek peered around the door. "I was waiting for you. In the hall. Is everything okay?"

She nodded, but it didn't feel honest. "I needed a minute."

Tarek inclined his head in a sign of understanding and crossed the room to stand beside her. "Do you need more time? I can tell them you're sick, or you've gone to get something from the room?"

"No, thank you." Her heart warmed. "I'm sorry about before. When I left, I went to meet Asher." Tarek waited for her to continue. "I was supposed to meet him in the library, but I got turned around." She told him about stumbling across Hedge Elmer and Camilla relieved to share the burden of what she'd witnessed and thankfully thwarted. Tarek went rigid. Kyra laid a hand on his arm. "No, Tar. You can't say or do anything. She made me promise. She's afraid she'll lose her job."

He pulled her into a hug. "Alright. For now," he sighed, pulling away. "If she won't come forward on her own, you know that legally there isn't much I can do, anyway. But there's something else bothering you."

"Mmhhmm. You know how people like Hedge Elmer are. This is probably not the first time he's assaulted someone. And it won't be his last. Asher and Loriann have a right to know what kind of person he is. Who they're getting into bed with. But if I tell them ... Asher would blow up the merger all together. And Loriann needs it. Omega Media needs Global's distribution to remain competitive. If I tell Asher and the merger collapses because of me, Assaf will have a conniption. He'll be furious. I'd be sacked, without question." Kyra rubbed her forehead. "I'm just not sure what to do."

"When will the merger be complete?"

"As far as I know they're quibbling over tiny, insignificant details. I imagine it'll be executed any day now."

"We'll keep an eye on Elmer and the staff. We'll make sure he doesn't hurt anyone else tonight. And the rest of it, we'll figure it out."

"Thank you." He gave her a quizzical look. "For listening. For helping."

"Always, Kyra." He glanced at the door. "Should we go in?"

Resigned, she sighed. "I suppose so."

When they arrived in the dining room, everyone was already seated. Cam raised his hand. "Tarek you're over here." He pointed to the seat between him and Ali.

Kyra shot him an apologetic look, and then another less friendly one at Loriann, who raised an eyebrow with a smug smile. Separating them would have been an intentional move by Loriann, but at least she'd sat Tarek near people he knew. He gave her hand a soft squeeze before leaving her to take his seat at the other end of the table.

The only empty seat left was between Hedge and Elise Elmer. *Fucking lovely*, Kyra groaned to herself. She walked to her seat and what was left of her smile fell away when she saw her name neatly printed on a sheet of cardstock cut out like a maple leaf. Assaf, stuck between Elise and poor Gerry, glared at her and gestured for her to sit down.

"Sit, Gibs," he grumbled under his breath.

Kyra mumbled an apology and fumbled into her chair.

She chanced a glance at Hedge from underneath her eyelashes, but he was staring across the table, his mouth turned down in distaste. Elise, too, was watching Chase, who sat across from them. Chase was leaned back in his chair, lounging. He held a full wineglass aloft by the stem. His mouth was pulled into his trademark smirk, all smarmy self-indulgence. Kyra wasn't sure what game he was playing, but his mask was firmly in place.

A swinging door, camouflaged into the wainscotting and wallpaper flew open with a soft *pfft* and Camilla and the bartender, the woman Asher called Tali, entered the room, carrying trays of food and bottles of wine. They set them on the long buffet table, sitting against the wall between the two fireplaces that flanked each end of the room.

Tali began distributing small appetizer plates, starting with Loriann.

"You all will be delighted with the menu tonight, I'm sure." Loriann clasped her hands together. "I asked the chef to serve all local and traditional New England fare."

Aysha pinched her perfectly glossed lips together and stared at her plate.

Kyra suspected Loriann had little to do with the menu.

"So," she said, her eyes on Tali. "Tell me, what is this?" She pointed to her plate.

"Oysters," Aysha said with uncontained annoyance. "You order them all the time." This earned a warning look from Loriann.

Camilla set a plate down in front of Kyra and she eyed the four gooey blobs, each in its own shell.

"Yes, fresh local oysters. *Mãe* ordered them special from Mackey's," Tali said, placing a plate in front of Cam. "They were brought in this morning from Duxbury."

Mom? Kyra's heart sank. *Oh no. It couldn't be.* She tried to catch Tarek's eye, but he wasn't looking her way.

"I'd heard the Mackey women were finally importing after closing down that little operation in Menemsha," Elise said in her sandpaper voice. She sounded like a lifelong smoker after a screaming match. "Everyone knows Duxbury has the best oysters in the region." Elise made a *tsking* sound. "I'd told Mackey Senior for years that his silly oyster farm was a poor investment." She shook her head.

Hedge grunted and plopped the white relish-looking

stuff on top of one of his oysters and slurped it back.

"But Loriann," Elise rasped, looking down her nose at her untouched plate. "What nonsense has your chef been telling you? Oysters? Traditional? I've never heard of such a thing. Have you, Hedge?"

Hedge didn't bother acknowledging his wife. He continued adding dollops of sauces to his oysters and tossing them back. Kyra sat as far back in her seat as she could, putting as much distance between herself and the Elmers as possible.

"Oysters and other shellfish—clams, mussels, maybe lobsters all would have been a part of the first Thanksgiving meal." Chase said, letting his mask slip and catching the attention of their side of the table. Chase shrugged at their surprise. "Seafood would have been plentiful in 1621. They probably would have steamed them, though."

"Hmmm, how interesting." Elise pushed her untouched plate away. "Miss?" She raised her hand and waved her thick fingers; each stub nail painted a garish magenta. "Take this away. I don't want it."

Tali reached out to pick up the plate.

"No," Hedge barked. He reached across Kyra's chest and grabbed the plate from Tali's hand. "I'll take it."

Tali froze, but she recovered quickly, releasing the plate before it sloshed onto Kyra's lap. "Can I bring you something else, Mrs. Elmer?"

"Yes. Something cooked. And more chardonnay." She tapped her wineglass.

"Right away." Tali retreated a step just as the door swung open.

Kyra's heart sank further when her speculation was confirmed. Julia Silva, Wes's mother, stood in the doorway, the lavender Verinder House apron tied around her waist. In her hands, she held a large basket, and Kyra recognized the scent of Julia's homemade bread. Her stomach gave an involuntary growl, no doubt the definition of a Pavlovian response.

Julia's brown eyes narrowed on Tali, her daughter. "Is something wrong, Talita?"

Standing side by side, Kyra wondered how she didn't make the family connection immediately. Tali was smaller, and her features more delicate than her mother's or brother's, but the resemblance was unquestionable. They all shared the same cheekbones and wide-set eyes.

When Grace mentioned that Julia had taken a catering job for the holiday, leaving them to fend for themselves, Kyra should have guessed Loriann would have hired her. After all, she'd given Aysha Grace's contact information, and Grace would sing Julia's praises to anyone who'd listen. Even if Grace hadn't recommended her, Julia was reputably the best chef on the island, and Loriann would accept nothing but the best.

Grace must not have mentioned that Kyra and Tarek would be attending the event. She didn't think Julia would have agreed had she known. As if reading her thoughts, Julia's gaze found hers, and her expression soured.

"No, *Mãe*. Mrs. Elmer has asked for something else."

Julia harrumphed.

Kyra shifted out of the way so Tali could refill Elise's wineglass. Julia eyed the table. She reached between Gerry and Assaf and dropped the basket, causing the glassware to clatter.

"We will bring you something else, Mrs. Elmer. Does anyone else have a special request?" Her scowl landed on Kyra's untouched oysters, and Kyra tried not to shrivel under Julia's blatant disdain.

"No, thank you, Julia. This is perfect."

She heard Chase smother a snicker. He knew she didn't care for oysters and probably found her discomfort hilarious. She met Julia's icy gaze, hoping her smile didn't appear as strained as it felt.

Julia pointed to the basket. "Bread. For the table. Talita, Camilla. I need you in the kitchen." Julia stomped away and disappeared through the door.

Tali and Camilla scrambled to follow.

The guests stared after them. In the silence, the soft *thwap* of the double-sided door swinging back and forth could be heard like a hammer on wood.

Assaf cleared his throat and picked up his glass. "Testy old bat, isn't she? I'd be wary of what else she serves tonight." He forced a guffaw, but no one else joined in. "Oi, Cam, let's have at that, shall we?" He gestured toward the breadbasket.

Cam pushed it across the table closer to him, and Assaf unwrapped the linen from the fresh rolls.

"Doesn't smell poisonous." He put one on his plate. "Elise?" When she didn't respond, he placed a roll on her plate, then passed the basket to Gerry, who mumbled a thanks.

Kyra wondered what the mild-mannered doctor made of the motley group. Sitting between Assaf and Loriann, he was likely getting quite an earful.

Elise sniffed and picked up her butter knife. "I swear the help on this island gets worse every year."

"The woman can cook. And we forgive a genius her shortcomings, don't we, Loriann?" Assaf said, tearing into his roll and slathering it with what Kyra knew was Julia's homemade herb butter. "Gibs, on my soul, you lot should have been here last night. That lovely woman made us a proper English roast. With Yorkshire pudding." Assaf dropped a hand to his stomach. "I've never tasted anything better in my life. Even Asher was impressed. Loriann, wherever did you find her? We must have her to London."

Kyra would pay good money to see Assaf on the receiving end of Julia's ire if he asked her to cater a dinner in England. Just the idea made her hiccup back a laugh and her water went down the wrong tube. She started coughing.

"Are you alright?" Elise hissed and Kyra patted her chest.

Chase cocked an eyebrow, and she shook her head. *I'm fine*, she mouthed to him, blinking back tears, and tried to swallow some water.

"Julia Silva came highly recommended by Verinder House management as well as independent third parties," Aysha said, her tone clipped and defensive. "At first, she declined, because she had other clients, and she no longer does overnights. Omega Media is paying her well above her standard rate to give you the best possible experience. We're lucky to have her."

"You chose her?" Elise's penciled eyebrows flew up. "Loriann, I live on the island. You should have asked me. I know all the best caterers. Or we could have flown in a chef from the city. Nothing up here compares to what we have in New

York."

"Seriously?" Chase scoffed just loud enough that their side of the table heard.

"I appreciate the offer, Elise. Aysha, we will keep Elise's counsel in mind for next time, won't we?"

"Of course." Aysha's mouth stretched into a tight-lipped smile. "For next time."

Kyra picked up on the undertone of scorn and maybe something else. Elise wasn't making friends at Loriann's little family dinner.

Kyra turned her wrist to check her watch.

"Kyra, love," Asher said, leaning forward. "It's best you don't look. Knowing won't help. Tonight will be the longest night of your life."

She slumped against the back of her chair. It already was.

Chapter Eighteen

DINNER PROGRESSED AT a snail's pace. Tali and Camilla removed and replaced plates with each course. They filled wine and water glasses again and again. Julia remained in the kitchen, but her ire was felt with every dish Elise sent back, and she sent back most of them or demanded a change or substitution. After the fourth course, they waited for the longest twenty minutes of Kyra's life before Loriann broke down and sent Aysha to the kitchen to inquire about the delay. When Aysha slunk back in, she said that because of unscheduled changes to the menu, the next course would be served when it was ready. Loriann's smile was brittle when she thanked her assistant.

If Kyra hadn't been the demilitarized zone between the Elmers, she might have found the whole thing funny. Chase, at least, was enjoying it. He could barely contain his smirks and snickers each time Elise got into it with Camilla or Tali. From their whispers, she suspected he and Ali were taking bets.

Bits and pieces of her companions' conversations drifted down the table. Gerry and Assaf questioned Cam about the restoration efforts on his ancient MG MGB. He'd been tinkering with that thing for as long as Kyra had known him.

Last she heard; he'd removed the passenger seat but wasn't able to get it back inside.

Hedge droned on comparing the political environments in the United States and the United Kingdom. Asher muttered ambivalent responses during pauses in Hedge's tirade, but he had the decency to look appalled when Hedge suggested the US would benefit from having enlightened, effective leaders like those who devised Brexit.

Aysha prattled on about her stay on the island. She'd had a *fab bit of fun* in Oak Bluffs and was hoping to see more of Edgartown.

"Does Martha's Vineyard have a vineyard?" Aysha asked Chase. "A wine tasting would be divine. We could make a day of it."

Kyra moved her food around on her plate, half listening to the small talk around the table and willing time to move faster. She caught her aunt's eye. Ali smiled sympathetically and mouthed, "Thank you."

Kyra smiled back and inclined her head in a nod. Even if this small dinner was not the elegant gala they'd been expecting, Ali seemed to be having fun chatting with Tarek, Chase, and Gerry. Gerry's stories about late-night emergency room visits were unbelievable, but he swore they were true.

"Were you able to call Iggy?" Kyra asked Ali when the conversation lulled.

"Yes, Cam called Grace, and they got him on video chat right before we came downstairs. He was already ready for bed. Grace and Charlie bought him these precious jammies from the Sea Dog. I'd completely forgotten about the shops. We'd eat at the tavern in Vineyard Haven all the time. Dad would take your mum and I when we were little." Ali's smile turned soft with nostalgia. "Is it still open year-round? I remember it being one of the few options when we came in autumn."

"It is," Tarek said. "I haven't been in years either. We should all go while you're still in town. I don't think Kyra has been yet."

Kyra shook her head. "I haven't been. I'd like to."

"What *is* that?" Elise's gritty voice interrupted their conversation. She eyed the bowl Camilla held above Elise's charger. "More seafood? No. Take it back." She turned her nose away from the creamy soup. "I don't want it."

Kyra shifted in her seat. She glanced at her aunt. Ali's hand was covering her mouth, barely containing her giggles, relishing in Kyra's secondhand embarrassment. The door opened, and for a moment, everyone's attention was off Elise. Wes Silva backed into the room, pulling a dining cart. It contained the largest turkey Kyra had ever seen, as well as dishes of sides not unlike the ones her aunt had made yesterday—lots of mashed starches.

"Is something wrong?" Wes asked Camilla, his eyes narrowing on Elise then flicking to Kyra as his frown deepened.

"Yes. Something is wrong. I don't want that," Elise snapped and pushed the bowl Camilla still held midair.

Hot liquid splashed onto Camilla's hand. She flinched back with a sharp yelp. The bowl fell to the floor. It shattered, splattering Kyra with scalding soup.

"Shit!" Kyra shot back, pushing her chair from the table and jumped to her feet. Her napkin fell to the floor.

"Look what you've done!" Elise shrieked and waved her

hands at Camilla.

"Oh, my god. I'm so sorry." Camilla stooped to help pick up shards of bowl.

Wes disappeared and returned with a roll of paper towels.

"Here," he said, thrusting it into Kyra's hands.

"Thank you." Kyra dabbed at her dress, her legs, her soup-drenched shoes, in dismay. There was no way she'd get the smell of shellfish out of the suede. "It's fine, really. I'm fine," she muttered, handing the wet, dirty towels to Camilla.

Camilla gave her a doubtful look, but took the trash. Kyra climbed back into her seat. Everyone at the table was staring. She attempted a smile.

Loriann gave Kyra an annoyed look, like she was somehow at fault for being covered in soup. Then she turned her attention on Aysha, apparently deciding that it was best to pretend the accident hadn't happened.

"Aysha, what were you saying? About visiting Edgartown, was it?"

"Kay, are you okay?" Ali whispered across the table, concerned. "Do you need to change? I can come with?"

Kyra shook her head. *No, thank you.* She hadn't brought another dress with her, and Loriann wouldn't stand her sitting at the table in jeans. The dinner couldn't possibly last much longer. At least she hoped it couldn't. How many more courses could there be if the turkey was already out? Kyra glanced at Loriann at the head of the table. She was speaking to Camilla, pointing to the sideboard.

"I should be able to escape in a bit," she whispered to her

aunt.

Kyra's toes slid uncomfortably against each other and against the wet leather soles.

Wes took a position behind the cart and brandished a long, serrated knife. He began carving the turkey.

"Think Julia deep fried it?" Chase asked with a smirk as Tali placed an artfully arranged plate in front of him. Kyra appreciated his attempt at humor, but didn't feel much like laughing.

"Can you tell us about the different dishes, Mr. Silva?" Loriann asked.

Wes pointed to the plates with the tip of his knife and listed off the names of dishes with no explanation. Loriann attempted follow-up questions that were answered in monosyllables until she finally gave up with a huff and glared at her assistant. Aysha stared at her plate.

Dinner was served, and the conversation resumed, albeit more subdued. Asher explained the rivalry between the English and Welsh rugby teams to Chase and Ali. He'd been born in Cardiff and was a staunch supporter of Wales's national team. Ali, it turned out, was a big fan of brawny rugby players, period.

Kyra moved the food around on her plate, her appetite gone. Her dress clung to her. The sticky, slimy sensation of her thighs sliding against each other had her cringing whenever she shifted. The scents of wet suede and lobster bisque mixed together, making her stomach roil. Even if the meal in front of her had been appetizing, she wouldn't have been able to stomach it. Her feet *squelched* in her ruined shoes, and she resisted the urge to pull them off, worried she wouldn't be able to get them back on. *Although they're going straight into the rubbish bin.* But walking out of this terrible dinner barefoot, leaving streaks of soup behind her, was an indignity she wouldn't survive.

After what felt like hours, but was probably just one, Talita and Camilla cleared away their plates. Kyra watched Julia's bread disappear into the kitchen. She hadn't even tried any, which only rankled her already sullen mood.

At last, the never-ending dinner was over. Kyra set her napkin down and pushed away from the table. She needed to be out of her ruined dress and shoes, and into a hot shower immediately. Loriann made a soft coughing sound, requesting the table's attention. *Oh, for fuck's sake.* Kyra closed her eyes to gather what was left of her patience. She gritted her teeth and dropped her hands to her soup-damp lap.

Loriann coughed again and pushed herself to a standing position. She raised her glass. "Honored guests, I want to express my gratitude. I know this was not the event we'd planned." She side-eyed Aysha, who flushed. "But I am still so pleased we were able to come together tonight to share this time-honored American tradition with our friends, our family, and our new family at Global Media. I know our new venture will be a wild success. To the new Omega Global."

"Hear, hear!" Assaf crowed and slammed his palm down on the table. Asher rubbed his eyes with his thumb and middle finger.

"Getting ahead of ourselves, aren't you, Loriann?" Elise asked.

"Pardon, Elise?"

"Nothing's been signed." Elise shrugged.

Loriann's face went red under her mask of foundation and powder. "Whatever do you mean? I gave you the papers this afternoon." Slowly, she placed her glass down on the table, lining it up with the edge of the table runner. Out of the corner of her eye, Kyra noticed Assaf freeze.

"Can you get nothing right?" Loriann snapped at Aysha.

Aysha scrambled to her feet.

"I handed them to Hedge myself, Loriann," Asher broke in, his jaw clenched as he stared down Hedge.

"I read them." Elise raised her penciled eyebrows primly and reached for her wine.

She took a long sip, stretching out the moment. Loriann's expression hardened with each passing second.

"The price is a little low, given how desperate Omega is for Global's North American access." Elise's frosty lips twisted into a self-satisfied smile. "Was that your intention, Loriann? Are you trying to acquire Global Media at a discount?"

"The pricing was adjusted. I didn't realize you were interested in the particulars." Loriann shifted her gaze to Hedge. "Hedge?" Hedge sputtered, looking embarrassed, but before he could respond, Assaf's chair skidded back and toppled to the ground as he shot up. The force of his retreat upset his wine glass, raining drops of Barolo on his sleeve.

"What the fuck are you on about?" He glared at Loriann, swiping at the wine stains. "The price has been adjusted? That wasn't the deal I brokered. And I haven't seen any finalized documents." He turned on Kyra. "What did you do?"

"No, Assaf. We didn't need you or Kyra's services at this

stage. The deal had some minor changes that were handled this morning. Sit down."

Assaf's hand fisted his napkin at his side.

When he spoke, his words were measured. "You didn't need our services? You *are* working with someone else. Who is it, Loriann?" Loriann eased back into her chair and pursed her lips in annoyance. "Tell me who you're replacing me, *me* with."

Loriann leveled him a bland look.

"Loriann, Assaf, perhaps now is not the time," Asher warned. "We can discuss it tomorrow. We wouldn't want to bore our guests."

"Or perhaps it's the perfect time, Asher. The offer was finalized, the boards approved. Hedge, what's the delay? Why isn't my acquisition executed? What are you waiting for? You gave me your word it would be done today."

"My husband gave you his word?" Elise made a dry wheezing sound that had a loose resemblance to a laugh.

Hedge Elmer grunted and his jowls shifted, like he was grinding his teeth.

He eyed his wife with blatant disgust. "It's a holiday, things are delayed, but it is forthcoming, I assure you."

Elise muttered something under her breath. She'd spoken so softly, Kyra could have been mistaken, but it sounded like, *We'll see, you bastard.*

Kyra caught Chase's eye. He wore a half bored and half amused expression, but she knew he was listening, taking everything in.

"What sort of minor changes, Loriann?" Assaf demanded.

"Assaf, sit down. I won't ask you again."

"I demand to know. What changes? Asher?"

"Ugh, for the love of Pete, Assaf!" Loriann snapped. "Fine, because you are insisting, let's discuss the new entity, shall we?" Loriann steepled her fingers.

"Loriann, perhaps…" Asher tried again.

Kyra's head ping-ponged between the two, sitting at opposite ends of the table.

"Nonsense, Asher. Now's as good a time as any. As you know, at the Elmers' request." She dipped her chin in their direction. "The new company will be headquartered here, in the States, in the Global Media building in Manhattan. And, of course, since we will be a brand-new American company, we will be severing our contract with you, Assaf, and engaging local legal counsel."

Assaf sputtered, "Beg your pardon?"

"What don't you understand, Assaf? We will no longer require the services of Downe Mastiss." Her mouth twisted, and Kyra went still.

Her firm had New York offices. She'd worked in them for years before moving to London. Whatever this was, it was personal. The chairwoman's smile turned feline. Kyra knew that smile. Loriann had more to say, and it would be brutal.

Assaf glared at Loriann, then turned to Asher. "You," he snarled. "This is your fault. You've wanted me out from the moment she brought you in."

"It's no secret that I think you're too rash." Asher's gaze found Kyra's, and now he was speaking to her. "But I assure you, this was not me."

A red flush climbed up Assaf's neck and he sucked in a

sharp breath. His gaze fell to Kyra, then jumped back to Asher. "Too rash? Too *rash*?" His voice rose with each word until he was shouting. "What game are you playing? Why drag me here just to sack me?"

"For the record, Assaf, you were adamant about attending tonight's event. Aysha told you it was a social engagement, and we didn't require external counsel. I did not drag you here."

He stared at Kyra. Betrayal written across his face.

"Assaf, I..." Kyra was at a loss as to what to say.

She hadn't seen this coming. She'd been finalizing documents only forty-eight hours ago. Was this what Asher had wanted to tell her? That she was being fired?

Assaf's dark eyebrows hitched together, and he spun around to face Loriann. "If it wasn't for me, Omega would still be a two-bit production company doing advertisements for dentists and kebab shops. *I* brought in the investors. *I* convinced the talent, the channels, to take a risk on you. *I* backed you, Loriann, when no one else would. And this is how you repay me?" He sucked in a ragged breath. "Then why insist Kyra attend? Do you get some sick pleasure from humiliating us? Her?"

Kyra felt like she was on the outside looking in, an attendee at a play—one of those pseudo avant-garde ones that insisted on audience participation.

"Assaf." Loriann heaved a sigh. "You're making a scene."

"This is entirely out of order, Loriann. You can't abuse my people."

"Calm down. We have no intention of abusing our dear Kyra. This was an informal interview, of sorts. I wanted to get a feel for our new executive leadership team. Of course, I won't be relocating to New York." She gave a dramatic shudder. "I wanted to ensure she was the right fit." Loriann's smile was triumphant. "That she'd get along here, and of course that she was comfortable to stay in America. I don't want her running back to London." She said the last bit with a dismissive wave.

The room was so quiet Kyra could hear the soft click of a clock.

"Ah well," Loriann continued conversationally, as if she hadn't shocked everyone speechless. "Now that the cat's out of the bag and all that. No point in waiting. Kyra, I want you to join us."

What?!

"Excuse me?" It came out like a squeak.

"We were going to discuss it with you next week." Loriann stared down Assaf, challenging him to say anything. "But as it's already come out. What do you say? Come work for me? Head up the new US-based organization with Asher?" Loriann sounded gleeful.

"Kyra?" Asher's voice broke through the roaring in Kyra's ears.

But she couldn't look at him. Her shock had dissolved into fizzing anger. She raised a hand, silencing him.

"Loriann, I—"

"You'll regret this, Loriann. And you, too, Owen." Assaf threw his napkin on the table and, turning on his heel, stormed from the room.

"And that," Asher said, his voice carrying over the stunned silence. "Is exactly why I warned you not to discuss it tonight." His dark eyes flashed.

"It's done now." Loriann sat back in her chair, untroubled.

"And when were you going to discuss it with me, Loriann?" Hedge spoke up.

"The terms of the deal were that Omega would establish the leadership team, Hedge. As you can see, I've established it."

"Omega may establish it with Global approval, and I do not approve."

Loriann's eyebrow rose at the challenge. "Your approval was a courtesy. One that still may be revoked."

"This..." Elise looked down her nose at Kyra. "This is the person you were talking about? I thought..."

"Shut up, Elise. No one here gives a shit what you think," Chase snapped, and Kyra's heart thumped. His voice reminded her she wasn't here alone.

Elise sat straight, or as straight as her bent body would allow, and pointed a thick gnarled finger at him. "How dare you, Chase Hawthorn! Hedge, do something."

"I think a break is in order." Asher stood up.

He slid his hands in his pockets.

"Splendid idea. Aysha, please notify the staff we will take our coffee and dessert in thirty minutes and then meet me in my rooms. We have much to discuss. This went splendidly, don't you think? Kyra, I'll have Aysha email you the paperwork. No point in delaying."

Kyra could only gape at Loriann. She'd been played. This was why Loriann had insisted she attend this absurd event. She'd wanted to parade Kyra in front of the Elmers, show them who would be in when they'd been pushed out, with the added bonus of humiliating and discrediting Assaf.

"Loriann, I had the staff already set up the Bride's Parlor for after-dinner drinks and dessert. You can go when you're ready. I don't think…"

"Nonsense, Aysha," Loriann cut her off. "I need you with me tonight. Come." She waved her hand at her assistant and stood up. "Thirty minutes," she said and left the dining room.

Aysha muttered something in French and threw her napkin on the table before stomping out after her boss.

Ali's blue eyes were round. *Are you okay?* she mouthed, and Kyra returned her aunt's concern with a helpless gesture. She glanced at Tarek, who inclined his head toward the door, a signal that they should leave.

"I'll text you," she whispered to her aunt and pushed out of her chair.

Her heels clicked on the wood floor, drowning out the soft *squish* of her foot in each bisque-sodden shoe.

Chapter Nineteen

"WHAT WAS THAT down there?" Tarek asked, closing the door to their suite.

Kyra stood on the patch of hardwood floor, reluctant to step on the carpet with her soup shoes. Tarek stripped off his jacket, tossed it on the chair, and loosened his tie. She was at a loss, unsure how to explain being caught in the fallout of typical Loriann pandemonium. Kyra kicked off her ruined shoes and threw them in the waste bin.

"I've no bloody idea," she said, settling for righteous indignation.

She stared at her ruined heels, the cream-crusted suede. She'd walked miles in them over the years to and from client dinners and nights out. They'd remained in near perfect condition. One night with Loriann Oma, and they were destroyed.

"Kyra?"

She shook her head, slowly. Her hair slipped across her shoulders, and she shuddered. Although the spill was contained to her bottom half, her skin itched all over.

"I didn't know. When Loriann mentioned I could remain in the States during the merger talks, I thought it was because I was meeting so often on New York time, and they had me traveling into the city. And I wanted to be here, so I didn't question it. I didn't know she was conducting some sort of clandestine interview process or that she manipulated us to get me into the same room as Global Media's controlling shareholders." She heard her voice shaking and swallowed.

Looking back over the past few months, she should have seen this coming. This was classic Loriann. Everything she did served her own purposes. "Assaf will think I've betrayed him."

Her boss could be a pompous ass, but he didn't deserve to be collateral damage in Loriann's machinations. He was an excellent lawyer, and he hadn't exaggerated his involvement in Omega Media's success.

"Assaf knows you didn't betray him," Tarek said.

Kyra looked up. "You think?"

Tarek's mouth dipped to the side in a sad smile.

He reached up and ran his thumb along her cheekbone. "Your face. You were shocked. Everyone in that room could see you were stunned." He gestured to her legs, her feet. "You weren't burned, were you?"

"No." Kyra looked down at her bare legs. The red splotches had already faded. "I'm more embarrassed than hurt."

She clenched her teeth. She still couldn't believe that Loriann simultaneously fired her and bullied her into taking another job. If she wasn't so angry, she might have been impressed with Loriann's audacity.

"I need to get this smell off me." She reached for the zipper at her back.

"Let me." Tarek made a motion for her to turn around.

She stood still as he unzipped her dress. She peeled it from her torso and threw it into the bin on top of her shoes. Tarek watched his expression doleful.

"What?" she asked, clasping her arms over her breasts.

He stepped back, a soft pink warming the tops of his cheeks. "It's nothing. It's just that I liked that dress."

"Me too." She let out a long sigh.

"Go get cleaned up."

Kyra trudged into the bathroom, careful not to tread on the rug with her bisque feet.

"Hey." He followed her, pausing in the bathroom doorway. "Are you hungry? You barely ate anything."

He smiled when she said, "I could eat."

"I'll get us something from the kitchen." Kyra thanked him and he shut the door, leaving her alone.

Kyra stood under the massaging spray. The drops pelted her skin with a fleeting burning sensation. The water pressure at Verinder House alone warranted its five-star rating. She languished under the scalding water. She grabbed the small bottle of body wash and scrubbed at her shins, between her toes, behind her knees and all the way up her thighs, washing away the remnants of cream and lobster, the memory of that humiliating dinner, and leaving behind the cloying scent of Verinder House's signature fragrance.

Hidden away from the rest of the guests, and Tarek's acute observational skills, she let herself get properly pissed off. Loriann had gone too far this time.

Her law firm would probably terminate her. Omega was her biggest client. If they were firing her firm, Downe

Mastiss, LLP had little reason to keep her on. Kyra squeezed her loofa with more force than necessary and watched the suds swirl down the drain.

It was all by design. Even if none of this was her fault, Assaf would never forgive her. By offering her a new career in the same breath as destroying her current one, Loriann had effectively backed Kyra into a corner, forcing her hand to accept the job Loriann offered. And Loriann no doubt believed Kyra would accept it. Gratefully. That she would pack up her small insignificant life on the island, move to New York, and dedicate herself to Loriann.

Kyra cursed out loud. She should have seen this coming. It wasn't so different from how Loriann had strong armed Asher into replacing his grandfather as CEO three years ago.

Asher. He normally acted as a ballast point. His reserved pragmatism balanced Loriann's outlandish capriciousness. That he'd been complicit in Loriann's scheme didn't make sense to Kyra.

But had he been? Was this what he'd been trying to tell her? Had he been trying to warn her? Even so, she wasn't sure it changed anything. Perhaps she'd have avoided being held captive to Loriann's theatrics, but Kyra would still have found herself in the same position. Unemployed.

Kyra turned off the water. She wrapped herself in one of the hotel's soft cushy robes. She combed her hair, carefully detangling the knots. Loriann had miscalculated, though. She hadn't considered that Kyra had made a home for herself on Martha's Vineyard and that she'd been toying with the idea of staying. And after tonight, nothing could convince her to go work for Loriann.

She met her own gaze in the mirror. The prospect of being unemployed, of taking some time to figure out her next move, wasn't frightening. She wasn't sure if she was just numb from that disastrous dinner, or if she really didn't mind the idea.

She padded back into the bedroom. Tarek had removed the wastebin with her ruined clothes and, with it, the horrible smell. She was probably turned off lobster for life after tonight. She pouted, giving herself a moment to mourn the loss of her favorite heels. *As soon as I'm home, I'm ordering a new pair at retail and sending Asher the bill.* He owed her that, at least. She smiled to herself. Her plan, as petty as it was, gave her a sense of vindication.

Kyra pulled on a pair of jeans and the thick fleece pullover she'd added to her bag at the last minute. She hoisted herself atop the enormous bed. It had one of those feather mattress toppers that felt like being cradled by a warm, smooshy cloud. Even the pillows were soft and forgiving. She propped herself up and flicked through channels, looking for the sports game-not-match.

Her phone buzzed. Asher. This time from his Omega Media account. Kyra stared at the phone for a moment before opening the app.

"K-Dinner was a total cock-up. Loriann was out of order. But the job offer stands. Think about it. When you're ready to discuss particulars, find me. XX A."

Kyra snorted. Asher assumed she'd jump at the opportunity, too. Her thumb hovered over the delete button, then paused. She tossed the phone to the side and sagged back into the pillows. *Tomorrow. I'll deal with them tomorrow.*

Kyra settled for watching the highlights of the Macy's

Thanksgiving Day Parade. She had vague memories of it growing up, flimsy and hazy, and she couldn't say with certainty that she'd actually seen it or if she'd only heard about it when she was a child.

There was a soft knock, and Tarek opened the door. He carried a plate piled with fruit and cheese. Under his arm, wrapped in a tea towel, he held one of Julia's baguettes.

"You look like you're feeling a little better."

Kyra climbed to her knees and reached for the bread. Her mouth watered. *Please say there's a pot of her butter in here, too.* She found the tiny ramekin nestled between the brie and grapes and let out a soft hum. *Yes.* She sat back down, the plate balancing on her thighs. She slathered a warm chunk of bread with Julia's butter and stuffed it into her mouth. *So good.* Tarek chuckled.

"Much better now," she said between chews. "Was this Julia?"

"No, Talita, or she goes by Tali. Julia's daughter. Wes and Julia weren't in the kitchen. I'm not sure they'd have given me anything." Tarek mock grimaced.

He toed off his shoes and slid onto the bed beside to her, stretching out his long legs and crossing his feet at the ankle. He was wearing socks embroidered with tiny turkeys. She huffed a soft laugh. *Ali.*

"How many turkey-themed things did she buy you?"

"You'd be surprised." Tarek picked up the remote and began flipping through the channels, searching for football, no doubt.

Kyra ate. Tarek must have told Tali what he wanted, since the plate held a selection of her favorites. She spread a slice of apple with brie and honey. She held it out, offering it to Tarek, but he declined with a shake of his head.

"Do you know the rest of the Silva family?"

Tarek had grown up off the island, but he'd spent much of his youth there, and when he worked for the state police, he often handled cases on the Cape and Islands.

"No, not personally." Tarek picked up a grape, rolling it between his fingers before popping it into his mouth. "Tali was chatty while she put the plate together. She doesn't seem to have the same aversion to me as her brother, or maybe she doesn't know that he hates me.

"She told me she usually spends the winters in Brazil, but this year Julia took on so many catering jobs, she asked her to stay on the island to help. She's still planning to go back for a few weeks after the New Year."

"The Silvas are from Brazil?"

"I asked the same question. Tali and Wes were born here, on the island. Their father came to the States as a child and grew up in Fall River. It's South Shore." Tarek said *South Shore* like it should have meant something to Kyra. "Julia immigrated when she was in her early twenties. They both still have family there. When Tali goes back, she stays with her paternal aunt and cousins. She's trying to convince her brother to go with her this year. She thinks he could rebuild his construction business there."

"That could be good for him," she said, but with a tinge of uncertainty.

She didn't care for Wes Silva, but she didn't like the idea that she could have played a role in his exile to another country. The island was his home, and it should be big enough for them both.

Finding the game he wanted, Tarek settled back against the plush pillows. Kyra set her plate to the side and curled up beside him, resting her head on his chest.

"Thank you for the second dinner." Her voice came out muffled.

"You're welcome. Second dinner is a Thanksgiving tradition. I'm surprised I didn't see Chase scrounging for scraps."

A soft buzzing came from beneath the piles of blankets and pillows, and Tarek shifted. His hands patted the blankets until he recovered her phone.

Ali.

"Babes. Are you OK? That was fucking mental." Kyra glanced at Tarek, but he was intent on the football game, giving her privacy.

"Not really."

"Do you want to talk? I can come to you. Or you here? I'll kick Cam out."

Ali was Kyra's best sounding board. She'd listen to Kyra's complaints, let her analyze all the available options. She'd ask the right questions without offering any useful advice. All the while knowing what Kyra wanted before Kyra knew herself. Then she'd grin her stupid, smug face off when Kyra finally figured it out. It was annoying. And incredibly helpful. But Kyra didn't need her aunt's help this time. She was pretty sure she knew what she wanted.

"No, thank you. I think I'm just going to stay upstairs. Watch telly. I want to get out of here first thing in the morning. But you should stay as long as you want."

"Fuck that. We can go now. Cam and Tarek are strong swimmers. They'll cart us over."

Kyra snickered at the image.

"That Ali?" Tarek asked, like he didn't know exactly who she'd been texting.

"*Mmhhmm.* We're sorting out the plan for tomorrow. When can we leave in the morning?"

"The ferries start up around six thirty."

She relayed the information to Ali, and they agreed to meet in the front foyer at six. Kyra promised to text if she needed anything.

"You don't want to go back downstairs?" Tarek asked.

Kyra shook her head and Tarek pressed his lips together, studying her.

She thought he was going to argue with her, but he just turned back to the television. "Wanna let Chase and Gerry know?"

Kyra shot off a text to Chase and Gerry. Chase responded with a few suggestive GIFs that had her giggling. She felt lucky to have them, Tarek, her aunt, Chase. Each, in their own way, had known how to improve her mood.

"Ger and I are going back to the game room. When you get bored with T, come play."

"Are you ready to become a real football fan?" Tarek asked, increasing the volume when she set her phone aside.

"As I'll ever be."

Chapter Twenty

TAREK WAS EXPLAINING the different backs to her—quarterbacks, running backs, tailbacks, halfbacks... It was all very confusing and, in her opinion, unnecessary. He was so enthusiastic, though, talking with his hands, pointing at the screen. It was cute.

He knew all the players' names, their jersey numbers, and bizarre statistics that didn't seem significant, like *most completed passes over ten yards in snow games*. Tarek's voice was deep, and melodic, almost musical. Even if the content wasn't exactly riveting, Kyra enjoyed listening to him.

He nudged her.

"What's that? They score?" She shifted and squinted at the television.

"You're not paying attention," he accused her, but his tone held no venom and his green eyes sparkled. "Did you fall asleep?"

"No! I was listening."

"Then tell me what I just said."

She glanced at the screen. It was playing a deodorant commercial. *Shit.* She gave him a blank look. She had no idea what he'd been going on about.

"I knew it. You were asleep."

She might have dozed off. She shrugged.

"I asked if you were considering the job with the new company in New York?"

"Oh." Kyra sat up.

That was not what she'd expected him to ask, but she was glad he did. She wanted his perspective. She wanted to be a part of a team, one where decisions were made together, and she hoped Tarek wanted the same.

He waited, watching her, his eyes clear, patient.

"I'm not sure. I thought, maybe…" A soft knock on their door interrupted her.

"Hello? Kay?"

"Cam?"

Tarek muted the game and slid off the bed to open the door.

"Hey, Cam, come in." Tarek waved Kyra's uncle inside.

"Is Ali here?" He glanced around the room.

"No," Kyra said. "It's just us. She's not with you?"

Cam's expression was tight, like he hadn't decided whether he was worried or annoyed. He'd changed out of his suit and was back in that ridiculous flannel shirt from yesterday, the buttons done up wrong.

Cam shook his head. "We were watching TV. I may have fallen asleep." His mouth stretched into an embarrassed grimace. "When I woke up, she was gone. I texted her, but she left her phone in the room."

"And you don't know where she'd have gone?" Tarek asked.

"She'd mentioned she wanted to see some architectural thing. I came here first, though."

"If she went downstairs, she may have been caught by Loriann." Kyra drummed her fingers against her thigh. "Or she found the desserts." Ali was a bloodhound where chocolate was concerned, and there was no reason for her to avoid the rest of the guests.

"I forgot about dessert." Cam rubbed his forehead.

"I bet she's eyeballs deep in an éclair," Kyra said, and Cam chuckled, but it sounded forced. "Is everything okay? Is something wrong with Iggy?" Kyra asked, unnerved by her uncle's overreaction.

"Iggy?" Her uncle shook his head. "No. Grace messaged during dinner that he'd gone down with no trouble." He yanked off his glasses and cleaned the lenses with the tails of his shirt. "It's this dreich place. It's put me out of sorts."

"You grew up in Scotland. In the highlands."

"I know. It reminds me of home. Why do you think I moved?" Cam's mouth stretched into a sheepish half smile. "Where was dessert served again? I'll try there."

"I'll go with you," Tarek said. "Just give me a minute."

"Right, sorry. I'll be just outside." Cam backed out of the room.

Kyra scooted off the bed. "You're going downstairs?"

"*Mmhhmm.*" Tarek stooped to tie his shoes. "It's easier than explaining how to get anywhere in this house."

True. Kyra rummaged in her bag for socks.

"You don't have to come."

"Eclairs," Kyra said, tying on her sneakers.

"Liar. You don't eat sweets." He saw right through her.

Her uncle's behavior had made her uneasy, and she wouldn't be able to sit up here and relax while they were searching for Ali. Tarek pulled on his suit jacket and slipped his phone into his pocket.

Cam was leaning against the wall next to their door when they came out. He'd fixed his shirt. Tarek led them down the hall to the front staircase. From the bridgeway, they could hear voices speaking in hushed, clipped tones, distorted by the cavernous space. Tarek threw them a look and stepped a little heavier on the tread to announce their presence.

Julia Silva moved into the light and her gaze met Kyra's. Even from a distance, Kyra saw the woman's expression harden before she disappeared into the shadows of the lower south hall. Kyra couldn't see who Julia had been talking to, but she heard heavy footfalls retreating into the interior of Verinder House.

"Who was that?" Cam whispered, and Kyra snickered. Who knew he was such a scaredy cat?

"Julia. The chef," Tarek said.

Cam stared down the hall where Julia had gone. A loud *whoop!* came from the darkened hallway and he jumped back with a gasp.

"What was that?" Cam's eyes went wide behind his glasses.

Kyra gave him a playful shove. "It's just Chase, you big baby. Come on. Ali may be with them."

"It's just so dark," Cam grumbled. "You won't tell your aunt?" Kyra gave him a look, and he heaved a resigned sigh. Of course, she was telling Ali.

They rounded the southern side of the grand staircase to the hall behind. A rectangle of light cast out into the hallway about two-thirds down.

As they drew closer, Chase's voice became louder and clearer. "I swear. I called the right pocket."

A low response came from whomever he was speaking with. Probably Gerry.

"I think we found the Billiards Room," Tarek quipped.

Every light in the room had been turned on. Chase and Gerry stood on opposite ends of a pool table. They'd abandoned their jackets and ties, their shirts undone at their necks. Gerry's arms were crossed over his chest, and he was giving Chase an exasperated look that melted away when he saw them. There was no sign of Ali.

"Hey, I thought you were staying in," he said kindly.

"We were, but we lost Ali." Kyra splayed her hands, palms up. "We heard your voices and thought she may be with you, but she's probably at the dessert table."

Chase whirled around. "Oh right. Dessert." He tossed his cue onto the felt. He grabbed his jacket, stuffing his tie in his pocket. "I could eat."

"You can always eat," Tarek deadpanned.

"I'm growing." Chase puffed out his chest and grinned.

"You're twenty-six. You are not growing."

Chase and Gerry followed them back through the foyer and down the north hall. The doors to the Garden Room and the other rooms in the north hall were closed. Without the ambient light from the rooms' open doors, the hall was dark. Kyra's skin felt clammy and chilled under her thick pullover, and she shivered.

The darkness was suffocating. It reminded her of being lost in the cave system underneath the lighthouse. She and Chase had wandered around for hours. She could almost taste the stale air.

Chase's pinky finger linked with hers, and she looked up. His blue-green eyes were narrowed with concern for her and etched with his own discomfort with dark, enclosed spaces. Her nerves settled, and the creases at his eyes smoothed out. He let her go, and he fell a step behind, stopping under a flickering sconce.

"Did they run out of budget before upgrading the lighting?" Chase asked and prodded the dying lightbulb with his finger. It glowed bright with a *sizzle* before dimming. "Did they talk about the historical significance of walking around in the dark on the tour, Cam?"

"By the time Ali and the tour guide had gotten to the topic of electrical upgrades, I'd zoned out." He gave them a shrug and took a step closer to scrutinize the sconce. He ran his finger along the patinaed brass. The fixtures were rather unremarkable, which was strange in a house so lavishly decorated. "These may be original. It looks like they were modified, converted to electrical."

"How can you tell?" Chase asked, squinting at the sconce.

"He tinkers with old cars."

Cam threw Kyra a withering look. "I am an electrical engineer. See here." He pointed to the wires running along the base. "Odd choice. Why not just replace them with all the other upgrades they've done?"

They reached the end of the hall. A thin line of light shone from underneath the door to the back parlor. Kyra raised her fist to knock, but when her knuckles hit the wood, it swung open with a *creak*.

The room was empty.

A table holding trays of desserts, and the makings for coffee and tea, had been set up and tucked away to the side. A few cups and saucers lay abandoned on side tables, evidence that at some point someone had been there.

"She's not here," Kyra said, glancing around the room.

Chase was already surveying the dessert table and picked up a lemon bar. "Not much has been touched. Do you think they all went to bed already?" he asked.

Kyra glanced at her phone. It wasn't yet ten. She knew Assaf would be up for hours and Aysha struck her as more of a night owl.

"I doubt it. Loriann's parties often go late. Was there anything else on the agenda after dessert?" Kyra's question was met with blank stares.

"At dinner, Ali was talking about the widow's walk," Chase said.

"Do you think she'd have gone up?" Gerry's gaze traveled to the ceiling.

"Ben told us it wasn't safe during the tour." Cam rubbed his forehead and his gaze followed Gerry's.

"Hmm. Ger and I can check. Kay, you and Tar stay here in case she comes back. Does anyone know how to get up there?" Tarek explained about the back stairs across the hall, the tight stairwell, and the third floor.

"Just don't go outside," Tarek warned.

"I'll go with you," Cam said. "Can we stop at my room first? She may have gone back, and we missed her."

Once the door closed, Kyra's eyes went to the ceiling, to the window's walk two stories above. She worried her lip, a nervous habit.

She doubted Ali was up there. Her aunt was an architect. She spent half her time on construction sites. She didn't mess around with safety protocols. But if not there, where was she?

Kyra shivered and rubbed her arms. The room was cold, colder than the hall. The fire had burnt out, and only embers remained, glowing a faint orange. With each gust of wind, smoke puffed out into the room.

Tarek tossed another log on the grate and squatted down. "It's fucking freezing in here," he mumbled, poking at the fire.

He blew on the embers, trying to coax out a reluctant stuttering flame. Something caught the corner of Kyra's eye. She stared at the floor-to-ceiling brocade drapes. The ones Tarek drew across the doors hours ago. *Are they moving?* She couldn't quite tell. It looked like the curtains were shifting or it could be an illusion, cast by the tiffany lampshades and the fire. She crept closer.

"Kyra?"

An icy draft hit her ankles. She reached for the fabric panel and pulled it aside. The doors were open.

Or the right one was. It was no longer latched, and it swayed in the wind, letting in bursts of frigid air.

"Tar," she whispered his name and pulled the curtain all the way back, uncovering the doors.

Kyra reached for the door handle. The metal was cold and covered in icy condensation, like it had been exposed to the freezing temperatures for a while. She looked out, past the patio to the long, dark garden, and Cape Poge beyond.

Loriann wouldn't have stood for a draft. So, either she'd demanded they change rooms, or the door was opened after the guests had departed.

Foreboding settled like a brick in Kyra's stomach.

"Ali wouldn't have gone outside, would she?" Her voice came out hoarse.

To see the widow's walk from the back lawn? Kyra looked over her shoulder at Tarek. He'd already pulled his phone from his pocket, the flashlight app turned on. He tilted his head toward the door. Kyra stepped through.

The wind cut through her fleece, leaving her skin stinging and raw.

"Fucking, fuck." She gasped and wrapped her arms around herself.

The straight lines of Verinder House offered no protection from the gusts, and sand pelted her cheeks and hands. Outside, the howling was much louder, and the tree branches creaked and rattled under the onslaught. She hunched her shoulders against the wind. Tarek's hand found hers and he pulled her close. In nothing more than his suit jacket, he must have been freezing.

"Stay close."

He guided them down the path, shining the light on the ground. Kyra looked up at the sky, but the stars weren't visible. Wispy clouds glided in front of the gibbous moon. It brightened the gloom just enough to enhance the shadows, turning the patches of solid black mass to gray-scale. They followed the stone path as it snaked around the planting beds and down to the water. The crash of the waves against the packed sand grew louder as they got closer to Cape Poge. Kyra could hear the soft gurgle of the swash as the water was sucked into pockets on the shoreline.

Tarek stopped, and his hand tightened around hers. He turned around, pointed the beam of light up at the roof of Verinder House. Kyra's hair snapped against her face, and she held her hands against her head, trying to keep the strands away from her eyes. Tarek's phone's flashlight wasn't strong enough to light up more than a few feet in front of them. The first floor of the house was dark, but for the meager light from the back parlor's open door. One of the second-floor balconied rooms, below the end of the widow's walk, was just visible.

Kyra squinted. The clouds covering the moon shifted, and the roofline emerged, a black outline against a dark sky. But it was enough. She could make out the lines of the widow's walk. It was empty.

"It doesn't look like anyone is up there," he said.

"No." Kyra turned her back to the house, and let the wind push her hair away from her face, but facing into it, the wind stung her eyes, causing them to water. She blinked against the blurring, swiping her tears away with icy fingers, until the edges and lines of the landscape took shape. Empty rock and plant garden beds were separated by low brambly hedges in grids along the walkway. It would be lush with greenery in the warmer months, but was now barren. Her heart rate quickened. Her feet moved, as if propelled or summoned, further down the path to the beach.

"Kyra?"

But she didn't answer. She couldn't tear her gaze away from the strange shadow, dark against the moonlit sand.

Her heart stopped. "Oh, my god." Kyra tore down the path.

Chapter Twenty-One

"K YRA!"
She scrambled down the path to the beach. The pale blue lump lay half in the shadows, just above the waterline, but Kyra knew that blue. Knew the camel color of the faux fur trim that was shifting in the wind.

"Ali!" It came out shrill and choked.

Kyra fell to her knees beside her aunt. "Ali? Ali?" The pitch of her voice rose. "Ali!" She reached for her aunt.

"Wait, Kyra." Tarek stopped her, with a hand on her shoulder. "Let me." He squatted down beside her and gently turned Ali onto her back. He pushed her hood back. Ali's eyes were closed. Her face was colorless except for her lips, still stained red from her lipstick. His fingers went to Ali's pulse point. "She's alive."

Kyra's entire body spasmed. *Of course she's fucking alive.* Tarek's hands moved over her aunt, checking for injuries. He checked her neck, her shoulders, then the back of her head. He let out a hiss and pulled away. Something wet and dark covered his fingers. Kyra froze. The roaring in her ears drowned out everything. *No.*

"Kyra." He grasped her chin with his other hand, forcing her to look at him. "Kyra, listen to me." His voice was calm, commanding.

She blinked, nodded.

He thrust his phone into her hands. "Take this. I need you to shine the light."

Tarek picked up her aunt, cradling her to his chest as he stood. Ali let out a soft whimper and her eyelids fluttered, but didn't open. Kyra hiccupped back a sob. Even with that ridiculous coat, Ali looked so small.

"Kyra, go on. Lead us back."

Tarek laid Ali down on the settee in the parlor. He smoothed the hood away from her head. "Call Chase. Get Gerry down here."

Kyra fumbled with the phone; her thumbs too fat, too useless for the miniscule icons on the touch screen.

"Hey, you guys find her? She's not up—"

"Chase," Kyra interrupted, her voice breaking and too high-pitched. "There's been an accident. We're in the dessert room. Bring Gerry. Hurry."

"Wha—" His breath caught. "On our way."

Not nearly soon enough, Chase burst through the door, followed by Gerry and Cam.

"Kay, what's happened?" Chase froze.

"Ali—" But she didn't finish.

Cam pushed past Gerry and dove toward his wife.

"Cam," Tarek intercepted him. He took him by the shoulders and steered him to a chair. "Gerry," he said over his shoulder. "Looks like a head wound. Can you take a look?"

"Chase, get my bag from upstairs." It was like a switch flipped. The sweet, shy Gerry was gone, replaced by the imposing authority of Dr. James.

The doctor kneeled by Ali's head. He ran his hands over her body, just like Tarek had outside, checked her neck, the base of her skull, her spine, and limbs. He spoke as his hands moved, using words Kyra's brain recognized from binging medical dramas. She didn't really understand them though and didn't know if what Dr. James was saying was good or bad.

"Gerry," she whispered, but he ignored her and continued his ministrations.

She felt oddly separated from the scene around her, like she was underwater. Her hands fisted the bottom of her fleece, pulling it taut against the back of her neck. Cam was still in his chair, perched on the edge, gripping the armrests.

"Kyra?" he whispered, and her heart stuttered at the fear in his voice.

Ali was his whole world. *Their* whole world. Kyra should go to him, comfort her uncle, but she couldn't make herself move or take her eyes off her aunt.

"Gerry," she said louder. He would not ignore her again.

"Got it." Chase ran inside with Gerry's backpack.

Gerry unzipped it. He pulled out a stethoscope and a blood pressure cuff.

"Help me get her coat off."

Tarek held his hand out, halting her before Kyra could even step forward. He and Chase followed Gerry's instructions, leaning Ali forward to carefully remove the coat, one arm at a time. Gerry took her blood pressure, listened to her lungs, her heart. He prodded the wound on her head. Checked her eyes.

Gerry rocked back on his heels and slipped his penlight back into his bag. He looked at Cam, his expression grim.

No.

"Gerry?" It was barely a whisper.

"She needs stitches. She's concussed. I'd recommend an MRI and a few more tests. Can we get her to the hospital?"

"Will she be, okay?" Cam rasped.

He shifted forward in his seat, a request to let him go to his wife. Gerry stood, giving him permission.

"Chase," Tarek said. "Can you get someone from the staff? The property manager." Chase disappeared out the door.

Tarek pulled out his phone and moved across the room. His voice grew harsher with each word. He was arguing with someone. Gerry motioned for the phone and Tarek handed it to him. When he came back, his mouth was pressed in a line. Kyra had never seen Gerry look so serious.

"She's stable, so they won't come get her. They'll have an ambulance waiting first thing in the morning, or as soon as the wind dies down." He addressed Cam. "I can stitch her wound here, but there's not much else I can do except keep her comfortable."

Cam's hands were wrapped around Ali's. He was so pale.

"Will she be okay?" he asked again.

Gerry let out a breath through his nose. *Why won't he answer?*

"Gerry, please." Kyra begged.

Gerry finally looked at her, and the sympathy Kyra saw in his eyes made her want to scream. To run.

"We'll know more when she wakes up, but her reflex responses are good."

Something in Kyra's chest cracked. *No, not an answer.* Her nails bit into her palms.

"What's happened?" Tali ran into the room a half-stride in front of Chase. Her eyes fell on Ali, and she froze. Her hands went to her mouth.

"Tali, Mrs. Babcock has had an accident," Tarek said. "Dr. James is taking care of her, but he needs some supplies."

Gerry spoke quietly to Tali. Her gaze kept darting to Ali, but she nodded. Gerry gave her shoulder a squeeze, and she retreated to fetch whatever Gerry asked for. Tarek joined him in the corner. Kyra couldn't hear what they were saying. Her attention was focused on her aunt's prone form, the slight rise and fall of her chest.

"Cam," Gerry said gently, returning to Ali's side. He put his hand on Cam's shoulder. "We should move her back to your room. I'm going to give her something for the pain while I do the sutures. When she wakes up, she'll be more comfortable there." Gerry shared a look with Chase in a silent communication. He tilted his head toward Tarek, and Chase nodded.

"Cam, do you think you can help me get her upstairs?"

Cam nodded, like he couldn't trust himself to speak. With shaky hands, he carefully gathered Ali in his arms. She moaned again and Cam gasped.

"You're not hurting her. I promise." Gerry slung his bag over his shoulder and murmured something to Chase as he followed Cam out.

Kyra forced herself forward, intending to follow them, but Gerry put his hand up.

"Kyra, stay," he said in a voice that would brook no argument. Then he said softer, "I'll let you know when she's awake. Promise."

She watched helplessly as Gerry pulled the door closed behind them. She felt Chase and Tarek watching her.

When she'd seen Ali lying on the ground like that, she'd thought… Her stomach dipped in a wave of nausea, and she pressed her hands to her chest. She didn't want to acknowledge what she'd thought. Tarek gently guided her into a chair. He squatted down in front of her and took her hands in his. He peered into her face, his jaw set. She looked into his green eyes. His thumbs stroked the back of her hands.

"Is she alright?" Chase asked.

Even through her haze, Kyra caught the edge to his voice.

"She's shaking like a leaf."

"Kyra, Gerry's going to take care of her. Ali's going to be fine." Tarek pushed a tendril of hair over her ear.

Chase approached the drinks cart. He poured a measure of whisky, brought it back, and held it out to her.

"Drink this."

Kyra tried to accept it but her hands were shaking so bad, Chase passed it to Tarek, instead. He helped her take a small sip of the peaty liquid. It warmed her from the inside.

Chase sat on the arm of her chair and draped his arm across her shoulders. He gave her a tight squeeze.

"Ger's got this, Kay," he said, his chin resting on the crown of her head. "He's a superb doctor."

She looked up at him.

"Apparently? I've never checked his reviews." He grinned when she huffed a strained laugh. Chase somehow knew exactly what to say to pull her out of a spiral.

"He is," she said. Kyra had looked Gerry up when he and Chase began spending more time together. Dr. Gerry James was an excellent doctor.

There was a knock on the door and it creaked open. Asher slipped inside. Tarek stood up and slid his hands in his pockets.

"Tali found me. She said there was some sort of accident?" His tone was calm, but his gaze jumped all over the room before landing on Kyra. Alarm flickered behind his eyes, then disappeared. "Were you hurt?"

"It wasn't me. My aunt. She fell and hit her head." As she said it, it didn't sound quite right. "The ambulance won't come until morning. Gerry is with her. He's an A&E doctor."

"Convenient."

"Where is Ms. Oma?" Tarek asked.

Asher's eyebrows stitched together before his countenance smoothed out. "Her rooms?"

"And Ben, the property manager?"

"I believe he left for the night. I can ask Tali or Camilla to call him. Although I'm not sure what more he can do." Asher pulled his phone out and started typing on the screen. "Will Alicia be, okay?"

Kyra shook her head. *I don't know.*

"And there's no way to get her to hospital?"

"Not without a boat," Chase said. "The Chappy ferries are closed for the night, and with the wind." He motioned toward the windows.

"They won't put the first responders at risk," Tarek explained. "And according to Gerry, Dr. James, she's stable."

Asher stopped typing and his head whipped up. "There are no medical services available on this island?" Asher's dark eyes flashed.

"No, only a small fire station on the other side of the bridge. She's in better hands with Dr. James," Tarek said.

"You're serious?" Asher snapped, his expression incredulous. "What the fuck was Aysha thinking? This house is overrun with octogenarians and you're saying we've no access to medical? Jesus, fuck."

The room went quiet. Asher was right. It was irresponsible for them to be so far from emergency assistance. The irony was it was Ali who needed that assistance, not one of the elderly visitors. Kyra's laugh came out more like a hiccup and Chase rubbed her shoulder. She reached up and took his hand. Her gaze caught on her blue coat lying discarded on the floor. Kyra could see the dark bloodstain on the inside of her hood. That niggling, unsettled feeling returned.

Chase's phone buzzed, and he pulled it from his pocket.

"It's Ger. He says Ali's awake."

Chapter Twenty-Two

"Ali." Kyra burst through the door the second Cam opened it.

She pushed past him. Ali was in bed, propped up against the headboard. Her skin was paler than usual, tinged an acidy green. Her hair hung damp and limp around her shoulders. The smells of rubbing alcohol and nitrile burned Kyra's nose.

"Always the life of the party, right?" Ali's mouth stretched into a weak smile.

Kyra edged closer. "How are you feeling?"

"Like I was caught on the pitch during a Tottenham/Arsenal match."

"That's absurd." Kyra slid in next to her aunt and gave her a hug. "Everyone knows you're for Chelsea."

Ali laughed through her nose, then groaned. "Don't make me laugh."

Kyra pulled away. "Does it hurt?" She turned to Gerry. "Gerry?"

"She'll be fine, Kyra. We just need to keep an eye on her for a few days to rule out any complications." Kyra's head jerked up in alarm, and Gerry raised his hands. "Standard protocol with head trauma. I really don't think there's anything to worry about."

"See?" Ali squeezed Kyra's hand. "I'm fine."

"You scared the shit out of me."

"I knew you cared."

Kyra closed her eyes. Now that her initial terror was waning, her relief shifted, chafed. She was livid. She stood up from the bed and turned around, her hands going to her hips.

"What were you doing out there, anyway? Ben said not to go outside."

"Yes, well, I didn't think he meant out of doors. I thought he meant don't wander off the property."

Kyra frowned. *If we're being technical, that is what he said.* "Still, Ali! What the hell?"

"I wanted to see the widow's walk. Since we're not allowed to go up there, I thought I'd get a view from the beach."

"And did you?" Kyra snapped, earning a glare from her aunt.

"Ali," Tarek said, interrupting the brewing argument. "Do you remember what happened?"

"Tarek, maybe now isn't the best time," Gerry said, looking between Kyra and her aunt.

"No, no, it's fine." Ali's brow furrowed, and she winced. "Cam and I were watching telly, and he fell asleep. I wasn't tired yet, so I went to the parlor where dessert was being served, but no one was there. The drapes were open. And the lights were on down by the water. It looked pretty. I thought I'd take a walk to the back garden, see the house lit up. See the widow's walk. We don't see them often in England." Ali pressed her lips together, her brow furrowing. "It was cold and windy, so I got my jacket from the front closet and wandered down the garden path."

She cleared her throat, and Chase disappeared into the en suite. He returned with a glass of water.

"Thank you." Ali took a sip. "I couldn't really see anything from the garden, so I went further down to the beach. It was windier down there. And then..." She blinked, frowning. "I must have tripped and fallen. Struck my head. That's all I remember. I'm sorry."

Kyra bit into her bottom lip. When she and Tarek had gone down the path, it'd been pitch black, but unobstructed. Had she missed a hazard in the dark?

"Ali?" she began, but a hand came to rest on her hip, pulling her back.

Tarek gave the tiniest shake of his head, silencing her.

"Don't apologize, Ali. Get some rest," he said. "We'll check in on you later."

"I'd prefer someone stay with her," Gerry said.

"I'll be here." Cam slipped onto the bed and took his wife's hand. He pressed a kiss to the back of it.

Ali leaned into him, letting her head rest against his shoulder. Kyra's throat tightened, and she rubbed her chest.

Kyra could only remember Ali being sick once in all the years they lived together. She'd gotten the flu or some such and had been stuck home for days. She'd been a complete pain in the ass—refused to take the medications the doctor prescribed and complained constantly about her runny nose and cough. But despite feeling like shite, Ali insisted they stay up late watching bad rom-coms, snacking on ice cream—for her sore throat—and popcorn—for fiber. Even then, Ali seemed strong, unshakable. Kyra didn't like seeing her like this, small and vulnerable. It brought back memories of her mother wasting away from cancer.

"If you need to leave for more than a few minutes, text me. One of us will sit with her. If her breathing shallows, she sounds delirious, or has trouble with her vision, find me immediately." Gerry paused packing his backpack to take Cam's phone and enter his number.

Cam swallowed, the color draining from his face.

Gerry put his hand on his shoulder. "Cam, it's just a precaution. Her vitals and reflexes are good. She's in good spirits, all things considered." He smiled at Ali, who gave him a weary thumbs-up. "It's just a safety measure until we rule out anything more with the imaging tests tomorrow."

Cam nodded, but he didn't look convinced. In fact, he looked terrified, which only increased Kyra's anxiety.

"Maybe I should stay, too."

"No, Kay. I'll be fine. Gerry said I need to sleep, and if you and Cam are hovering, I won't be able to."

Kyra fidgeted. "Do you want for anything?"

"Tea?"

Kyra glanced at Gerry, who nodded his approval.

"I'll have some sent up."

"And biscuits."

"And biscuits." Kyra breathed out a relieved laugh and let Tarek guide her out. Once the door closed, he hugged her close, running his hand up and down her spine.

"You heard Gerry. She's going to be fine. She just needs rest and he's being cautious."

"I know," she mumbled against his shirt. "But knowing doesn't make me feel better."

Chase offered to run down to the kitchen and have tea and cookies sent up and disappeared down the front stairs.

"Do you want to go back to the room?" Tarek asked against her ear.

Kyra felt exhausted and wired all at once, but the last thing she wanted to do was sit in her room and worry about Ali.

"No."

"Okay. Come on. Let's go back downstairs." Tarek gripped her hand as they made their way to the main floor.

He brought them back to the Bride's Parlor. He guided Kyra to a sofa near the hearth and added logs to the flames. Kyra raised her hands to the heat. Tarek stood up and walked to the French doors. He ran his fingers along the door handle.

"What are you doing?" she asked.

"Nothing." He shook his head and flipped the bolt. With a soft smile, he pulled the drapes closed. "It'll warm up soon," he said and moved across the room to the bar cart. "Do you want anything?"

"Just water, please." Kyra heard the soft *tinks* of ice hitting glass. "What time is it?"

"Quarter to eleven."

Seven more hours.

Kyra ran her hands down her thighs. She wanted to be off Chappaquiddick. Now. She wanted to be home. The main island still felt like part of civilization. She had neighbors, access to shops and businesses, an airport. But Chappy?

She felt weighed down by the isolation.

Kyra let her head drop against the sofa back. She drew her feet up and wrapped her arms around her knees.

Tarek returned. He handed her a glass and sat beside her. He shifted her legs, so they draped over his lap. She sipped her water while he sipped on something that looked stronger. They gazed into the fire. The flames snapped and crackled, fighting the chimney's down drafts, but the room already felt warmer. Tarek ran his thumb along her shin.

Just then, the door opened, and Gerry walked in. He dropped his doctor's bag on a table and rubbed his temples. Kyra shifted, as if to get up.

"No, stay." Gerry waved her back down. "She's fine. I checked her bandage. Room service had just arrived when I left."

Kyra slumped back. "Thank you, Gerry. I don't know what we would have done if you hadn't been here."

Gerry gave her a tired smile. "No, thanks necessary. She really will be fine, Kyra. She just needs to rest. Is there still coffee?"

"I'll get it." Tarek patted her leg and Kyra shifted her weight so he could stand up. "How do you take it?"

"Milk and sugar, please." Gerry took a seat across from her. He stretched out his legs and leaned back in the chair.

Chase slipped inside. He'd changed into jeans and a thick fisherman's sweater. He held a fleece pullover in his hand.

"Here, I brought this for you." He tossed it to Gerry, who quickly swapped it with his suit jacket. Kyra noticed the drops of blood stark against his white shirt cuffs.

Tarek handed Gerry a mug and retook his seat. Chase fussed at the bar cart and returned with his own cup, although Kyra couldn't tell what it held. He flopped down in the chair next to Gerry and his gaze shifted between Kyra and Tarek.

"Are you going to tell us?" he asked.

"Tell you what?" Tarek asked.

"Whatever you're thinking. You both get this look." He pointed to his face and made a strained, pinched expression.

Kyra wanted to make a snappy comeback, but lacked the energy. And Chase was right. She was thinking. She couldn't stop thinking. Kyra pressed her lips together, debating whether or not to share what was bothering her.

"Spit it out," Chase urged.

"I don't understand how she fell. She said that the paths were lit up, but when Tar and I walked down, it was dark. There were no lights, but the paths were clear. It wasn't icy or anything. She's not clumsy."

"She did have a lot to drink tonight," Tarek said, but his gaze was on Chase, who was frowning.

"No," Kyra shook her head.

"Nah, Tar. Ali wasn't drunk."

Now that she'd started voicing her suspicions, she couldn't stop. Her voice pitched higher. "When we found her, she was lying face down. But the injury was to the back of her head…" She paused. *Maybe I'm remembering wrong.* She'd panicked when she saw her aunt lying there. "Could she have fallen, struck her head, then attempted to get up before passing out? Is that normal?"

"Kyra," Tarek gripped her knee.

"It does sound strange, though. Ger, what do you think?" Chase asked, sitting forward.

"I'm not trained in forensics," Gerry said, stirring his coffee.

"But..." Chase coaxed.

"No, buts. The laceration was caused by blunt force trauma, which is consistent with falls. I really can't speak to more than that."

Chase leaned forward. "Humor me, Ger." When Gerry tilted his head in a go-on motion, Chase asked, "What else is it consistent with?"

"Chase." The warning in Tarek's tone was clear, and Kyra knew it was for her benefit. He didn't want their conversation to upset her. Meaning Tarek was already considering whatever Gerry was going to say.

"No," Kyra said, placing her hand on top of Tarek's. "I want to know. Gerry?"

Gerry blew out a breath, eyeing Kyra. "Being struck. But—" He rushed, holding up his hand. "I can't tell you what happened from her head wound."

"You think someone could have hit her? On purpose?" Chase's gaze drifted to the couch where Ali had been laying. His expression grew more troubled.

"No, I didn't say that. I'm just saying her injuries were likely the result of an impact. That's all."

Tarek stood up. The muscle in his cheek twitched. "I'd like to check in with the other guests and the rest of the staff."

Kyra frowned. *Why?* There was no reason to check in with everyone else.

Someone knocked on the door. "Kyra, it's me."

Asher.

When Kyra nodded, Chase yelled, "Come in."

Asher pushed open the door. He took them in sitting close to the fire but directed his question at Kyra. "Tali said Alicia's awake?"

"Yes. Cam is with her now."

Asher nodded. He'd lost the jacket of his three-piece suit and had rolled his shirtsleeves up his forearms. "Is there anything I can do? Does she need anything?"

"No. We sent up some tea, but Gerry said she just needs rest. We'll take her to hospital tomorrow."

"Have you spoken to the other guests?" Tarek asked.

Asher's brow creased for the barest second before smoothing out. "I messaged Aysha. She'll notify our insurance company and will file a claim with the facility."

Chase and Tarek shared a look.

Asher narrowed his eyes and crossed his arms over his chest. "Kyra?"

"We want to make sure everyone's safe," Tarek said.

Asher's shrewd gaze shifted to Tarek. Kyra thought he resembled a miffed hawk. "Is there a reason they wouldn't be?" Tarek didn't answer, and Asher's mouth ticked up in a smug smirk. "In that case, I'd rather not raise an alarm unnecessarily."

Tarek crossed his arms, mirroring Asher. "I wouldn't say it's unnecessary."

"Assaf would want to know," Kyra said. "I can call him."

Asher raised a shoulder in a half-hearted shrug. "If you must."

Kyra pulled out her phone and dialed. It went straight to voicemail. "His phone is off." She redialed, frowning, but again the voicemail clicked in before it rang. For as long as she'd worked for him, Assaf's phone had only ever been off when he was on a plane, and even then, it was only with his loud objections.

"Still in a strop, eh? Always has been a moody bastard." At Kyra's unconvinced look, Asher said, "If it were anything more, you'd be the first person he'd call to sort it, no?"

Yes. Still, it was strange. Kyra rubbed the space between her eyes. *I'm just being paranoid. Ali had an accident. Assaf is throwing a tantrum. I'm overtired.*

"You're probably right."

"Of course I am." Asher dropped into a chair.

Under the glow of the firelight, she noticed the dark circles under his eyes, the rough stubble on his jaw. He looked like he hadn't had a good night's sleep in weeks.

"Mr. Hawthorn?" Asher called to Chase, who was back at the bar cart. "Be a chap and pour me one of those?" Chase pulled down a glass and poured Asher a whisky. "My thanks." Asher raised it and drank down half. He cleared his throat, and a smile ghosted across his features as he turned the glass in the light. "Kyra, I am glad Alicia wasn't seriously hurt. Truly."

Kyra looked up, surprised, but Asher's expression was sincere. She opened her mouth to thank him, but before she could, a guttural howl tore through the night.

Chapter Twenty-Three

THE CRYSTAL GLASS in Asher's hand fell to the floor and shattered. He jumped to his feet.

"The fuck was that?"

Tarek was already out of the room. Kyra chased after him, down the hall to the front of the house.

"Where did it come from?" she asked, looking behind her to see Chase, Asher, and Gerry.

"What was that?" Talita appeared at the other end of the foyer. Her eyes were wide. "It sounded like a scream." Her voice came out raw and breathy. Her chest heaved.

"Chase, you and Gerry check the north side. Kyra, with me."

"What about me?" Asher asked, falling into step beside Kyra.

Tarek threw him an annoyed look and led them through the foyer to the south wing of the house. Kyra had to jog to keep up with their long strides.

Tarek stopped at the first door and tried the handle. Locked.

"Shit."

"I can let you in," Tali said, stepping forward with a keycard. She looked to Asher, who nodded. She pressed the card to the keypad, and the door unlocked with a soft *click*. Tarek pushed it open and swept inside. Kyra followed, sliding her hands along the wall, searching for the light switch.

She found it, and murky light bled from the central chandelier. It was another parlor, similar to the Garden Room but with a piano. Floor to ceiling curtains concealed the view of the front yard.

"Nothing's here," Asher said after a cursory search.

Tali unlocked the doors of the next two rooms. The doors to the Billiards Room were still open, but it was empty.

The dining room was next. They filed into the long, grand space. Dinner had been cleaned up, the fires extinguished. The only evidence that the room had recently been occupied was the faint scents of roast turkey and Loriann's perfume.

Kyra didn't know what they were looking for. That sound they heard? It could have come from anywhere. An animal outside? Or even a loud television. It had been so strangled and raw. It hadn't sounded human. But something about Tarek's instant reaction made the hair on her arms stand on end, and her heart bang against her ribs.

"Tar, what are we looking for?" Kyra asked, standing at the head of the table, where Asher had been sitting.

He didn't respond. Whether because he didn't hear her or he didn't want to answer, she didn't know.

"Where haven't we searched?" he asked Tali, who was hanging back in the hallway, as if afraid of what they might discover.

"On this side? Just the kitchen." Tali's voice cracked, and she pointed to the service door across the room. "Through there." She crept into the dining room, her gait stiff. She used her card to open the door.

"You didn't come from there?" Tarek asked, pushing it open. Tali shook her head.

Unlike the rest of the house, the kitchen was sleek and modern. It hadn't been renovated with regard to historic or period details, but only to accommodate the state-of-the-art equipment. The stainless-steel surfaces reflected the bright overhead lights with a sterility Kyra associated with hospitals. Side-by-side industrial stoves mirrored the double glass front refrigerators on the other side of the room. Tea towels covered trays of baguettes on the metal island, and the air was heavy with the musty, warm scent of rising bread. There were no windows, but another door was in the far corner.

"What's through there?" Asher pointed.

"Basement access," Tali said.

Kyra's phone started buzzing.

"Chase, you're on speaker."

"We're at the back staircase. It's Elise."

Kyra's gaze locked on Tarek.

"We're coming." Tarek headed back toward the dining room.

"The service hall is faster," Tali said.

"Show us?" Tarek asked.

Tali went a little pale, but she swallowed and said, "This way." She pushed open the heavy-looking doors to the hall.

Across the south hall was another one of those doors styled to blend in with the wall. Tali held her keycard up to the panel and the electric lock disabled. She pushed it open and slid her hand along the wall for the light switch. Two ancient wall sconces flickered on, cloaking the room in soupy shadows.

"The back service staircase is on the other side of the ballroom."

They followed her through the butler's pantry, then through another set of doors to cut through the ballroom. Asher's dress shoes echoed in the vast, empty space. Milky moonlight shone through the wall of glass doors. Tali stopped at another camouflaged door and used her card to open it. Kyra heard voices.

Gerry.

Tali pushed it open and walked through. She stopped short with a cry. Her hands covered her mouth.

"Wait, don't!" Asher grabbed her by the elbow, and pulled her out of the way, leaving the view open for Kyra.

Gerry was kneeling at the base of the spiral staircase. He was leaning over Elise Elmer. Her cane lay abandoned to the side.

Gerry looked up when he heard them. His brown eyes were wide.

"Dr. James?" Tarek said.

Gerry blinked and his features shifted, smoothed out. He cleared his throat and pointed to her neck. "Cervical fracture." Then to the back of her head. "And a laceration here."

"Is she okay?" Tali asked, her voice muffled.

Kyra stared at the woman on the floor. *No.* Elise Elmer wasn't at all okay.

"I'm very sorry. She was already gone when we arrived,"

Gerry said. His gaze shifted to Chase, and he looked up at him, his expression full of sorrow. "There was nothing I could do."

Chapter Twenty-Four

TALI'S BREATHS CAME in short, wheezing gasps, too loud in the eerie silence. Asher pulled her further away from the body.

"Don't look. Breathe, Tali."

Kyra wished she could take Asher's advice, but she couldn't pull her eyes away from Elise's body crumpled at the bottom of the stairs—the odd slant of her neck, her blouse askew, pulled from the waistband of her full satin skirt. Even under the fabric, Kyra noticed her left leg was bent at an unnatural angle. Her eyes, empty and wide, stared up where the stairs disappeared above.

Tarek squatted down next to Gerry. The movement snapped Kyra out of her daze.

"Did you see what happened?" he asked.

"No." Chase's voice was gritty and hoarse.

He'd gone white as a sheet, making his eyes look too bright in contrast.

Chase swallowed and pointed up the narrow staircase, winding counterclockwise to the floor above. "But there's that." Kyra followed the line of sight to where he pointed. "She must have lost her balance. Hit her head there."

About a third of the way up, she saw it, a swipe of red,

glistening on the dark wood paneling. *Oh god.*

Tarek stood and pulled his phone from his pocket. He moved away, as far as he could, in the tight space and spoke with someone at emergency services.

"You want me to do what?" he seethed. "You have got to be fucking kidding me." Cursing again, he hung up.

He pushed his hands through his hair and turned back to them. He looked sick.

"You can go back to the parlor. Gather the rest of the guests. And we need the property manager. Tali, were you able to reach him?"

"No, I left a message," she said, her voice still strained.

"What? Why? What did emergency response say?" Kyra asked.

Tarek scowled. "Emergency services won't come to move a body. They'll send an ambulance over on the first boat to take her to the morgue."

"What?" Kyra asked. "What are we supposed to do with her? We can't leave her here."

"No. We can't." Tarek sighed and stared at the floor. His shoulders rose and fell with a deep breath, like he was steadying himself, and Kyra's confusion deepened. "Tali?" His voice was soft and gentle as he made his way to stand in front of her.

Tali's face was white, her breathing labored. Her gaze slowly focused on Tarek.

"I need your help."

Tali smoothed her apron, her hands shaking. "I … I…" She blinked against tears, but one still slid down her cheek. She took a breath and wiped it away. "What do you need?"

Kyra's heart went out to the poor woman who was putting on a brave face.

"We need to move the body. Do you know where we can put her for the night?"

Tali's eyes widened. Kyra's mouth fell open. *What?*

"The fuck you say?" Asher demanded. What little color was left on his cheeks drained away. His gaze shifted to Elise Elmer. His throat bobbed with an exaggerated swallow.

"You won't have to do anything more than show me a place. Somewhere out of the way. Cold."

Tali blinked. Again. She seemed to mentally shake herself. "The basement? It stays cold down there. And there is the wine cellar."

"Okay." Tarek's smile was reassuring. "That's good. Can you show me where it is?"

Tali wrapped her arms around her body, but she nodded.

"Asher, can you stay here, keep people out of this hall? I'll find a place and then come back. Gerry?"

"I'll stay with her." Gerry's voice was grim.

He unzipped his medical bag and rummaged through it, pulling out a sleeve of sterile gloves. Kyra's stomach turned. She forced herself to look anywhere but at the body.

"I can help," Chase said, throwing back his shoulders.

"We can handle it, Chase. You, go," Gerry said without looking at him.

Chase looked like he was going to object when Tarek shook his head and nodded toward Kyra. The intent was clear. *Take care of her.* Kyra stiffened, objections on the tip of her tongue, but to what end? She couldn't help carry Elise. She'd only be in the way while her friends transported a corpse. Ashamedly, she was relieved she didn't need an excuse not to be a part of such a macabre progression.

"If you need us..." Chase let the words linger and reached for Kyra's hand. He gripped it tight in his and ushered her around the crumpled body.

"I'll call," Tarek promised.

When the door shut behind them, Kyra leaned against the wall, staring into the parlor across the hall. Chase strode past her, into the familiar room and beelined for the bar cart. He sloshed whisky into a glass and drank it back in one gulp.

"Chase?"

He pushed his hair out of his eyes. "May come as a surprise to you and those who accused me of murder, but I've never seen a dead body before." He poured another measure, and sipped it, more slowly this time.

"Me either."

"Not even your mom?"

"No. My father didn't let me see her."

The fire crackled. The room finally felt warm, but Kyra still felt chilled down to her bones. She toed the carpet with her sneaker. Someone had cleared away Asher's broken glass, leaving just the damp spot. Someone had been here to tidy and refresh the dessert tower while Elise lay at the bottom of the stairs across the hall. The thought made her feel ill. Verinder House had continued to function, a well-oiled machine unbothered by the body of a dead woman lying on its floor.

Chase poked the fireplace, fussing with the embers. "I didn't like Elise. But I'm not sure she deserved tonight."

Kyra held her hands to the fire and shifted on her feet.

She hadn't known Elise Elmer before that afternoon, and that brief experience had been unpleasant, but she didn't wish the old woman dead. "What do you mean?" she asked.

Chase glanced over his shoulder and stood up, wiping his hands on his thighs. "All of it. Taking a digger down the stairs and cracking her neck. Her bastard husband selling her family's company from underneath her." He shrugged. "I guess that doesn't matter much now, though, does it?"

"What are you talking about?" Kyra asked, confused.

"Oh. You're still up." Wes Silva's voice startled them, and Kyra spun around. His large body was framed in the doorway. He nodded toward the drinks cart. "Can I get you anything else?" He spoke through his teeth, his tone dripping with sarcasm.

Kyra's temper flared. It wasn't her fault they were under the same roof.

"Just leave it," Chase said and turned away, dismissing him.

Kyra faked a smile. "You can leave everything. We'll be up for a while. There's been an accident."

Wes's forehead creased. "Did something more happen to your aunt?"

Kyra paused. Wes's question sounded genuine.

"No, not Ali. Mrs. Elmer. She fell down the service staircase. She's…"

"Elise is dead," Chase said.

Wes didn't so much as blink. He shifted his weight and the creases in his forehead deepened. "Dead? Are you sure?"

"Dr. James confirmed it," Kyra said. "We'll need to notify Mr. Elmer and Loriann. Do you know what rooms they're in?"

"I don't," Wes said, shaking his head slowly. "But Camilla or Tali would know. I'll ask." He walked over to a table with a small display of brochures and a phone. He lifted the receiver and dialed a short extension.

"Camilla, what rooms are Loriann Oma and Mr. Elmer staying in?" He gave Kyra a long look. "Come to the Bride's Parlor. And call Ben. There's been another accident."

Another accident.

His phrasing discomforted Kyra. It seemed a strange coincidence that two guests at Verinder House would take such terrible falls, but the house was a strange building full of hazards.

Wes set the receiver down. "Ms. Oma is in room 202 and Mr. Elmer is in 206. Mrs. Elmer was in 210. All even numbered rooms are on the south side." He crossed the parlor and pushed back the drapes covering the French doors. He turned a knob to the left. Kyra hadn't noticed it earlier. Flood lights brightened the patio. "I'll get more firewood, then see to the refreshments."

The doors clicked shut. Kyra sat down and pulled out her phone. She stared at the screen. She was debating her next step. Call Loriann? Assaf? Mr. Elmer?

Chase sat down next to her and dropped his head to her shoulder. She smoothed back his criminally soft hair and rested her cheek against him.

"You don't want to wait for Tar and Gerry?"

"Hedge could be looking for his wife."

Chase scoffed. "Doubtful."

Kyra flipped through the contacts on her phone. Loriann

wouldn't respond. Aysha would. She texted Aysha, telling her to call her or Asher immediately. She tried Loriann, but unsurprisingly, the call went to voicemail.

Kyra stood up. She dialed Assaf. The call went straight to voicemail. Again.

"Assaf, it's Kyra. Call me as soon as you get this. It's urgent." Kyra rubbed her forehead in annoyance. "Why won't he fucking answer?" she muttered. She tried texting him.

They waited ten more minutes. Nothing.

Kyra sighed. She used the desk phone and dialed Hedge Elmer's room extension. He didn't pick up. "Elmer isn't answering," she said, replacing the receiver. "I'm going to try his room."

Chase stood up and pushed his hair off his forehead. "I'm coming with you."

"It's not necessary," Kyra objected, but he cut her off, "I'm coming, Kay."

His tone was serious. It was so unlike him to make a demand. It gave her pause. She frowned, but dipped her chin. "Okay. You can come."

Chapter Twenty-Five

SHE AND CHASE walked back up the north hall to the grand staircase at the front of the house. Wes had said the even numbered rooms were on the south side. At the top of the stairs, they checked the placard.

"Looks like his room is this way," Chase said, pointing to the left.

"Mr. Hawthorn?" A woman's voice came from behind them, and they turned around. "Kyra?" Loriann assessed them, not bothering to hide her annoyance. "What are you doing here?"

Loriann had changed out of her evening dress into trousers and a cashmere turtleneck. Her large diamond earrings twinkled in the meager light. She had her laptop clasped to her chest in one hand, the charger in her other.

Kyra glanced at Chase. His shrug was more like a twitch.

"There's been an accident," Kyra said.

Loriann's expression darkened, and she sucked in her cheeks. "Yes, I'm aware. Aysha will have notified the insurance company, but I'm not sure why I should be held responsible for a woman wandering around at night."

Kyra started, taken aback by Loriann's insinuation.

"I'm not here to negotiate a settlement," Kyra snapped,

losing her patience with the old woman. "It's Elise Elmer. She fell down the stairs." Kyra pointed toward the back of the house. "Gerry, er, Dr. James thinks she hit her head."

"Dr. James?"

"Gerry, you know the man sitting next to you at dinner? My plus one." Chase leaned against the wall and crossed his arms over his chest. "He's an emergency medicine physician."

"I didn't realize he was a doctor. How fortunate. That is terrible for poor Elise. The staff can get her some ice. I'm sure she'll be right as rain in the morning. Have you seen Aysha? I sent her to fetch—"

"No, stop, Loriann." Kyra put her hand up and Loriann's mouth fell open, shocked. Kyra was probably the first person brave or stupid enough to interrupt her. "She's dead. Elise Elmer is dead."

Loriann just stared at them. Her mouth closed, then opened again as she searched for words. Finally, "I beg your pardon?"

"Elise is dead. She fell down the stairs. Broke her neck." Chase ran his finger across his throat. "Dead."

Kyra shot Chase a look. *Seriously?* He shrugged.

She turned back to Loriann. "Chase is telling the truth. Dr. James confirmed it."

"Dead." Loriann pressed her lips together, and her eyes slid closed. Her mouth twitched at the corners. Then her eyes popped open, bright and blue. She didn't look upset at all. In fact, she looked relieved. "Oh, a real shame that." She didn't bother to sound convincing. "Have you alerted Hedge?"

"We were on our way to his room." Kyra pointed behind her.

"Ah. Very good. Very good indeed. Have you seen Aysha or Asher? I need them both right away."

"Not Aysha, but Asher is meeting us in the back parlor. Where dessert was served."

"Excellent. Let Hedge know I've gone there. And find Aysha." Without another word, Loriann hurried down the stairs.

It wasn't until they heard the clap of her heels receding on the floor below that Chase pushed himself off the wall.

He moved to the railing and peered over. "Your boss isn't a big fan of Elise, huh?"

"Ex-client. And no, it appears not." Kyra frowned. "What even was that?" But she didn't wait for Chase to answer. "Come on."

Mr. Elmer's room was the front most room on the south side. It probably had views of the front lawn, like her aunt and uncle's suite on the north side. Kyra knocked softly. Nothing. She tried again, a little harder this time.

"Mr. Elmer? It's Kyra Gibson and Ch—" But Chase shook his head and she grimaced. She knocked again, wondering whether the old lecher would bother answering her. "I'm sorry to disturb you, but it's important," she called through the door. She heard rustling.

"Goddammit, what is it now?" he demanded, yanking the door open. Hedge Elmer lowered the phone he had in his hand and scowled at her. Then his eyes traveled to Chase, and the scowl shifted into fury. "What do you want? I'm busy." He held the phone against his chest.

"Mr. Elmer, I'm sorry to disturb you."

He gave her a condescending look. "I bet. What. Do. You. Want?"

Right then. Just get to it.

Kyra straightened her shoulders. "Mr. Elmer, your wife had an accident. We found her at the bottom of the service stairs. I'm afraid there was nothing we could do." Mr. Elmer stared at her. "She's dead. I'm so sorry."

They stared at each other until Kyra looked away.

Hedge Elmer glanced up at Chase, who affirmed the news with a nod.

"Is there anything else?" Hedge asked, lowering his phone and checking the screen.

What? "I … no." She stared at him, unsure of her next move.

"Thanks." He stepped back, letting the door slam shut in her face.

Kyra hopped back, and Chase grabbed her arm, steadying her.

"And what the hell was *that?*" she asked, pointing to Hedge's door, bewildered.

Hedge hadn't so much as blinked when she'd told him of his wife's death. *But it's exactly how I reacted when I learned about my father.*

When she'd received the news from her father's attorney, she'd sent back a terse thank you, and instructed him to take care of it. She'd felt guilty about her behavior, but pretending not to care about Ed Gibson had been her best coping mechanism. Now, on the receiving end of that conversation, she realized just how callous she'd been, and her shame burned anew.

Chase's grip on her biceps tightened, and he pulled her toward the stairs. He rolled his shoulder as he ushered her toward the foyer.

"What is it, Chase?" she asked. "What aren't you telling me about these people?"

"I don't know what's up with your boss, sorry ex-client, but I know some things about the Elmers."

Kyra pulled her arm from his grasp and waited for him to continue.

Chase shifted on his feet, uncomfortable. "Elise was the heiress to Global Media, and its fortune. Their marriage isn't exactly conventional. As you've seen, she's nearly old enough to be his mother. No one knows how he convinced her to marry him and turn over the management of her company. A little while ago, though, there was a scandal, and Elise took the reins back.

"It was a poorly kept secret that Hedge had mismanaged the finances and had done a bunch of other shady shit during his leadership. It's less well known that he'd been using the company's resources to cover his shady shit up, paying people off and the like. His failings at Global were bad, but the effect on the stock price would have been worse if he was fired publicly, so he's remained the CEO, but it's mostly been as figurehead."

"How do you know this?"

"Mommy Dearest. How else?" Chase started walking down the stairs again, leaving Kyra no choice but to follow. "With Elise dead, Hedge will regain control of the company. He probably isn't all that upset. I'd bet he's elated." Chase stopped on the bottom tread a few feet below her and looked back. "It's all his now. Well, his and his daughter, El's."

"When was the scandal?" Kyra asked, having guessed the answer.

"About a year and a half ago, it came to light."

Hedge's boat. The one Chase was blamed for sinking.

Chase heaved a sigh and glanced at Hedge Elmer's closed door. "Mazie, their granddaughter, was living with them that spring." Chase's expression looked pained. Kyra's hand tightened on the railing. "Her grandfather took an *interest* in her. Elise and her mother, El refused to interfere. She asked for my help. The plan was to steal Hedge's boat, throw a party on it, make some noise to draw the paparazzi. We knew once my name was leaked in connection with a stupid incident, the press would go nuts. They'd look into Mazie and then her family connections. Or maybe Hedge and Elise would be so pissed that they'd send her home. It wasn't the best-conceived plan, but she was desperate.

"But Mazie didn't know the harbor, and her boyfriend didn't know what he was doing. We hit something, and the boat sank in fifteen feet of water. I took the blame. It was essentially the same plan, just a much bigger and stupider incident.

"The press came sniffing around about my relationship with Mazie. She alluded to having troubles at her grandparents' home and seeking me out. Elise needed her silenced before the reporters dug into Mazie's story and found out she wasn't lying about her grandfather, nor was she the first, and that Elise had been turning a blind eye to her husband's activities for years."

"He sexually abused his own granddaughter, and her grandmother allowed it to happen? Covered it up?" Kyra's skin crawled.

There was no way she wasn't telling Asher. Hedge Elmer was a monster.

"I don't know how far it ever got." Chase shook his head. "Mazie promised the family she wouldn't tell if they handed over her trust fund and left her alone. We leaked the story of a falling out or a break-up, depending on your tabloid of choice. I did another stupid thing and the attention on Mazie died off."

"Chase." Kyra's heart broke for him.

"She's safe now." He shook his head, brushing off her concern. "I told you it's better if everyone believes it's me. We should get back. Tar and Gerry are probably looking for us." Kyra moved to step down, but Chase put his hand on her arm, halting her. "Just promise me you won't let yourself be alone with him."

Kyra put her hand over his. "I promise."

Chapter Twenty-Six

When Chase and Kyra entered the Bride's Parlor, Loriann was standing in the center of the otherwise empty room, her hands on her hips. She spun on her heel and leveled Kyra with a glare.

"Where is everyone?" she demanded.

"I'm sure they're on their way," Kyra said, rubbing her temple, but Tarek and Gerry had been gone a long time. They should have been back by now.

Chase gave Loriann a lazy shrug and pasted on his trademark smirk. He flopped onto the chaise in front of the fire.

Loriann threw her hands up. "Did you at least tell Hedge I was here?"

"It slipped my mind while I relayed the death of his wife," Kyra snapped.

Loriann gaped at her, her mouth ajar.

At that moment, the door opened. Tali, Camilla, and Asher entered, followed by Julia and Wes, who was carrying a heavy-looking firewood caddy. He set it down next to the hearth with a *thud*.

"Asher." Loriann pressed her hands together. "Thank goodness. Where on earth have you been? You've heard about Elise?"

Asher cocked an eyebrow at his great aunt's unsympathetic tone. He slid his hands into his pockets as he nodded. "I have. The police detective and the doctor moved her body to the cellar. An ambulance will be sent to retrieve her in the morning."

"Oh, yes. Unpleasant business that." Loriann's mouth twisted in an exaggerated grimace. "But there's much to discuss. I need a call with the financiers immediately. And our firm in New York. We can assemble the new board on one of those video call things you use." Asher tensed and something that looked like disappointment shifted behind his eyes. If Kyra hadn't known him as well as she did, she'd have missed it. "And for the love of Pete, where on earth is Aysha?" She spun around, her hands in the air.

She was met with silence.

"Have you tried her room?"

Loriann blinked and turned around. "What?"

"Have you tried Aysha's room?" Asher repeated his tone polite, but the tick in his cheek, visible when he clenched his teeth, revealed his irritation.

"Are you mad? That would be entirely inappropriate. You, there." She pointed at Camilla, who froze, a deer in headlights. "Yes, you. Go find my assistant. And get me a meeting room. One with media support."

"Now, hold on," Wes interjected, standing up from where he'd been stacking firewood.

"Wes, it's fine." Camilla put her hand up. "Yes, ma'am. I'll prepare the room you were using earlier."

"See that you do. And quickly."

"Loriann, it's almost midnight. On Thanksgiving. It's not yet six a.m. in England." But Kyra's protest died under Loriann's withering stare. "Fine." Her hands raised and dropped in defeat, and Kyra turned away.

Loriann might look like a gentle old woman, but one doesn't beat out three older brothers to turn their family's small video production business into a multibillion-dollar company without being ruthless. If she wanted something, she took it, with little regard for others. Asher was often the voice of reason talking Loriann back from potential public relations nightmares. *Like hosting a death dinner.* Kyra wondered what the investors would say when it got out that Elise Elmer had died at Loriann's dinner. Then she realized it wouldn't be her problem to deal with. She almost smiled.

Asher cleared his throat. "Right, well. I hate to be the barer of bad news and all that, but we have another issue." Loriann huffed her irritation but sat down in a chair. She crossed her feet at the ankles and motioned for him to continue. "We can't reach Ben."

"The property manager?" Kyra said at the same time Loriann asked, "Who?"

"Camilla tried his house," Wes said. He wiped his hands on his jeans. "His wife said he wasn't home. She thought he was still here."

"I don't see how their marital miscommunications are an issue for me."

Asher ignored Loriann's dismissal. "I am quite certain he said goodbye after the house tour. He said he would see us at breakfast."

"Could he still be here?" Kyra asked.

"I haven't seen him. Have you?" Tali asked Wes.

"Not since before dinner, when he gave me the keys to lock up."

Kyra didn't find the idea of Wes Silva being in charge of their safety comforting. At all.

"Where does he live?" Chase asked, sitting up.

"I think he said by the Mytoi Gardens," Tali answered. "On the other side of Dike Bridge. Camilla would know for sure."

Dike Bridge. Kyra shivered.

"Fuck. With this wind, if the tide came in, he may be stranded. The road was already washing out when we came in earlier." Chase stood and rolled his shoulders. "We should go look for him. I've got my car here."

"Chase." Kyra's voice came out hoarse. *No.*

"Right then. I'll go with you." Asher turned to Tali. "Tali, we need torches, er, flashlights. Do you have any here?"

"*Mãe*, do you know where we have flashlights?"

Julia was standing by the wall. Kyra had forgotten she was even in the room. Her hands were clenched in her black apron. She looked pale and drawn.

"There may be some upstairs."

"Bring whatever you can find." Asher turned to Chase. "Are you ready?"

"I need to grab my jacket and keys from the front closet."

"Tali, we'll meet you in the foyer."

Tali nodded and pressed her keycard against a camouflaged panel on the wall and slid open a pocket door, similar to the one in the room at the front of the house. With a nod, she disappeared into the corridor and the door slid closed.

Kyra watched them, feeling helpless. She wanted to dissuade them from going. Earlier, the road had been nearly undrivable. If the tide was as bad as Chase made it sound, they could be stranded or, worse, swept out into Cape Poge, but Chase knew this island better than anyone here. He'd have the best chance of finding someone out there.

"Please, just be careful."

Chase's expression softened. "I will." He glanced at Wes and the door, then back at Kyra. "Will you be okay?"

Wes snorted.

"Why wouldn't she be?" Tarek's voice carried through the room.

He held the door open for Gerry. The doctor looked exhausted.

"I'll be fine. Tar, the house manager, Ben, left the property a few hours ago, but he never arrived home. He lives on the other side of the bridge," Kyra explained.

"Owens and I are going to drive up to Dike Bridge, make sure he didn't get himself stranded."

"I'll go with you." Gerry hitched his bag higher on his shoulder.

"Thanks." Chase gave him a grateful smile.

Loriann made a disgusted noise in her throat, silencing the room. Asher stiffened. She was holding her phone close to her face, squinting. She dropped it in her lap and looked up at her nephew. "For the love of Pete. Where is that girl? I need my bloody reading glasses."

"Are we ready?" Asher asked, and Gerry nodded, his expression grim.

Chase nudged Kyra's foot with his own. "You won't be able to reach us once we're out of range of the Wi-Fi. I didn't have cell service when we were driving up. How about you?" he asked Asher.

"Not since I've landed on this bloody rock."

Tarek's mouth was set in a thin line, but he gripped Chase's hand. "Watch the water levels."

"I know."

Chapter Twenty-Seven

"Aysha?" Kyra called through the door of the room assigned to Loriann's assistant. She knocked again. "Aysha, it's Kyra and Tarek. Are you awake?"

Shortly after the men left to search for Ben, Camilla returned to the Bride's Parlor. She told Loriann she'd searched the entire main floor and wasn't able to find her assistant. Camilla called her room phone, but it had gone unanswered. Loriann demanded Camilla search everywhere else for Aysha and set up the meeting room she needed.

"My cousin can either help set up your god damned conference call, or search the property for your employee," Wes had growled at Loriann. "Pick one."

"Loriann." Kyra knew she was wasting her breath, but tried nevertheless. "A woman is dead. Let's find Aysha, and we can sort the paperwork tomorrow."

"For the love of Pete!" Loriann threw up her hands. "This is ridiculous. I need those signatures as soon as possible, Kyra. Meaning now. You go find Aysha. And you!" She'd glared at Camilla. "Get me my meeting space."

Only after Loriann threatened to sue, and Kyra promised she would be respectful, did Camilla program her a keycard and, noticeably relieved, retreated to set up Loriann's meeting room.

Kyra tried knocking on Aysha's door again. She cocked her head, listening, but she heard no sound coming from within.

"I don't think she's in there." She ran her thumb across the smooth plastic of the keycard, debating.

"Go ahead. Open it."

"Aysha, I'm going to open the door." She pressed the keycard to the panel and pushed the door open a crack. The room was dark. "Aysha? Aysha, are you in here?"

Tarek pushed the door open wider and ran his hand along the wall until he found the light switch. Aysha had one of the interior rooms. It was smaller but no less ornate than the suite Kyra shared with Tarek. The four-poster, king-sized bed took up most of the floor space. Sliding glass doors opened onto a Juliet balcony overlooking the grand staircase and the foyer below. A small desk had been pushed against a wall, and in the corner, behind the door, was a wardrobe.

The bed was neatly made, tucked in at the corners. A down comforter was folded across the bottom. The room smelled faintly of Aysha's perfume, something citrusy and warm. Kyra checked the en suite. The vanity was littered with cosmetics. A silk kimono hung from the hook on the door.

Tarek opened the wardrobe. Aysha's vintage-inspired luggage lay on the bottom, next to her laptop case. Her clothes were neatly folded and stacked on the shelves or hanging from the hangers. The blue dress she'd worn to dinner hung on the back of the door. Three pairs of pumps were lined up next to her suitcase. Kyra pushed aside the clothes, scanning the wardrobe's contents.

"Do you see her purse? Her phone? Her wallet?"

Tarek searched the desk, opening and scanning the drawers' contents. "She probably has her phone on her. Maybe her purse is with her coat in the coatroom downstairs?"

Kyra frowned. It was possible, but she thought it unlikely. In her experience, women weren't separated from their handbags. "Maybe. We'll check when we go back downstairs."

Tarek opened the top desk drawer. He pulled out a leather-bound folio stamped with the Omega Media logo.

"Look at this." He flipped it open and thumbed through the pages. "She has her and Loriann's passports and travel documents. The Verinder House contract. Oh, also this." He held up a thick manilla envelope, marked CONFIDENTIAL in thick black letters.

Kyra opened it and pulled out the sheaf of papers. "This is a copy of the merger agreement." She returned it to Aysha's folio.

She stared at their passports and the first-class tickets tucked into the retaining flap. *Wherever she is, she planned on coming back to her room.* The thought made her pause. She returned to the wardrobe, studied its contents. It was full of tailored business suits and formalwear, designer dress shoes. Nothing casual.

"Tar, do you think she could have left the property?"

His answer came quickly. "I don't think she's in the house. Unless she's hiding."

"But where would she go?" She remembered Aysha's

shortness with Loriann earlier. She'd protested her required presence at dessert service. "Do you think she'd have gone off with Assaf? Or Ben?"

The corner of Tarek's mouth hitched down. "You know Aysha better than I do. You tell me? Would she leave Loriann's party to go somewhere with the property manager or your boss?"

Kyra's relationship with Aysha had been mostly transactional. She really didn't know the girl that well. But she knew Assaf. He could be petulant, and it wouldn't be the first time he'd stormed out of a meeting to sulk somewhere.

"Maybe," she conceded. She couldn't shake the bad feeling that had settled on her since Ali first went missing. Something at Verinder House was wrong. She stilled. *Oh, no.* "Tar, didn't Gully say something about hunters?"

"No one is hunting in the dark in a windstorm on Thanksgiving." Tarek gripped her shoulders and turned her to face him. "And if Assaf or Aysha come across anyone, they'll be okay. Chappy is a tight-knit community. The neighbors support each other, especially those who live here year-round. They have to, with so few easily accessible resources. They're in good hands with the residents. And if they haven't made it across Dike Bridge, Chase will bring them back."

Kyra breathed out a long breath. Logically, she knew Tarek was right, but she didn't feel much better. This night had been one disaster after another.

"I'll try her mobile again." Kyra pulled out her phone. "Huh." She studied the screen, frowning.

"I don't have Wi-Fi service. Do you think we're too far

away from the router?" She checked her phone settings. "That doesn't make sense. Aysha would need internet access. Can you check your phone?"

"I don't have a signal either. Maybe whatever Loriann is doing is interfering with it? Or the wind could have knocked it out."

She gripped her phone. Her knuckles turned white. *If the wind knocked it out, we're totally stranded.*

"Hey," Tarek said softly and rubbed her back. "It'll be fine." He looked past her and his gaze snagged on the desk. He shifted away and pointed. On top of Aysha's desk sat an old-fashioned train-style cosmetics case, monogrammed with an *O*. "What's that?"

Kyra knew it was an attempt to distract her, but she nodded for him to go ahead. He zipped it open.

"What is it?" she asked.

He dumped the contents out. "Medicine." Tarek picked up the items, one by one. Prescription containers, supplements, over-the-counter pills and liquids. She picked up one of the prescription bottles, then another.

"They're prescribed to Loriann Oma. Do you know what these are?" she asked.

Tarek read the labels. "This one is for blood pressure. This one is warfarin. It's often prescribed to prevent heart attacks or stroke." Kyra gave him a surprised look, and he quirked his eyebrow at her. "You don't grow up with a cardiac nurse and not pick up at least a few things." He shook a container, rattling the pills inside. "Does Loriann have a heart condition?"

"Not that I'm aware of, but this would suggest yes." She

picked up one of the containers and examined the label. "Loriann has to take this one, three times a day. That explains Aysha feeding her pills this afternoon, and probably why Loriann is adamant we find her. She needs her medication, and apparently, she doesn't administer it herself." She tapped her nail on the plastic cap before replacing the container in the case. Kyra worried her lip, thinking.

"Kyra?"

"It's just... Do you think Loriann is hiding her heart condition?"

"Is there a reason she would?"

"Maybe? She's the heart of Omega Media. If the financiers knew she was ill, they may not back the deal. Asher is still too new and untested. Throughout the merger negotiations, Loriann insisted on handling the HR and employee due diligence on her own. Maybe she was trying to keep her health concerns confidential?" Kyra frowned, thinking of the demanding, impatient woman downstairs waiting for a conference room to be set up. Kyra reexamined the prescription bottles. She recognized the address of the prescribing physician as one of London's most exclusive and discrete private hospitals. The one preferred by a certain high-profile family. She shook her head. "No. Loriann uses private healthcare. Her records wouldn't be with the company. There must be some other reason she didn't want me or Assaf to see the employee files."

"Could it be because of the position she's offering you?"

Kyra repacked the case and zipped it closed. "Maybe, but that doesn't explain why she hid it from Asher."

Her hand went still. "Oh, no." Realization slammed into

her. "Loriann knows." It came out like a whisper. Tarek gave her a questioning look, and she grabbed his forearm. "Chase said Hedge has a history of sexual harassment and assault. That he used his position at Global to shield himself. What if he'd harassed or harmed employees and covered it up? Look what he did to Camilla right here. Chase said an investigation into Global Media might uncover things that the Elmers didn't want made public. Loriann insisted on doing all the HR review herself. She knew, Tar. She knew what Hedge Elmer did and how Elise covered it up and she hid it from Asher, from Assaf, and from me."

Chapter Twenty-Eight

KYRA WAITED IN the hall while Tarek did a final sweep of Aysha's room. She was still reeling from the fact that Loriann had undermined her, Assaf, and her own nephew. What she'd done wasn't illegal exactly, but it wasn't ethical either. Kyra wondered if Assaf had known. *No.* If he had, Loriann couldn't risk firing him. But she'd have needed someone on Omega's side to help her, to review and update documents, add and remove them from the data room. *Aysha.* Aysha had helped Loriann hide it. That would also explain Loriann's fixation on finding the girl. She'd need her to finish the deal. What Kyra didn't know was what Aysha was getting out of it.

Tarek stepped into the hall, letting the door close behind him. "Kyra?"

She shook her head. She was angry with her client and disappointed in Aysha. Kyra pushed herself off the wall and uncrossed her arms. "I want to know if Assaf is still here."

"Alright. Do you know what room he's in?" She didn't. Kyra straightened her shoulders and knocked on the door across the hall.

"Assaf? It's Kyra." Nothing.

She debated opening the door. It would be a massive invasion of Assaf's or, if she chose wrong, someone else's privacy. She dragged her thumb across the plastic, then pressed the card to the pad. The door unlocked with a soft *click*.

Tarek's eyebrow quirked up. "She made you a master?"

"I promised to be respectful."

Tarek's nostrils flared as he tried not to laugh, but he indicated for her to proceed.

"Assaf?" Kyra cracked open the door.

The room was dark. She reached inside and turned on the light. It was empty and smelled slightly musty. She shut it and tried the next one.

"Assaf? It's Kyra. I'm coming in."

She tried, over and over, ping-ponging between the exterior and interior rooms. When she cracked open the fifth one, an exterior room, near the back of the house, light filtered through the seam.

"Hello?" She pushed it open further.

The lights were all on. Every single one. Even the bathroom was lit. Relief washed over Kyra, but it was short-lived. The room was empty. She stepped inside.

She recognized Assaf's designer roller suitcase sitting on the luggage rack. Beside it, a navy suit hung on the valet stand. Case files and a legal pad were stacked next to his laptop on the desk.

"I'll check the bathroom," Tarek said, heading to the en suite.

Kyra nodded and fanned out the files. Assaf's caseload. His phone charging cord sat coiled on the bedside table. She didn't see his wallet or phone.

"Tar, is the safe locked?" Assaf would have locked away anything highly confidential or important, like his passport.

Tarek checked the wardrobe and tested the safe. "It's engaged. We can't open it without the keycode or master." He nodded to the card still in her hand.

Kyra slipped it into her pocket. She couldn't justify opening the safe. It wasn't like he was hiding inside.

Kyra walked around the bed and pushed the maroon damask drapes aside to peer out the window. Assaf's room overlooked a small garden and, beyond that, the parking and pool areas. She could just make out the outline of her Range Rover in the dark, and the empty spot beside it, where Chase's Bronco had likely been. She couldn't see the entire parking lot, but she counted at least three more cars. Two sedans, and two pickup trucks. One she recognized as Wes's truck, the other, based on its lavender color, could have been a Verinder House employee vehicle.

"What is it?" Tarek asked.

"Just the parking lot. I can't tell if any cars besides Chase's are missing, though." She pulled the curtains closed.

"Wherever they went, neither of them intended to stay away for long," Tarek said, pulling Assaf's door closed behind them.

He was right. Both Aysha and Assaf had left their luggage, their clothes, and their travel documents. Maybe they were safe on the other side of the island. Maybe they'd somehow made it to Edgartown.

She pulled out her phone, planning to text Aysha and Assaf again. The screen unlocked and Kyra frowned. "Still no Wi-Fi." She turned her phone for Tarek to see. He checked his.

"It must be down. Maybe the router needs to be reset? We'll ask Camilla. If the internet has been going in and out, that could explain why no one's been answering your calls."

Kyra hoped it was something so simple.

Chapter Twenty-Nine

KYRA AND TAREK walked down the long, dim south hall. She didn't believe they'd find Aysha's purse in the foyer closet, but they'd agreed to check just in case. And if they found it, she wasn't sure what that would mean. Her gut told her that Aysha wasn't at Verinder House, but that didn't explain where Assaf was. She couldn't reconcile that they'd gone off together, especially after learning Aysha had been lying for Loriann for months. Kyra felt like she was missing some crucial piece of information.

"Tar," Kyra said, putting her hand on his arm, halting him on the grand staircase bridgeway. "Don't you think this is all ... I don't know. Wrong? First Ali, then Elise, and now all these people are missing?"

Tarek's gaze shifted from her face to the floor and back.

"What are you two doing skulking around?"

Hedge Elmer stood at the top of the stairs, glaring down at them. He was still in his tuxedo, his dress shirt untucked, his mermaid tie hanging undone around his neck. After what Chase had told her, it took all of Kyra's self-control not to strangle him with the damned thing. He tucked a folder under his arm and started stuffing his shirt into his pants. Kyra swallowed back a wave of disgust.

WIDOW'S WALK

"Do you have any idea what time it is?"

Tarek ignored his question and instead answered with one of his own, "Where are you off to so late, Mr. Elmer?"

Hedge's eyebrows hitched together as he looked down his nose at them. He raised his phone. "The phones aren't working, and I have business with Oma. Where is she?"

"We left her in the Bride's Parlor, but she's asked Camilla to set up a conference room." Kyra didn't feel like being helpful. She wanted to send him walking right into Cape Poge, but it was safer for them to know where the lecherous old bastard was, rather than have him wandering around.

"The *what* parlor?" Hedge swiped his hand down his face. "This house is a damned maze," he mumbled to himself.

"Mr. Elmer," Tarek said, slipping his hands into his pockets. He assumed a relaxed stance, leaning against the railing. "Why was your wife over in the service stairwell?"

Hedge's forehead creased in confusion. "Service stairwell?"

"There is a service staircase on the other side of the house," Tarek explained, and waved to the north hall behind him. Hedge's expression settled into a combination of irritated and bewildered. "It goes up to the third floor and down to the basement. Your wife fell down those stairs. I'm just wondering what she was doing all the way over there."

"The hell should I know?" Hedge opened the folder and thumbed through the pages.

"Aren't you curious?" Tarek asked.

Hedge snapped the folder shut and glared at him. "I am in the middle of a two-hundred-million-dollar merger." He waved the folder at them. "So, no, I do not give one shit why my wife was fucking around in a stairwell. Excuse me." He thundered past them, and Kyra had to step out of his way or get bowled over.

Kyra watched him go.

"Chase may have been correct about Hedge mourning his wife," Tarek said after Hedge was out of earshot.

"Why do you think Elise was over there?" she asked. It'd been niggling at the back of her mind, and she could come up with no good reason for the old woman to be in the service area.

"I don't know."

"And why would he lie about not knowing about the service stairs?"

"He lied?" Tarek frowned.

"He went on that tour. Remember, Ali and Cam said they talked about the service corridors? But he pretended he didn't know about them. Do you think he had something to do with it? Could Hedge have killed Elise?" Kyra pushed her hair behind her ear.

Had the last year made her so jaded that she saw murder and motives when there were none? Was she really accusing Hedge of pushing his wife down a rickety old staircase? He had a strong motive, but Kyra couldn't picture his hefty frame maneuvering through the narrow servants' corridors or the stairwell.

"It'd crossed my mind. And it's not a great look that, with his wife's death, Hedge gained control of the company." Tarek tilted his head to the side as they started back down the stairs. "But no," he finally said, shaking his head. "The guy's a dick and a sexual predator, but he's calculating. As you said, he has a history of assault, and he hasn't yet been exposed. I don't think he'd have attempted anything premeditated here. He had hundreds of opportunities to harm his disabled, elderly wife before today. Why would he do it now, in a house full of people, where there's a decent chance of being caught?"

"Elise said something at dinner. She implied she may not sign off on the merger. Maybe she was holding out?" Kyra frowned, trying to remember what Elise was mumbling about before she doused Kyra in hot soup.

"And he lured her across the house to push her down the service stairs?" Tarek pointed to the grand staircase behind them. "If it'd been a crime of convenience, or even a spontaneous, passionate one, he would have pushed her down these stairs."

Tarek had a point, but if it wasn't Hedge, then what was Elise doing on the other side of the house?

Chapter Thirty

THE FOYER CLOSET was packed with the guests' coats and luggage. Kyra couldn't tell if Aysha's or Assaf's coats were missing. Unsurprisingly, she didn't see a handbag. She shut the door harder than necessary, her frustration manifesting.

A blast of wind hit the house, and the tall windows rattled. Kyra jumped.

"It's getting worse," Tarek said, peering outside. They shared a look.

Kyra swallowed. "Chase and Gerry?"

Tarek's smile wasn't as reassuring as Kyra needed it to be. "They'll be fine, but we should get back to everyone."

Kyra nodded, but her gaze traveled to the ceiling below her aunt and uncle's room. "Would you mind if we stop in and check on Ali first?"

"Sure."

The north side of Verinder House felt darker and colder than the south side. It could have been the wind, or it could've been Kyra's imagination. She suppressed a shiver. At the top of the stairs, they took a right and Kyra knocked on her aunt and uncle's door.

"Cam? Ali?"

After a moment, Cam opened it, his face easing into a smile, despite the tired strain at the corner of his eyes. "Kay?"

"How is she?"

Cam opened the door wider and stepped to the side. "Come in. See for yourself."

Ali was propped up on the bed, the television remote in her hand. "Kay." Her smile was genuine, but the dark hallows under her eyes, and the pinched look to her mouth were evidence of her exhaustion and discomfort.

"How are you feeling?"

"Concussions are amazing. Cam called down for ice cream and he's given me full control of the remote." She brandished it like it was a priceless treasure. "I found reruns of *Love Island*! The one in Mallorca." Ali's eyes widened and her feigned innocent smile was pure mischief. "You've been, haven't you? What was that like, again?"

Kyra rolled her eyes. "She's clearly delusional," Kyra mumbled to Tarek, who let out a soft laugh. "I've no idea what she's talking about." Kyra leaned down to press her cheek against her aunt's. "How are you, really? Are you in pain?"

"Just a headache, but it's nice to be fussed over. Is that terrible?"

"Never." Kyra stepped back and Ali snuggled back into the pillows.

Kyra had the urge to slide in beside her like she had done when she was a girl. Ali had been a teenager when her parents, Kyra's grandparents, died, and then not long after, she'd been saddled with raising her young niece while finishing her degree at UCL. Kyra made a silent promise to never forget to fuss over her aunt.

"Cam, do you have everything you need?"

"More than. Camilla gave me her direct number if we needed anything. Gerry checked in on us about an hour ago. He said all her vitals were normal. I've been trying to convince her to go to sleep."

"I'm right here. And I can't sleep after all that sugar. You know that. And this is the episode where…" Ali broke off. She studied Kyra, her brow creasing, then glanced at Tarek and back. "What's happened?"

"It's nothing, Ali," Kyra said, not wanting to alarm her aunt.

"You're lying. What is it?" Ali grimaced as she pushed herself more upright. "Tell me."

"Mrs. Elmer fell," Tarek said from behind Kyra.

"Oh no. Poor woman." Ali's tone was sarcastic, and she made a face.

"She died," Kyra said almost apologetically, and Ali blanched.

"Fucking hell."

"She's dead?" Cam asked.

"Yes, Gerry saw to her, and Tar called the police, but they won't come until the morning. I didn't want to upset you."

"Oh, that's terrible. Her poor husband. He must be out of his mind." Kyra didn't correct her aunt.

"Is there anything I can do?"

"No, Cam, thank you." Kyra took a step toward the door Tarek was holding open.

"Kay, wait a second," Ali said, and two pink spots

bloomed on her pale cheeks, like she was a little embarrassed. "I don't know if it's important, but I remembered something. Before I fell, when I was down by the water, trying to get a better view of the house..." Kyra nodded encouragement. "I saw someone."

"Inside?" Tarek asked.

"No. He was near the gardens, right by the house."

"Did you recognize him?"

"Yes. It was the big man. The one who carved the turkey at dinner."

Wes.

"And you're sure you saw him?" Tarek asked. Ali nodded. "Did he say anything to you?"

"I don't think so. I wasn't really paying him any mind, you know? And it was so windy, I probably wouldn't have heard him had he said anything." She attempted a smile. "Does that help?"

"It does." Tarek's smile was encouraging, but Kyra knew by the set of his jaw he was bothered by the news. "You should both get some rest. We'll come by to get you in the morning."

Cam walked them to the door. "Thanks for stopping in. She's putting on a brave face, but I think the fall gave her a fright."

Not just her. Kyra glanced at her aunt, whose eyes were already closed.

"Cam," Kyra said, her words hushed. "The internet and Wi-Fi are out. You can't reach us on our mobiles. We'll be in the Bride's Parlor downstairs. Use the house phone to call there."

"The Wi-Fi is out?" Cam asked, his nose scrunching under his glasses. "Kay, the house phones are VoIP. No internet, no phones."

Kyra gaped at him. *What?*

"Oh, but honestly, I wouldn't worry," he said, and gave her shoulder a reassuring squeeze. "Ali will be asleep soon. We shouldn't need for anything, but I'll come find you if we do."

"Thanks, Cam." Tarek shook his hand. "Goodnight." He pulled gently on Kyra's elbow, guiding her into the hall.

The door closed clicked closed, but Kyra barely heard it. She was trying to wrap her mind around what she'd just learned about the phones, about Wes Silva.

"Do we really have no way of contacting anyone inside or outside Verinder House?"

Tarek nodded, and he ran his hand through his hair. His jaw flexed like he was grinding his teeth.

"Tar, tell me."

He pulled her away from the Babcock's door, closer to the front staircase. When he spoke, his voice was low. "You asked me before if I thought something more was going on here." He glanced down the hall to the service stairs and back. "I do. There are too many things going on at once. And now with the internal communications down? It feels deliberate. Like we're being cut off." Kyra's eyes went wide. He ran his hand through his hair again, making it stand at odd angles. "I'd be a lot more comfortable if I knew where everyone was."

He was worried, and with his concern Kyra felt a surge of validation. She wasn't being paranoid. Something more was going on at Verinder House.

"Tar," she said, and he looked up, meeting her gaze. "Before we go back, I want to see the stairwell."

Chapter Thirty-One

THE DOOR TO the back staircase was locked. Kyra used her keycard and pushed the door open. Tarek pulled out his cellphone and turned on the flashlight app. He shined it along the walls, the stairwell, down the stairs.

"I don't understand why she chose to go down these stairs," Kyra murmured, following the beam of light. There was no railing, nothing to offer a disabled old woman support.

"Maybe she was trying to climb up?" Tarek mused. "If she was in the Bride's Parlor downstairs, maybe Elise thought she'd take a shortcut instead of going all the way around to the foyer?"

Tarek turned in the stairwell. His light danced over the floor, the wall, the ceiling.

"Wait." Kyra grabbed his arm and dragged the light along the back wall. "Are those ... cupboards?" She opened the closest one.

Tarek had to take a step back to allow the door to open. "Whoa!" He made a squeaking noise as his heel slipped off the landing.

His phone fell as he grabbed for the wall. Kyra's hand grasped his shirt, and she yanked him toward her. He stumbled forward.

His hands came to her hips. "That could have been bad." He tried to make a joke, but his eyes were too wide. He looked over his shoulder and back. "Thank you." He pried her fingers from his shirt and stooped to retrieve his phone.

"Be more careful." Her heart pulsed in her throat.

"It's really narrow up here." He had the grace to look embarrassed. "I guess falling isn't all that unlikely."

No, Krya agreed. Falling, in fact, was very likely. The landing wasn't safe. Nothing about this house was.

"What's in there?" he asked, jerking his chin toward the wall of cabinets.

Kyra turned back to the row of doors, keeping one eye on the narrow landing. She pulled them open one-by one. "Linens." White towels and sets of sheets were neatly stowed next to extra comforters and coverlets. "And toiletries." Baskets of hairdryers and curling wands, sewing kits, and the fancy toiletries she'd seen in their own bathroom lined the rest of the shelves. "Guestroom supplies."

"Could she have come here to get some extra towels and slipped?" Kyra asked, watching Tarek run the light back and forth.

He looked up, his expression doubtful. "You think Elise Elmer, the woman who knows all the best *help* on the island, deigned to fetch her own towels?"

"Fair point."

He took a tentative step toward the stairs. "You said that Chase helped their granddaughter escape Hedge. Elise seemed pretty antagonistic toward Chase. Maybe she was seeking him out? She came up here to find him, and when she couldn't, she didn't want to go all the way around?" Kyra considered it. The idea that Mrs. Elmer was seeking out Chase wasn't unbelievable, especially if she thought Chase was still in touch with her granddaughter.

"Maybe?"

Tarek shined the light down the stairs. "No. That's not it," he mumbled to himself.

"No? Why not?"

"The timing would be tight for someone with mobility issues. Elise fell while we were all in the Bride's Parlor, after Ali's accident. She'd have had to walk right by us to get to the stairwell. I don't think we wouldn't have noticed. Her walk is distinctive."

Kyra remembered the heavy thud of her cane on the floor.

"No," Tarek said, sweeping his light along the landing. "Elise was up here while we were downstairs."

"She was coming down, then."

"She must've been." Tarek stepped down onto the first tread. "Come on. I know just enough about forensics to make an educated guess about her trajectory. Keep your hand on the wall."

Tarek moved slowly, pausing on each tread. His light moved across every surface.

Kyra cursed under her breath. Even in sneakers navigating the narrow stairwell was treacherous. She kept one hand on the wall. The other gripped Tarek's shoulder, tight enough it must have been uncomfortable for him.

"Elise wasn't a small woman," Tarek said. "Her body weight was uncentered because of her stooped stature. She'd have had to crab walk or shuffle down the stairs. She was right-handed. She could have used the wall for support and held her cane in her nondominant hand, or she used her cane and walked more in the center of each tread."

They completed a half circle, and Tarek stopped. His light floated across the dark wood paneling. It stopped on the dark smear. The blood had dried and oxidized, turned a rust brown. Kyra's grip on his shoulder tightened.

"She may have struck her head there. Stay here." Tarek moved closer and squatted down to get a better look. He stood and shined the light back up the stairwell. "There."

Kyra turned her head. Just behind her, there was a scuff mark on the paneling.

"Switch places."

They maneuvered until Kyra stood in the first-floor stairwell. Tarek climbed back up and crouched down for a better view. "It's a mark, about three and a half inches long, about two feet above the tread."

Kyra realized he wasn't just talking for her benefit. He was recording himself.

"The paneling is chipped. Based on the light coloring of the damaged wood, it could be fresh."

He made his way down until he was standing beside her.

"What does that mean? That the paneling is chipped?"

Tarek took a moment, his eyes unfocused, contemplating, and Kyra wondered if this was what he was like when he was working on a case. It was both impressive and frustrating to watch him as he silently processed.

"Gerry said she suffered from a cervical fracture. Her neck snapped." He pointed the light at the bloodstain. "She was probably dead before she hit the floor."

His light swept to the base of the stairs where her body had been discovered. He squatted down, one finger on his lip, as he swept the light across the floor. Tarek unlocked his phone, and his thumb passed over the screen, again and again. He'd angled it away, so she couldn't see, but Kyra was certain he was looking through photos of Elise lying at the base of the stairs. His gaze switched back and forth between the images and the area around him. Minutes passed.

She couldn't hold it in any longer. "Tarek?"

"I'm just thinking." Finally, he looked up at her, his lips pressed together in a line. He shut off the screen. "She not only broke her neck. She also dislocated a shoulder and had a broken femur. Gerry said she could have more internal injuries, but those couldn't be confirmed without an autopsy.

"If she fell from the top stair, I think she struck her shoulder there, where the paneling is chipped. That would have altered her momentum, and she could have struck the back of her head there." His light went back and forth twice more.

"Tar? What is it?"

"I'm just thinking out loud." He stood up. "Elise moved slowly. She wasn't running up and down the stairs. Her injuries are consistent with a fall, but not a short one. To suffer the injuries she sustained; to damage the paneling like that, she'd had to have hit the wall with incredible force." He frowned.

"You think she was pushed."

"I think it's more likely she was propelled than she

tripped, or lost her balance. Or she could have an underlying medical condition that affected her bone density. Or the paneling is rotted. I can only do so much without a forensics team. And none of this explains what the hell she was doing over here in the first place." He shoved his hand in his hair again.

Tarek pulled his phone back out and reviewed the photos and videos he'd taken of the scene. He made a frustrated noised in the back of his throat.

There was nothing more here that could explain why Elise Elmer was in the corridor, or whether she'd fallen or been pushed. Kyra turned in a circle, scanning the hallway that led to the ballroom, the door to the north hall, the stairs spiraling down. They hadn't searched the basement. Maybe Elise was looking for something down there.

She pointed down. "This continues down to the basement?"

Tarek gave it a cursory glance. "*Mmhhmm.*"

"Show me."

Chapter Thirty-Two

TAREK WENT FIRST, keeping his flashlight trained on the steps. Kyra assumed the descent position, one hand gripping Tarek's shoulder, the other on the wall, as they spiraled down.

"Did you really bring the bod—Elise this way?" Kyra couldn't imagine how they'd have maneuvered it.

"No. We used the entrance through the kitchen. It was added during the renovation. I haven't been this way."

Kyra thought about carrying a body across the ballroom, through all those corridors and into the kitchen, past Julia's bread, rising for the morning. Her stomach soured. Part of her wanted to ask how Tarek and Gerry had managed it, but a much bigger part didn't want to know or think about it at all.

"Have you done it before?" she asked, dreading the answer.

Tarek cocked his head to the side. "Moved a body?" Kyra nodded, even though he couldn't see her. "No. Under normal circumstances, it's recommended to leave it for the investigation. But in this case..." His voice trailed off. *Leaving her there would have been worse.* "But I've seen ... dozens." Tarek's voice was soft, tinged with regret.

She knew he'd seen terrible things with the Massachusetts State Police, and now, as a consultant with a private security company working with all levels of law enforcement to solve complex violent crimes, he saw worse. She couldn't imagine what he'd been exposed to.

Upstairs, he had been so calm and clinical as he walked her through the sequence of Elise's fall, her injuries, her death. He'd seemed so unaffected.

"And before you ask, no, it never gets easier or any less horrifying." Tarek stepped to the side and Kyra clambered down the last two stairs to stop beside him.

"I'm sorry, what?" she asked.

"That's normally the next question. Does it get easier to see death? Or do you get used to it? It doesn't. And I hope I never get used to it." Kyra's heart broke for him. She looked up, but he was already looking away. He pointed. "This is the maintenance hallway."

They were in a wide hall. The tile floors and cement walls glistened with moisture. She heard the soft mechanical whir of dehumidifiers fighting against the insidious damp of the island. Kyra rounded her shoulders against the chill and rubbed her arms.

"It's freezing down here."

"It is. This way."

Kyra was all turned around thanks to the spiral staircase, but she thought they were walking toward the kitchen. Squares of light from open doorways slanted on the concrete floor, breaking up the dark.

"Tali said they keep the doors open to keep the basement as dry as possible." Tarek ran a finger down the wall, then rubbed it against his thumb. "I'm not sure it's working."

"Do you know where you're going?"

"I've a general idea." They turned down another hall. "Do you think one of your colleagues or clients would have killed Elise Elmer because of the merger?"

Kyra considered it. "Loriann needs the merger. If her illness or Hedge's illicit activities are disclosed before it's finalized, the financiers may backout. She needs it signed. But I don't think she'd kill anyone." As Kyra said it, she felt it to be true. "Even if she was strong enough, Loriann isn't one to get her hands dirty like that. She has people." *Like Aysha.* Kyra grimaced.

"And your boss? Assaf?"

"Assaf's not a killer, and he gains nothing from Elise's death. Especially now that Loriann's sacked him." They stopped at a T. Kyra peered down both dark corridors. "Are there no bloody lights down here?"

"If we are where I think we are, there is a switch at the other end, right next to the wine cellar." Tarek cleared his throat and directed her to the left. "I think this side is all storage area."

Kyra peeked inside an open door. The musty smelling room was packed full of banquet tables and chairs. Arbors in different shapes were stacked against a wall.

"Wedding stuff."

"*Mmhhmm.* Tali said they have a workshop somewhere back here. There's also the gun storage locker, and the utility room is down that way. I think."

"Wait." Kyra pulled him to a stop. "Gun storage?"

"Yeah, there's a shooting range on the property. Don't

worry, I checked. The room is locked." Kyra held up her keycard. Tarek shook his head, and he began walking down the hall. "It requires a physical key."

"And who has that?" she called after him, but he was stopped, standing in an expanse of dark hallway. "Tar?"

"This door is shut. They're all supposed to be open." He tried the knob, but it was locked.

Without really thinking, Kyra pressed the keycard against the panel. The locking mechanism disengaged.

She gave the door a push. It creaked open on rusty hinges. A beam of flickering light appeared on the concrete floor, widening as the door swung open. Kyra's body reacted before her brain made sense of it. Her hands lifted to her mouth to cover her scream.

Chapter Thirty-Three

TAREK PUSHED HER aside and rushed inside. "Stay back!"

"Ohmagod." Kyra's words were muffled by her hands still pressed against her mouth.

Tarek squatted beside the body. "He's dead."

Kyra wasn't hearing him. Her eyes were glued to her boss. To the black handle protruding from his neck, just below his ear.

"Assaf!" she wheezed.

She stepped forward, but Tarek raised a hand, stopping her. Her spinning brain processed his red, shining fingers. *Oh god. Blood. So much blood.*

She choked on a strangled sob. "Assaf."

"Hey, hey." Tarek was standing in front of her. He reached for her with bloody hands and pulled back. "Fuck." He spun in a slow circle.

Kyra heard water splashing.

The room slowly came into focus from the periphery in. Her mind's aperture narrowing, sharpening every detail. Shelves. Racks. Large white machines. Washing machines and driers. A steamer. Tarek was at a utility sink, washing his hands. They were in a laundry room.

Then the smell hit her. Lavender, the acrid smell of

burnt lint, and something more caustic. *Bleach?*

She looked down at the shining concrete floor. She stepped backward, leaving a bright red footprint. Kyra gagged. She'd been standing in his blood.

"Tarek." It came out like a sob.

He pulled her against him and pushed her out into the hall, out of sight of her boss's corpse. Tarek stooped so they were at eye level. His gaze jumped back and forth between her eyes, her face in his hands.

"I'm ... I'm okay." She wasn't.

Her gaze wandered involuntarily back to the door, as if her subconscious had some morbid need to resee the body on the floor. His stupid purple dinner jacket still clutched in his hand. His red-stained Prada sneakers.

"Kyra?" Tarek's grip on her face tightened. "Eyes on me."

Her gaze snapped back to Tarek.

Without breaking eye contact, he pulled his phone out of his pocket and dialed. The phone made an alarm-like sound, and he cursed. "They still haven't fixed the fucking internet. Kyra, listen to me. I have to record this. And I'm going to need to take some pictures." Tarek looked over his shoulder. "Just ... just wait here."

"No." She couldn't be alone in that dark hallway. She shook her head and stepped closer to the door. "No," she said again, her voice clearer. "I'm fine. I'll be fine."

His expression was wary, but he didn't object. "Don't come in. We can't disturb the crime scene any more than we have already." Kyra swallowed and stood in the threshold. She gripped the door jamb tight enough to cause the tendons in her arms and wrists to ache. She told herself it wasn't to keep from passing out.

Tarek pulled out his phone to record a video. He crouched near the body.

"Victim is male, early fifties."

"He's fifty-two. Fifty-two last month," she whispered.

"Fifty-two. Stab wound to the neck. Weapon appears to be a kitchen knife. Blood congealing on the floor suggests death occurred within the last few hours." He glanced at Kyra and then back. He pointed the camera at the blood. "Blood pooling on the floor and on the victim suggests he was killed on site. No scuffing on sneakers or streaks on the floor. Body was discovered at 12:37 a.m. by Tarek Collins and his partner Kyra Gibson."

Tarek took video of the body, their footprints, and the room. She stopped listening as he quietly described the crime scene in specific, scientific detail. He never once used Assaf's name, always referring to him as *the victim*.

Assaf would hate that. Hate being reduced to a common noun. He'd hated anything as mundane as common. She swallowed against the painful tightening in her chest.

"Kyra?" He had to say it twice more before she acknowledged him. "Take off your shoes."

"What?" Her body was numb. She couldn't even feel herself trembling.

Tarek kneeled and worked her bloody sneakers off her feet. He set them inside the door next to his dress shoes. Some far part of her brain acknowledged she'd lost two of her favorite pairs of shoes in one abysmal night.

Tarek guided her out into the hall. "We need to notify

the others. Make sure everyone is accounted for." He shut the door behind them, making sure it was locked.

Her muddled brain understood what he didn't say out loud. *We have to tell them one of us is a killer.*

Chapter Thirty-Four

TAREK'S HAND WAS wrapped tightly around Kyra's as he pushed open the door to the Bride's Parlor. They'd taken the long way up from the cellar, through the kitchen, stopping there just long enough for Tarek to request from a bewildered Tali to gather everyone, guests and staff, in the Bride's Parlor. Immediately.

Kyra was hardly aware as they walked up the south hall, through the foyer and down the north hall. She only knew where she was by the textures under her feet. Concrete, tile, textile, tile, wood floor, and textile again. Her teeth were clenched together so tightly an ache was forming in her jaw. Her mind just played over and over the image of Assaf lying in a pool of blood.

Seeing Elise sprawled at the bottom of the stairs had been unsettling. But it was nothing like this. It was nothing like seeing Assaf, his skin pale and waxy. His features twisted in agony. The knife stuck in his neck. Murdered. She wasn't equipped to deal with it. Her breathing came faster. She felt like she couldn't get enough oxygen.

"Kyra. Sit." Tarek pushed her into a chair by the fire.

He added a few more logs to the flames, causing sparks to fly up the chimney. He'd said it never got easier seeing the dead, but he at least was functioning. Kyra was spiraling. He bent down in front of her.

He held both of her hands in his. "Hey."

Kyra blinked at him. He squeezed into the seat beside her, pulling her against him, and she let him hold her. His thumb traced her spine between her shoulder blades. His chin rested on the crown of her head. Her eyes burned, and she blinked back tears.

"Kyra, breathe."

She took deep inhales and slow exhales, willing her heart rate to slow. She needed to calm down, needed to keep her wits about her.

There was a knock on the door.

"I'll get it." Tarek unfolded himself from the chair and crossed the room to open it. Wes and Cam were supporting Ali. Seeing Wes holding her aunt sent a jolt of a different kind of panic through her. Kyra wanted to scream at him to get away from her.

Kyra swiped at her cheeks.

Cam settled his wife on the chaise. Wes handed Cam a blanket, then he retreated to the other side of the room. He eyed Kyra and Tarek with distaste and suspicion.

Cam tucked the blanket around his wife's legs. "Kyra?" he said, looking over at her. "Mr. Silva said there was an emergency, and we needed to come downstairs. What's happened?"

"We'll explain once everyone's here," Kyra said. She didn't trust herself to tell them about Assaf and not break down in tears.

"Explain what?" Ali asked, but Kyra just shook her head.

"Kay, what's happened?" Kyra looked away, her heart sinking, and Ali slumped back with an annoyed huff.

The door flew open, and Loriann barged into the room, her expression thunderous. "What on earth is happening? The house girl was adamant that we return here immediately." Loriann sniffed, displeased. "Like I don't have better things to do. I don't appreciate being summoned, Kyra. What is it?"

"Ms. Oma, please take a seat. I'll explain once everyone's arrived."

Loriann narrowed her eyes at Tarek. She made a show of looking around the room. "Has Asher not returned? And Aysha? And why, Kyra, is your guest telling me to sit down? What am I doing here?"

"You are sitting. Quietly," Tarek snapped.

The room, already quiet, went utterly silent. Kyra had never heard Tarek speak to anyone like that. His tone was commanding, an unsaid dare to test him. It worked. Loriann fell into her seat. If looks could kill, Loriann's qualified as a war crime, but she only sniffed again and opened her laptop.

Cam sat beside his wife and murmured, "About time someone put that old witch in her place."

There was another knock on the door, and Camilla slipped inside. She was in her black trousers, and she'd pulled on one of Verinder House's lilac fleeces. She was no longer wearing the apron. Her face was scrubbed clean, and her thick dark hair was in a messy topknot.

"Dr. Collins? Tali said there was an emergency." She looked around the room. "Is everyone alright?"

Kyra realized Camilla had probably been off work for the

night, getting ready for bed. Her heart sank as she took in the tired woman, who'd been nothing but gracious since they'd arrived.

"Are Tali and your aunt coming?"

"Yes, sir. Tali's on her way. Aunt Julia said she'd be downstairs in a moment. She'd already gone to bed."

Camilla sat down next to her cousin. When Wes noticed Kyra watching, his mouth twisted in a sneer, and she looked away.

Asher, Chase, and Gerry hadn't yet returned with news of Aysha and Ben. Kyra shut her eyes tight. She hoped Ben and Aysha were on the other side of Dike Bridge. Being stranded somewhere on Chappy would be less terrifying, and safer, than being stuck in this house.

But wait. Where was Hedge?

"I'm going to get a glass of water." Kyra whispered to her aunt and uncle, needing an excuse to talk to Tarek without alarming them. "Do you want anything?"

Cam shook his head and tightened his hold on Ali's hand.

Kyra made a pretense of pouring a glass of water. "Tar, want anything?"

He gave a slight nod, understanding her silent request. "I've got it." He moved close so they were standing side by side. He poured a cup of cold coffee and made a face as he drank it. "What is it?"

"Hedge Elmer. He's still wandering around."

Tarek put the cup down and surveyed the room. "Shit."

"Do we need to go find him?" she asked. She was more concerned for anyone who came across him than for Hedge

Elmer's well-being. "Even if he's not the killer, we probably can't leave him out there, can we?"

She hadn't been ready to dismiss Hedge as his wife's killer, but he couldn't have killed Assaf. It'd come to her when she saw Camilla changed for the night. Assaf had been killed sometime after dinner. It was a messy, violent death. Whoever killed him would have been covered in his blood. The killer would have had to change their clothes.

"His tuxedo?" Tarek asked.

Kyra nodded and shuddered at the thought of bloody clothes hidden somewhere in Verinder House. She glanced around the room. Nearly everyone, save Tarek, had changed from dinner. *Shit.* It really could have been any of them, except Hedge Elmer. She set her water glass down with force.

Tarek turned to Loriann. "Ms. Oma, have you seen Hedge Elmer?"

Loriann eyed him over her laptop screen, then turned away. He stepped closer and snapped it shut.

Loriann pulled her hands out just in time. "I beg your pardon?" she sputtered, then glared at him.

"I said, have you seen Hedge Elmer?" his tone was so polite it bordered on threatening.

"Yes, of course. The girl..." She squinted at Camilla. "The other girl came and found us in the room we were using. We were waiting *patiently* for the internet to come back so we can witness the rest of the signatures. Hedge said he needed something from his suite. I'm sure he'll be here shortly." Her eyes narrowed to slits. "Although you have still not told me why any of us are here."

Tarek cleared his throat and turned back to Kyra. She

couldn't help but smile as Loriann's eyes bugged out of her head at Tarek's obvious snub.

Tarek rubbed his forehead and met Kyra's gaze. "No, you're right. We can't let him wander around, but I don't want to leave you here alone." He cast a glance at Wes, who was still glowering in the corner.

"I'm not alone. We'll be fine."

Tarek didn't look convinced, but he dipped his chin in a reluctant nod. "Lock the door behind me. Don't let anyone in. *Anyone*, Kyra. If someone knocks, tell them to wait until I return." He leaned in close to her ear. "And keep your keycard hidden."

Chapter Thirty-Five

"OH, FOR THE love of Pete!" Loriann snapped her laptop shut.

Kyra stiffened. Tarek hadn't been gone for five minutes.

Loriann pointed at Camilla. "I've asked you multiple times. There is no internet. I am paying a fortune for this house, and I need to get this bloody deal signed. Now."

Kyra grit her teeth to keep from lashing out at Loriann.

"I'm sorry, ma'am." Camilla's eyes went wide, and she clasped her hands together in her lap. "The wind has probably downed the lines. The company will be here in the morning."

Next to Camilla, Wes straightened and pushed off the wall. He glared at Loriann and opened his mouth as if to say something when a gust of wind blasted the back of Verinder House. Logs toppled from the fireplace grate with a flaming crash. One tumbled out, rolling past the hearth, spewing sparks.

"Christ and shite!" Cam scrambled to stamp down the embers, smoldering on the rug. Kyra hurried to help, but he waved her away. "No, stay back. You don't have any shoes."

Wes's thick boots stomped across the floor.

Cam's hair flopped over his glasses as he said, "Find us a

broom, would you?"

"Right here." Wes held out a brass-handled fireplace brush. Using the tongs, Wes restacked the wood and pushed the fire as far back against the firebricks as it would go, while Cam gathered up the ashes.

Cam wiped his hands against his pants. "Maybe we should put it out?"

"I'll keep an eye on it," Wes said, standing up. "The room will get cold if we don't keep it going. The heat here is garbage."

Kyra felt Wes's stare, daring her to say something. His Ponzi scheme involved installing faulty heating systems, but Kyra didn't take the bait. She backed away, reclaiming her space near the door.

"Or." Loriann's sharp voice cut through the room. "We hang the blasted fire and go back to our rooms and about our business." Loriann was standing now, with her hands clasped in front of her waist, ever proper. "Really, Kyra, I don't understand why your man has us all gathered here, like some Yankee Inspector Poirot. The old woman fell down the stairs. It's not some big mystery." She threw up her hands. They froze in the air before dropping limply to her sides.

The room went quiet, the crackling of the fire the only sound. They saw the facts in a new light—a dead woman, people missing, and an ex-policeman who wanted to keep track of the guests and staff.

"Kay, what's going on?" Ali asked, her voice wavering.

The doorknob jiggled.

Loriann made a gasping sound, and her hand went to her heart. For all her posturing and sputtering, Loriann was frightened. Kyra inched toward the door.

"Kay," Ali whispered, her eyes a little wild. She gripped her blanket, her knuckles white. Cam stood.

The doorknob jiggled again. Kyra stared at it. Her heart banged against her ribs. Whoever was out there could have killed Elise. Killed Assaf.

Someone knocked. "Hello? Kyra? Tar? You in there? Anyone?"

"Chase!" She scrambled to unlock the door.

"Wait! Don't!" Loriann yelled.

Kyra threw it open. Chase stood on the threshold, one arm raised, mid knock. He was soaked through. His thick sweater dripped water on the floor. His jeans clung to his thighs. He was shivering.

"What happened?" She grabbed his forearm as she took in his cold, wrinkled fingers, his colorless lips. She hauled him to the fire, practically pushing him inside the fireplace. Her nose filled with the sharp scents of sea salt and ice.

Chase tried to pull the sodden sweater off, but his fingers couldn't seem to grasp the drenched fabric. Kyra reached for the hem. "Cam, help me."

Together, Kyra and Cam peeled the sweater off him. Camilla handed them bar towels and Kyra used them to blot up as much water as she could.

"Kyra, give him this." Ali handed her the blanket, and Kyra pulled it around Chase's shoulders with some difficulty. He was just so damned tall. Chase didn't object to her administrations. He held his hands to the fire, rubbing them together. All the while dripping on the rug and shivering.

"Chase, what happened? Where are Gerry and Asher?"

WIDOW'S WALK

"Parking. They let me out." At her alarmed expression, Chase shook his head. "They're fine. Gerry made me promise to go straight upstairs."

"He's right. You need to get dry. You could be hypothermic."

"And you sound just like him." Chase attempted a smile, but his lips barely moved. "Are you going to tell me why you're all locked in here?"

Kyra ignored him. She didn't like the blue tinge to his lips and cheekbones, and he was still shivering—and not the delicate little shivers when one had been outside too long, but bone rattling ones that spasmed through his whole body. His jaw was clenched, and Kyra wondered if it was to keep his teeth from rattling.

Kyra deliberated her choices. Chances were that there was a murderer in this room, or just outside. Hell, Chase could have spent the last hour with one. Kyra didn't want to leave the safety of the Bride's Parlor, but she didn't see a better alternative. Chase needed to get dry and warm immediately and she didn't trust him to get upstairs on his own with the way he was shaking. But she also didn't want to come face-to-face with the killer in the hallway. Kyra swallowed. She understood why Tarek wanted everyone together. Keeping track of them, when she couldn't see them, was like playing blind chess, and she sucked at regular chess.

Kyra bit her lip and turned to her uncle. "Cam, I'm going to take him upstairs. Lock the door behind me. Don't let anyone in but Tarek. Tell everyone else they can wait in the hall."

Cam gave her a wild look, but he didn't argue.

"Absolutely not. You can't leave us here!" Loriann shrieked.

For a split second, Chase's shudders stopped. Kyra dragged him toward the door.

"Loriann, how will it look if Chase-fucking-Hawthorn dies at your murder dinner?" Kyra asked, her voice sharp. "How will that make your precious company look? What will you say to the senator? To his *wife*?"

Loriann blanched. Kyra yanked open the door and pushed Chase into the hall. She used the keycard to gain access to the service stairs.

"Look at you being all formidable," Chase said. "And when did you get a skeleton key?"

At least that was what she thought he said. It was hard to tell with his teeth chattering.

"Can you climb the stairs?" Kyra half pushed Chase up the narrow staircase. She was careful to keep her eyes averted from Elise's blood still staining the wainscotting.

She unlocked Chase and Gerry's room. It was marginally smaller than hers, and some far part of her brain wondered why she'd gotten the preferential treatment over the senator's son.

Unlike her and Tarek's traditionally styled room, Chase and Gerry's was decorated in contemporary masculine navies and greens, with a giant flat screen television and a leather couch. She pushed him toward the en suite.

"Get out of your wet clothes and get dry."

That he didn't argue with her, caused her nerves to ratchet up. She found his overnight bag and rummaged through it, pulling out sweatpants and the sweatshirt he'd been wearing in the car. *Was that just earlier today?* Their short journey to Chappy felt like days ago, not hours.

"Chase?" She knocked. "Chase, I have your clothes. I'm coming in." The bathroom was smaller than hers, with only a large walk-in shower. He was inside, sitting on the tile floor, wrapped in a towel, his wet clothes discarded next to the drain.

"Hand me another towel?" he asked as he rose to his feet.

She yanked one off the rack and handed it to him, averting her eyes as he sorted himself. He chuckled, but it sounded hoarse and dry.

"I'm decent." She looked up. Chase had one towel wrapped around his waist, another around his shoulders. He looked like a terry cloth nun.

He wasn't shivering anymore, but his skin was still too white, almost a perfect match to the shade of the snowy towels. She set his clothes on the vanity.

"Put these on. I'll be outside."

She gave him privacy and waited, leaning against the sleigh bed. She picked at the contrast stitching in the churn-dash style quilt coverlet. Chase came out of the bath, drying his long hair. Kyra stood straight. She scanned every inch of him.

"How are you feeling?"

"Cold. Do not go swimming in November." He pulled a pair of socks from his bag and sat next to her to drag them on.

"I could fucking kill you myself for scaring me like that."

Chase huffed a soft, warm laugh.

She raked her eyes over him again, looking for any sign

that he was hurt. "I'm fine, Kay. Promise." At least he could smile now, even if his lips remained colorless. "She wouldn't care, you know," Chase said, his voice soft and rough and Kyra's gaze snapped up to his vivid eyes. "Margot wouldn't give a single shit if I dropped dead at your boss's front door. She'd probably relish it, use it as an opportunity to boost her image."

"I know." Kyra sat next to him and wrapped her arms around him.

For once, she was providing warmth to him. She'd banked on Loriann not knowing what a horrid bitch Chase's mother truly was, but she hadn't expected her threat to be so effective. She hugged him close.

"Why would Loriann be frightened of your mother?"

"Other than because she's terrifying, you mean?" Chase shifted beneath her chin. "Elise has, *had*, Margot's ear. You never know what my parents are involved in for their personal gain. And remember, Margot insisted I show up to this shitshow. I'd bet she's invested somehow." Chase pulled away and gave her a look. "Are you going to tell me why you're all locked away together? And what did you mean *murder dinner?*"

"Are you going to tell me why you went swimming in the middle of the night fully dressed?" she challenged. Chase tipped his chin, an acquiescence. She pulled back an inch. "You go first."

"Someone drove off the road, near the bridge, or got stuck in the sand. The car was half-covered by the incoming tide. I swam out to make sure no one was caught inside."

"Jesus, Chase!" She pushed him. "What the hell were you

thinking? Ben said the tides were dangerous. You could have been pulled out! You could have drowned."

"Calm down. I'm fine. And what choice did we have? If someone was stuck, we couldn't leave them out there."

"Was someone in the car?" Kyra already knew the answer.

"No, it was empty. We think it got stuck and whoever was driving just left it there. They were close enough to Dike Bridge that they could have walked over. At least I hope that's what happened. I checked around the car, but it was so dark, and the undercurrent was strong." Meaning if the driver didn't make it to the bridge, they could have been sucked out to sea.

Kyra's chest hallowed out.

"Asher and Gerry are going to call the police. They'll send a search team."

"They won't be able to. The phones, the Wi-Fi, it's all out."

Chase's eyes widened, and she told him in rushed hurried words about the phones, and the internet, finding Assaf, about her and Tarek's suspicions that Elise was killed.

"Tarek went to find Hedge Elmer. He wants everyone together to keep us safe. He should be back by now."

"Kay." Chase's tone made Kyra go still.

She took in the reluctant set to his mouth, pulled down in an embarrassed frown, and asked, "What is it?"

"Tar didn't want me to say anything. But what about Ali?" At her blank look, he continued, "She was wearing your coat. Tar wondered if maybe someone was trying to hurt you and hit Ali by mistake."

Ali had been wearing Kyra's hideous coat. The one she'd been seen all over the island in. Ali said Wes Silva had been outside with her. Was it possible he'd attacked her aunt, thinking it was Kyra? That he'd pushed Elise down the stairs, stabbed Assaf? Elise and Assaf certainly hadn't ingratiated themselves with him or his family. And everyone knew how much Wes hated Kyra. Suddenly, Tarek's overprotectiveness made sense. He thought she was a target. Kyra pulled away.

"Why didn't you tell me?" she demanded as a slew of emotions roiled insider her, hurt, anger, fear.

"He didn't want you to worry," Chase said.

"*You* should have told me."

"Kay, come on."

Kyra stood up and moved out of his reach. "We should get back downstairs."

Chapter Thirty-Six

WHEN KYRA AND Chase returned to the Bride's Parlor. Tarek was standing right inside the door. Kyra noticed the tense set to his jaw, the slight pulse in his cheek, his tells for when he was worried or just pissed off.

As soon as Chase crossed into the room, Gerry grabbed him by the forearm and hauled him to the nearest chair. He pushed Chase down and took his vitals.

"Ger, I'm fine..." Chase tried to push the doctor away, but when his protests went unheeded, he gave up with a *harrumph*.

"You're lucky," Gerry said, his voice low and gravelly. He rocked back on his heels and jammed the blood pressure cuff into his bag. "Your body temperature is low, but not dangerous. Blood pressure and heart rate are normal." He rubbed his forehead with his thumb and finger, as his shoulders rose and fell with a long breath. Kyra felt a pang of empathy for him. This wasn't the composed doctor from earlier. This was a man beside himself with worry for someone he cared about.

"Okay," Gerry said, dropping his hand. "We need to heat you up, but slowly. Find a seat near the fire, away from the drafts."

Chase rolled his eyes but let Gerry pull him closer to the fireplace.

Kyra felt a hand on her elbow. Tarek was looking at her with his own exasperated frown, but she shrugged him off and put a few feet of distance between them. She was upset with him. With Chase. She'd questioned Ali's fall. She hadn't considered that she was a target, but she also had never been convinced Ali's fall was accidental. It stung that Tarek and Chase had had their own suspicions but chose not to tell her. They let her doubt herself, and she wasn't ready to forgive them for it.

Tarek must have found Hedge Elmer because now he was sitting next to Loriann, reading through a stack of papers. He looked even more disheveled and rumpled than before. Kyra was curious where Tarek found him, but she didn't trust herself not to start an argument, and now was not the time.

"Right, Collins."

Kyra jumped at Asher's deep voice. In her irritation with Tarek and Chase, she'd nearly forgotten that Asher had been in the search party with Chase and Gerry. She gave him a cursory once over. But for his windswept hair, he was no worse for wear. He looked like Asher always did, a little bored, and a lot arrogant. Asher tilted his chin in her direction and slipped his hands in his pockets.

"Kyra and Hawthorn are back." He shifted his gaze to Tarek. "Care to explain what the bloody hell this is all about now?"

Tarek nodded, his expression grim, and he moved to the center of the room. "Excuse me. Can I have your attention?

Thank you for coming downstairs. I know it's late," he said smoothly, amiably, as if it was a normal occurrence for thirteen near strangers to be gathering in a too-small parlor in the middle of the night. "There's been a murder."

The room was silent for half a beat.

Then it erupted.

Tali made a choking sound. Cam's hands went to his wife's shoulders.

"What the fuck, Collins?" Kyra barely heard Wes over the racket.

Everyone was speaking over everyone else.

"Oi!" Asher rose his voice. "I said, oi!"

The room quieted.

He pulled his fists from his pockets and stared Kyra down. "Is this some sort of sick joke? What is your man on about?" His mouth pressed in a thin line, and his gaze swept the room, dislodging a lock of his styled hair. He pushed it off his forehead. "And where the fuck is Maloof? If he put you up to this, I swear to god, Kyra.—"

"He's dead, Asher. Someone killed him. Elise too, probably."

Whatever Asher was going to say next died on his lips. His mouth opened and closed. "When? How? What happened? Where are the authorities?"

Tarek explained how he and Kyra had found Assaf in the basement. That he was already dead when they found him. All the while, Asher watched her.

"But how do you know it's murder?" Loriann asked, ringing her hands together. "It was probably just an accident. Americans are so dramatic."

"He was stabbed. In the neck. I saw it myself." Kyra shut her eyes, seeing it all again. The blood. His dinner jacket. His mouth twisted in a silent scream.

"Fucking hell," Asher breathed, at the same time Tali let out a strangled cry.

Camilla hugged her cousin close.

"I need everyone to remain calm." Tarek raised his hands. "We'll stay here until the authorities arrive."

"Why!? So the murderer can kill us off one by one?" Hedge barked, glaring at Tarek. He jutted his chin out. "And under what authority? You're a nobody!"

Tarek's jaw clenched. Technically, without his police credentials, he had no official authority, but whether he held a badge or not, Tarek was the only person here who was trained to handle anything like this.

Kyra forced herself to set aside her anger. Not telling her their suspicions hadn't been the right call. She deserved to know if they thought she was in danger, but right now the people at Verinder House needed to listen to Tarek and trust his judgement. He was the only one here who could keep them safe. If they suspected a rift between them, it could undermine that trust.

"Dr. Collins's current role as a consultant does not negate the years of experience he has with law enforcement and your state police, Hedge. To my knowledge, he is the only person here equipped to protect us." Kyra straightened her shoulders, daring anyone to contradict her.

"Wesley?" Julia reached for her son.

She appeared so small, hunched on the bench against the wall. Her clean, black apron hung loosely on her neck.

"*Mãe?*" Wes went to his mother. He squatted down in front of her, taking her hands in his. Kyra turned away while they spoke softly in Portuguese. His tone was gentle, so unlike the rough, contemptuous growl he used with everyone else.

"And when will the police arrive?" Asher demanded, drawing Kyra's attention.

"The phones and internet are down." Tarek ran his hand through his hair. "I can't reach the Edgartown authorities or the mainland to inform them of the second victim. Edgartown PD said they'd be here on the first ferry over. So until then, to keep everyone safe, we'll wait here."

"What? Absolutely not." Loriann stood up. Her laptop clattered to the floor. "Asher, get Aysha. We leave now."

"Wake up, Loriann! Aysha is fucking missing," Kyra snapped.

Loriann gaped at her. "*Missing?* What do you mean she's missing? Where is she?"

"We don't know, but we are certain she's not at Verinder House," Tarek said. He turned to Asher. "Is there somewhere she would have gone?"

"One of the facility vehicles isn't in the lot," Wes said, straightening to his full height.

"Wesley." Julia shook her head and tugged on the hem of Wes's flannel. He patted her gently on her shoulder.

"What was that?" Tarek asked.

Wes let loose a loud sigh and turned around, scowling like this was all an incredible inconvenience. "The hotel keeps two cars for guests to use. When I was cleaning up after dinner, I noticed one had been taken."

"And you didn't think to tell anyone? You must have known we've been looking for her all evening," Loriann gritted out, her voice high pitched.

He responded with a bland look. "What the guests do or don't do isn't any of my business." He said it with so much disdain, Kyra suspected he knew in detail each of the guests' activities.

Asher made a choked sound, and he grabbed the back of the closest chair. "The abandoned car?" He shared a look with Chase and Gerry.

"There was no one inside," Chase whispered. "I searched it. What kind of car is missing?" he asked Wes.

"A white Tesla."

All the color seeped out of Chase's face, and Kyra knew that was the model of the car they'd found half submerged in Cape Poge Bay.

"Fucking hell," Asher swore. "Fucking hell."

"There's an emergency fire station by the Mytoi Gardens. We can go there," Camilla said.

Tarek rubbed his jaw.

"We can't," Chase said, his voice quiet. The corner of his mouth hitched up into a grim parody of a smile. "The tide is coming in and the winds are causing a surge."

"Nonsense. We're going. The firemen will arrange our departure. Asher, get the car." Loriann pointed to Wes. "You, get our bags."

"You won't get out." Chase shook his head. He looked between Asher and Gerry. "You both saw the condition of the road. It's only going to get worse. If we were going to leave, we should have left already." He raked his hand through his hair. "It's a miracle we got out and back without ending up in the bay ourselves."

"What are you saying, Chase?" Ali asked, her voice shaking.

"We're stuck. Until the tide retreats."

"What time is high tide?" Tarek asked.

"Around two."

The tide would be going out when the ferries started running again.

The reality of what Chase said sank in and Kyra's heart banged against her ribs. Her eyes found Tarek's, and she saw her own fear reflected back.

We're trapped.

Chapter Thirty-Seven

"WE'LL WAIT HERE, together. We'll be safe and we have everything we need." Tarek declared, speaking with a calm authority. "When Edgartown PD arrives, or the phones come back, we'll arrange for transportation off the island and a search party for Aysha and Ben."

Another blast of wind hit the house, causing the fire to crackle and sputter. Asher crossed his arms over his chest with an unhappy huff. Kyra didn't blame him. She'd rather be pretty much anywhere else in the world than in this room, with these people, one of whom was a murderous psychopath.

Tarek wasn't a natural optimist. He was putting on a show for the others, pretending everything would be alright, that Aysha and Ben weren't wandering around the island in the dark, or worse, dead—pulled out to sea and drowned. Despite her irritation with him, Kyra was glad he was with them. They needed his assuredness as the example to follow. She certainly wouldn't have been as convincing.

She took stock of the others, assessing who could have had the ability, access, and motive to shove Elise down the stairs, or a knife through Assaf's throat and, if Chase and Tarek were correct, had a reason to hurt her.

It dawned on her that she was at the center of this entire night. This was her job, her clients, her family, her friends. But for her connections, these disparate groups of people wouldn't have come together. She wasn't sure what that meant or how that factored into Elise's and Assaf's deaths, or Ali's injury.

The occupants of Verinder House settled into an uneasy inertness. Tali was sitting on the floor below Camilla. She rested her head against her cousin's knee. Ali was sharing her blanket with Chase. He looked like he was resting, his head back and his eyes closed, but Kyra knew he was listening, paying close attention to everyone around him. Gerry hovered, concern and exhaustion deepening the thin lines at the corners of his eyes. Wes prodded at the fire while Cam stood nearby. Loriann and Hedge were back in their chairs, Loriann gripping the arms, her laptop still at her feet. Hedge looked annoyed as ever. They were all quiet and in relative comfort. For now. But the Bride's Parlor wasn't intended to house thirteen people overnight.

"Tar," Kyra said, keeping her voice low. "If we're going to stay in here all night, we need supplies. Blankets, water, more firewood." She jerked her chin toward the pile to the left of the fireplace. It'd dwindled down to just a few logs, not nearly enough to see them through to morning.

Tarek's hand wrapped around her forearm, and he guided her to the corner, further away from the others.

"I know." He shifted on his feet and gave her an uneasy look. He'd probably been thinking it before she even approached him. Kyra debated who they could ask to go. Tarek wouldn't trust Wes where he couldn't see him. Cam wouldn't want to leave Ali. Hedge and Loriann were non-starters. Gerry wouldn't let Chase go without him, and selfishly, she wanted Gerry near her aunt, and if she was being benevolent, Loriann.

"Fuck," she hissed under her breath, and her hand went to her forehead. "Loriann's medication. It's still in Aysha's room."

Kyra blew out a shaky breath. It had to be her. There was no one else Tarek would trust out of his sight, and who knew what they needed and where to find it. She could probably accomplish it in a few trips.

"I'll go," she said, trying to keep from being overheard. The fewer people who knew she would be wandering the halls alone and vulnerable, the better. "I'll get Loriann's medication, and whatever else we'll need. I'll be back in a few minutes."

"No. We'll send someone else."

"Who?" she demanded, waving her hand at the rest of the room.

"Ben and Aysha aren't accounted for. I don't want you out there alone. It's not safe."

"Because you think I'm a target," she scoffed. "But not enough to actually tell me, so I could protect myself." She glared at him, and a soft flush crept over his cheeks.

His mouth turned down, but Kyra wasn't ready for his apology. She stared at her socks, the white clashing with the colors in the ornate rug. Could Ben or Aysha be behind all this? Ben certainly had opportunity, and the ability to hurt Elise, Assaf, and Ali, but to what end? And Aysha? What had she to gain from any of this?

"I'll go with her," Asher said, and Kyra startled.

She hadn't heard him approach. How much had he overheard? His expression remained coolly neutral, and Kyra suspected he'd heard the entire exchange. If he was the killer, he knew they thought she was a target. Without meaning to, Kyra took a step back and Asher's eyebrow went up.

"No, thank you." Tarek looked pointedly in the direction of Loriann and back, dismissing Asher.

"Come off it. I can help. Let me." He slid his hands into his pockets. "And *she* trusts me." He turned to Kyra, his head tilted to the side, assessing. "Don't you?"

She didn't answer. Instead, she studied Asher from under her eyelashes. He was still in his tailored waistcoat and matching trousers from dinner, but he'd lost the jacket, and his shirtsleeves were rolled up to his elbows. *To hide Assaf's blood?*

Before Loriann had whisked him away, Asher's life in Wales had been troubled. Kyra knew from her firm's background checks that he'd had a few run-ins with the law as a teenager, and she'd witnessed his nasty temper on more than one occasion.

Her silence went on for too long.

Hurt and anger flickered behind Asher's eyes, and he turned to Tarek. "We should also take one of the staff. They'd know where the things you need are." He turned his sharp gaze on Kyra. "And I'd be less likely to murder the two of you at once."

Kyra winced at his sarcasm.

Before Tarek could respond, Asher crossed the room to where Camilla and Tali were sitting. Kyra couldn't hear what they were saying, but Camilla nodded, while Tali shook her head.

"Wes?" Camilla said loud enough for her voice to carry.

Wes replaced the fire poker on the tool stand and went to his sister. Tali clutched him. And even from across the room, Kyra heard the poor woman's sniffles as she cried.

Camilla followed Asher back to the front of the room. Asher paused next to the door and nodded toward it. Kyra sighed. Not only was she going, but thanks to Asher, everyone knew.

"Kyra, no," Tarek said, his voice sharp, and Asher just raised an eyebrow at him.

"We've no better option, Tar. It'll be fine," she said with more confidence than she felt.

Tarek gripped her wrist, and when he spoke, his voice was low and hoarse. "If you're not back in twenty minutes, I'm coming for you." Tarek glared at Asher. "If anything happens to her."

Asher raised his hand and scoffed. "Spare me your intimidation tactics. Miss Gibson will be fine. Perhaps you can be a helpful chap and sort out the heating in the meantime?" Asher opened the door and bent in a mock bow. "After you."

Chapter Thirty-Eight

THE DOOR CLICKED shut behind them, immersing them in quasi-darkness. Even though Kyra knew her friends were just on the other side, she felt alone and exposed under Asher's cool stare. She raised her chin to meet his gaze.

Camilla pulled a lanyard containing her keycard and a set of keys from around her neck and stepped toward the service corridor across the hall.

"No," Kyra said, louder than she intended. "We'll take the front stairs. We need to go to Aysha's room first."

She didn't want to be stuck in that small, dangerous stairwell with them. The close confines and the narrowness of the treads made it too easy to incapacitate someone or throw them down the stairs. Camilla shrugged and began walking in the opposite direction, up the north hall.

Kyra fell into step behind her, hyper aware of Asher at her back and the prickling sensation on her neck. She jumped when she felt his hand on her arm, his touch feather light, a request, not a demand, that she stop.

She whirled around, stepping back, keeping distance between them. Asher didn't advance closer, but when he spoke, his voice was low and full of venom, "So, Kyra love, do you want to tell me what I've done to put me at the top of your murder suspect list?"

Camilla's soft footfalls stopped.

"I've no idea what you're—" Kyra stuttered.

"Cut the bullshit." He narrowed his eyes at her and then they widened. He took another step back, his mouth fell open. "You think I killed Maloof."

Kyra squared her shoulders. "Everyone saw you antagonize him at dinner. You hated each other. You were always at loggerheads." Asher recoiled. Disappointment and hurt flickered behind his eyes. "You didn't want me to contact him after Ali's injury, you knew about the cellar, and you changed after dinner."

"I see. And Mrs. Elmer? Did I kill her, too? Tell me. Do I also toss elderly women down flights of stairs? For what? Shits and giggles? To appease my villainous psyche? Curb some morbid compulsion?"

"Stop it," she whispered.

"Then what, Kyra?" Asher demanded; his hands clenched into fists by his sides. "What could make you think I've done this?"

"Elise was the holdout on the merger."

"I know. She had been hesitant for some months. Unlike her husband, the money wasn't her primary objective."

"What was?"

"I couldn't say. I never asked."

"But now, you don't need to. Hedge can, he *will* sign it." Kyra's voice rose.

"He already fucking did. Fucking hell, you really think I did it." Asher raised his hands to his head, before dropping them to his sides and with it went his anger. He looked bone-tired and older than his forty-three years. He'd aged a decade in a moment. "I didn't touch Elise Elmer. I wouldn't harm an old woman. I'd expect you of all people to know that."

Kyra swallowed and looked down at her socks. How many times over the years had Asher run back to Wales to take care of his mother? Failed to persuade her to leave whatever lowlife she'd attached herself to? More than she could count.

"And I certainly didn't kill Maloof. He was a hothead and, in my opinion, a poor lawyer who gave us shit advice. I prefer ... *preferred* your counsel. But disliking the man is a far cry from wanting him dead." His voice went soft and full of regret as he said, "He has two young daughters, Kyra. You think I would deprive them of a parent? Over a grudge?" Asher shook his head. He looked so pained.

"Show me your shirt cuffs."

"What?" he reeled back.

"Show them to me," Kyra repeated, holding his gaze.

Incredulous, he yanked down his shirt sleeves and held out his arms. He twisted them back and forth.

"See?" Asher's eyes flashed.

Kyra reached out to touch the cotton of his pristine white shirt.

"Satisfied?"

She bit her lip and nodded. Kyra hadn't really needed to see his shirt cuffs. She'd already known that Asher would never physically hurt anyone, had known as soon as he comforted Tali after finding Elise in the hallway. Underneath his pompous swagger, Asher was a good man.

"Camilla," he said, turning around. As he folded his left sleeve up over his forearm, he made a *carry-on* motion. "Let's go."

"Asher, wait." Kyra placed her hand on his arm, and he flinched back. Her hand fell to her side as she looked up at him. "I'm sorry. I misjudged. I apologize." Kyra threw a look at Camilla, then back at Asher. "But you need to know something. About Global Media." Asher blinked at her, waiting, his expression wary. "Hedge Elmer is a sexual predator." Asher went completely still. "I can't tell you the specifics, but I know of at least two women he assaulted. There were others. Global Media, Elise, they knew of it, covered it up. Loriann knows. She knows about all of it – Hedge, the women, and the cover up. She hid it from you."

"And how long have you known?"

"A few hours." That gave him pause. She hadn't deceived him, not really.

He stared at her for a moment. "Thank you for telling me." He smirked at her, but it was strained and humorless. "We'd best get on before your policeman goes all American and shoots me."

Chapter Thirty-Nine

CAMILLA OPENED AYSHA'S door and stood to the side to let them in. Kyra could have done it herself, but Camilla seemed to have forgotten she'd given Kyra a master key. Kyra suspected if brought to her attention, Camilla would ask for it back, and for some reason, Kyra felt safer with it.

Asher followed Kyra inside. The medicine case was sitting on the desk where she and Tarek had left it. Kyra zipped it open to double-check its contents. She wanted to ask Asher how serious Loriann's condition was, but after their conversation downstairs, she doubted he wanted to speak with her or discuss his aunt. Kyra placed the case in Asher's outstretched hands. She followed him out, shutting the door behind them. They crossed the bridge landing to the north side's second floor and followed Camilla back to the service stairwell. Camilla unlocked the door and propped it open.

"What will we need?" she asked. Kyra listed off supplies, and Camilla opened the cabinets, pulling down extra blankets, pillows, and two cases of bottled water.

"Do we need anything else?" Kyra asked Asher.

She turned in the narrow space. Her heel slipped, throwing her off balance. She yelped. Camilla grabbed her arm, steadying her.

"Thank you," Kyra wheezed, pressing a hand to her heart. She felt its wild fluttering below her fingertips, and in her ears. She shook her head.

"Are you okay, Ms. Gib ... Kyra?" Camilla asked, peering at her.

Kyra sucked in a deep breath and nodded. She refused to look behind her, see how close she'd come to repeating Elise Elmer's tumble. With every minute, her loathing for this house grew.

Camilla stepped an inch closer and Kyra tensed.

"We don't have extra shoes, but you can take these." She held out a pair of lavender-colored bath slippers.

"Oh, thank you." Kyra took them and maneuvered away from the landing to slip them on.

They were the typical hotel one-size-fits-all terrycloth slides that fit no one well, but they were better than nothing. Kyra was touched by Camilla's gesture. She'd expected the same combativeness she'd received from Wes and his mother, but Camilla Ramos and Tali Silva had been nothing but kind.

As if reading her thoughts, Camilla spoke, keeping her voice soft, "I didn't know what to think when I heard you would be here." She angled herself between Kyra and the hallway.

"Pardon?" Kyra's stomach dropped and her shoulders tensed.

"Renee said you weren't all that bad, but Wes didn't have anything nice to say about you."

"He wouldn't."

"They blame you for ruining everything. After what Wes did to the summer people's houses, he lost his contractor's license. No one on the island will hire him for any construction work. He can only get odd jobs and that's only if someone like me or my brother vouch for him."

"My cousin made a mistake, Miss Gibson. He took on too many projects, too quickly. He couldn't source the materials he needed and fell behind on his contracts." Camilla fisted the bottom of her shirt and she looked at the floor. When she looked back up at Kyra, her mouth was drawn and downcast. "He started taking materials from one worksite to finish another. And it got out of hand. He really didn't mean to hurt anyone."

At that, Kyra stiffened. "He broke into my house. He chased me down the street, ran me off the road. When the police came, they were his friends, and they insulted me, accused me of stealing from him."

"He was desperate!" Camilla's voice hardened. "Did you know he had to sell the company? His house?"

Kyra shook her head.

"He moved back in with Aunt Julia. Tali's taking extra jobs and every cent she makes she gives to him. Wesley made a mistake, and he owns that. He's doing everything he can to make amends. He's paying everyone back."

Kyra wasn't sure what to say. She glanced in Asher's direction, but he was staring at the medicine container in his hands, either not listening or not inclined to interfere.

Kyra swallowed. "That's great, Camilla."

"Having you as his enemy makes it so much harder for him. Everyone bends over to make you and your fancy, rich friends happy. Ben wanted to fire him when he found out you were coming with the Hawthorns. But then when you came, you and Dr. Collins were so *nice*. To Tali. To me." She shot a quick look at Asher and back, and she shrugged. "I thought maybe you're not as bad as my cousin and aunt say, and maybe you can see we're not as bad as you and your boyfriend think we are."

"I..." Kyra wanted to defend herself, but Asher cleared his throat and gave her the tiniest shake of his head, warning her not to engage. Apparently, he had been paying attention. He was right. Getting into an argument with Camilla over Wes Silva right now wouldn't help them get away from Verinder House and safely home.

"I... *we* don't think you're bad, but you're right. I'm sorry for the part I've played in all of it," Kyra said instead. "Thank you for the slippers, Camilla. And for helping us."

Camilla dipped her chin in a nod.

"Do we need anything else?" Asher asked and when Kyra shook her head, he hoisted up the cases of water, balancing Loriann's medication on top. Camilla and Kyra gathered up the stacks of blankets and pillows and they began their return to the Bride's Parlor.

Chapter Forty

VERINDER HOUSE WAS silent as they retraced their steps. Even the wind couldn't be heard from the interior hallway. Kyra hadn't realized that she'd taken comfort in the ambient noises from the house's occupants. Crashes from the kitchen, the squeak of a cart's wheels, or thumps from footsteps, laughter that carried. Even the hushed tones of an argument had all made the house feel alive and lived in. The quiet made it feel like a tomb. Gooseflesh broke out on her arms, and she clutched the blankets closer to her chest, holding in her shiver.

Outside the Bride's Parlor, Kyra fumbled with the blankets, trying to knock on the door.

"Tar?" she called. No response. "Tarek?"

"Oh, for fuck's sake." Asher huffed and kicked the door. Hard. "Oi! Open up!" he hollered.

There was rustling, and the door cracked open. Gerry's dark eyes peered at them, and the worry lines at the corners softened.

"You're back," he said, pulling it open and ushering them inside. He pulled the top case of water off Asher's stack and followed him to the drinks cart in the corner.

The back doors were open, letting in the cold. Tarek was

standing just inside, talking to whomever was out of sight on the back patio. Kyra did a mental roll call. *Wes.* The wind caused the heavy curtains to twist and flap, revealing a leather log carrier on the paving stones. Tarek had listened to Asher's request to see about the heat. Tarek held the curtains out of the way so Wes could pass. He held a carrier in each hand. His thick-soled work boots *thumped* on the floor. He caught Kyra watching him, and his mouth twisted. Kyra ignored him, and she carried blankets and pillows over to his family.

She helped Camilla pass out the rest of the bedding, making sure all the guests were comfortable and had what they needed. She brought the last set over to her aunt and uncle. Ali was still resting on the chaise, but now her eyes were closed, and her breathing was deep and regular. Cam had pulled a chair up beside her and was playing on his phone. She touched her aunt's arm, but Ali didn't stir.

"Cam?"

"She's fine, Kay." He took the extra blanket she handed him and tucked it around his wife's shoulders. "She was complaining of a headache." He pushed a tendril of blonde hair behind Ali's ear, and she made a soft sound.

"Headache?"

"She said the back of her head hurt. Gerry examined her. He said she probably had bruising where she was struck. He offered her something for the pain. It made her drowsy."

Oh. She reached out and rubbed her uncle's shoulder. "You can get some rest, too. I'll watch over her."

"I won't sleep." He shook his head. *No, none of us will.* She stepped back. "Wait, Kay?" Cam held up the mobile phone in his hand. He had one of those models preferred by techies. "I was thinking about the issue we have with the phones. I didn't see wires outside." Kyra gave him a blank look.

"No, they buried all the telephone and electrical lines on this side of the island a decade ago."

Chase's voice came from behind her shoulder, and she startled. Her nerves were fried. She narrowed her eyes at him. He'd wrapped the quilt she'd handed him around his shoulders.

"You need a bell," she said, repeating what he'd said to her last summer.

His mouth twitched in a tired, lopsided smile. He cocked his head to the side. His still damp hair clung to his temple. "Why, Cam? What's up?"

"I was thinking. Someone said the wind blows out the internet, but if there are no suspended lines or wires, then the outage probably isn't due to a downed cable. We still have the electrical. I was thinking it may be a hardware or a software issue."

"Like the modem or the router?"

"*Mmhhmm.* If so, I might be able to fix it."

If they could get the phones working, the authorities would have to come. The wind be damned. They could leave this nightmare behind them.

"Tarek?" Kyra called to him and waved him over. "Cam, tell him."

Cam relayed the information. "We just need to find the modem."

"Silva," Tarek called to Wes, who was by the fire. "Do

you know where the modem and router would be?"

"No," he said and walked away.

Kyra shared a defeated look with Tarek. Wes wouldn't help them. He hated them. Hated them so much he'd rather spend a night with a killer. Unless he was the killer.

Wes came to a stop next to his cousin. He spoke to her in hushed tones, in Portuguese.

She nodded and walked over. "It could be in the basement."

"The signal was strong when it was working. Concrete in basements cause interference." Cam shook his head. "No, I'd bet the router was on this floor."

"This floor?" Camilla pressed her lips together, thinking. "The only other place it might be is Ben's office."

"Ben has an office?" Tarek asked, catching Kyra's eye. "Where?"

Chapter Forty-One

"It's off the kitchen, next to the basement entrance," Camilla said. "But he keeps it locked."

Absently Kyra's hand went to her pocket, where she'd put her keycard.

"I remember where it is—on the other side of the house, in the south wing," Tarek said. "Cam, I'll go with you." Cam nodded and grabbed his fleece from the back of the sofa. "Kyra, keep the door…"

"No!" Hedge bellowed and smashed his hand down on a table.

The lamp jostled. The soft murmurs of conversation ceased. Kyra hadn't known he'd been listening to them. Casually, Chase angled his body in front of hers, and she gave him a nudge.

"One of you people is a murderer. You." Hedge pointed a fat finger at Tarek. "You wanted us all here to babysit us. For our safety, you said. You stay."

"Mr. Elmer, you'll be safe enough here. It's best if I go with Cam."

"Safe enough? *That's* your standard of care? Safe *enough?*" Hedge grunted and lumbered to his feet. "First my beloved wife, and now the lawyer! Someone is trying to sabotage the merger. I'm probably next! I am in danger. And I'm stuck on this godforsaken island. A sitting duck." His nostrils flared. "Who did it?" he demanded, spinning in a circle. His eyes narrowed at Chase. "It was you, wasn't it? You little shit. I should have pressed charges. You're a criminal, just like your father and that bastard sister. Damn your mother."

"Oh, stop it," Loriann snapped. "Beloved wife? You can't be serious." Loriann scoffed when Hedge looked affronted. "Come now, Hedge, how long after you found out she was dead did you wait to finalize the acquisition?" When he didn't answer, her mouth stretched into a cruel smile. "Let me remind you. It was immediate."

Hedge's bushy eyebrows flew up. "Should I have waited?"

"No, of course not, but do not attempt to exact any sympathy from these people, or from me. Dear Elise was hesitating. Everyone could see it at that dinner. Her very convenient fall, or murder, whatever it was, has made you a very rich man."

Hedge sputtered. "What are you implying, Loriann?"

"Whatever you want to infer, Hedge." Loriann stood up. "But we need the phones. Kyra, you and your uncle will go. Take the maintenance man with you. Mr. Collins and Dr. James stay with us."

Tarek stiffened, prepared to object, but Kyra tugged him away by his shirtsleeve.

"You won't win. She feels safer with you and Gerry here. It'll be fine, Tar. Cam and I will be fine. We'll sort out the router, call the police, and we'll go home."

"Kyra, no." His eyes were on Silva behind her. Tarek dipped his head and whispered. "I don't trust him."

Kyra didn't trust Silva either, but she sure as shit wasn't sending her uncle out there alone with him.

"And why's that, Collins?" Wes asked, his tone barbed and his sneer deepened. He did it so often, it had lost its impact. She bit down on the inside of her cheek to keep from snapping at him.

"Tar," Chase interrupted. "I'll go with them." He gave Kyra a gentle nudge and looked over at Cam. "I know a few things about computers. I may be able to help."

A muscle in Tarek's jaw jumped, and he ran his hand through his hair. He took out his wallet and pulled out a business card. He grabbed a Verinder House pen from the secretary desk by the door and wrote two sets of numbers on the back.

"This is the Edgartown chief's direct number."

Kyra took the card, ran a thumb over the subtle embossing.

"When they answer, give them my name, and read off this number. They'll send help." It was Tarek's card with the security company, the one that gave him security clearances well above normal law enforcement. He wouldn't have given this to anyone else, she realized. "And if they give you any shit, give Silva the phone."

That was why Tarek wasn't telling Wes to stay. He had friends on the police force, ones who were willing to bend the law to help him. If she wasn't able to convince them to come, Wes could.

Kyra nodded and slipped the card into her pocket. She reached up and gave him a soft kiss at the corner of his mouth, hoping it didn't come across as a goodbye.

"We won't be long."

Chapter Forty-Two

THEY FOLLOWED WES around the grand staircase and down the south hall to the kitchen. Kyra scrambled to keep up with the men. She tripped in her ill-fitting slippers and stumbled. Wes caught her by the arm, keeping her from sprawling to the floor. Once she'd found her footing, he let her go, glaring at her, like her near fall was a personal insult, before huffing and turning away.

Cam reached out, tapped her shoulder, and they slowed down enough to drop behind Wes and Chase.

"Kay, what is going on with the maintenance man? Why did Tarek say he doesn't trust him?" Kyra glanced at Silva's back. "Kyra?"

"He's Wes Silva. Julia's son." Cam nodded, not following, and Kyra explained in a rushed whisper. "He's the man who broke into my house last spring. He was stealing from me."

Cam's eyes went wide, and he let loose a violent curse.

Kyra winced. "I don't think he's a threat." *Right now.* It didn't sound convincing, and Cam frowned.

Wes used his keycard to open the doors to the kitchen and turned on the lights. The overhead fluorescents flickered, and the stainless-steel surfaces glinted in the harsh blue-toned light.

"Ben's office is this way." He crossed the kitchen to the door at the back. It opened into a small vestibule with the stairs going down to the basement and another door to the right. This door didn't have a keypad, but a normal lock requiring a key. Wes tried the knob. It turned. His eyebrows rose, and his expression darkened, like he wasn't pleased. In fact, Wes looked... *troubled*. Kyra's pulse quickened.

"What is it?" Chase asked, but Wes shook his head and gave the door a push.

It glided back on its hinges. Light from the interior shone out into the dark stairwell. The four of them crowded in the doorway. Chase let out a strangled noise, and Wes took a step back, bumping into Kyra. Kyra stared, trying to process what she was seeing.

No. No, no, no.

Ben was slumped in his chair behind the desk. His eyes were open, staring blankly at the desk blotter in front of him. His lips were white. In his right hand, between his index and middle finger, a ballpoint pen was propped at an angle.

"What in the actual fuck?" Chase's voice caught, and he rushed inside.

He rounded the desk, giving it a wide berth, and swore again. Kyra moved closer and Chase raised his hand.

"Kyra, don't. Stay there."

But she ignored him. She blinked, taking in the wooden handle protruding from the base of Ben's skull, the dark halfmoon stain between his lavender clad shoulder blades. She let out a gasp, and Chase spun her around, away from Ben.

He held her against his chest. "He's dead."

Wes swore.

"What ... what is that?" Kyra asked, untangling herself from Chase's embrace. She rubbed her eyes and swallowed, making herself look. "How?"

Chase crept closer. "An icepick?" Chase's voice rose. "Who fucking does that?"

"He was pithed," Cam said. His face was white, and his voice trembled.

"He was what?" Chase choked out.

"I've seen it before." Cam's voice was flat, his eyes behind his glasses too round. "With animals. On my family's croft." His shoulders fell, and he said in a whisper so soft it was nearly unintelligible, "It'd have been instantaneous, if done properly."

"Is that supposed to make us feel fucking better?" Wes seethed.

Cam's hands went up, and his features slackened. "No, no, of course not. I don't know why I—" He broke off.

"Where would the router be?" Kyra asked, trying to focus and looking anywhere but at the body. Another body. How many people would die tonight? "We need to call in the police."

They stirred.

"Kay and I'll take this side. Cam, Silva, you look on that side. The modem would be about yay big, black. Probably with coaxial cables." They searched, as if the task kept them from falling apart.

Kyra stooped, checking the shelves that ran along the wall. Ben's office wasn't neat. He'd shoved things onto the shelves with little rhyme or reason. Stacks of extra Verinder House swag in its signature color, binders of notes, sample menus, wedding and function materials, brochures, and empty boxes. Kyra pushed the clutter aside as she rushed to search the shelves.

"Shite." Cam's voice was hoarse. "Shite. Shite."

"Cam?" Kyra stood up and turned around. In his hands he held a black plastic box.

"Someone's cut the cables."

"Are you fucking kidding?" Chase scrambled to Cam's side for a better view. He grabbed the frayed cable ends, turning them in his hand. "These are shredded." His blue-green eyes, wide with terror, found hers. His face was ashen. Kyra's heart stuttered.

"Cam, can you fix it?" She knew the answer.

Her uncle shook his head so, so slowly, like he was dazed, trying to make sense of their situation. When he spoke, his voice was thick with apology. "No. I'm sorry, I can't."

"Someone's taken the cashbox."

Kyra's eyes snapped to Wes. "What?"

He pointed to a bare part on the shelf near his shoulder. "Ben kept the office locked because he had the cashbox in here." Wes's scowl deepened.

"What was in it?" she asked.

"Cash," Wes said like she was simple. "They kept some on hand to pay for local supplies, fish or produce at the farm stand."

"How much was in there?" Chase asked.

"Maybe three thousand minus whatever my mother

spent. Your host ordered as much local products as possible. And some suppliers prefer cash." Then he scowled and said, "We have receipts."

Did someone kill Ben for a few thousand dollars? It sounded ludicrous. Any one of the antique rugs or other furnishing was worth much more and could easily be squirreled out of Verinder House without murdering someone. And who here would be desperate enough to kill for whatever cash was in that box?

"We should go back," she said, her voice flat, defeated.

But Wes didn't move. He was still staring at the blank space where the cash box had sat. His forehead was beaded with sweat, and he looked very uncomfortable over the loss of a few thousand dollars. Did he think they would accuse him?

"Wes?" She tried to keep her tone as neutral as possible. "What is it?"

His eyes met hers, small and beady. "Ben kept cash in the box. But that's also where he hid the key to the gun lockup."

Chapter Forty-Three

TAREK FLUNG OPEN the door before Kyra could finish knocking. They'd practically run back, and Kyra was a little out of breath.

"What happened?"

"Hand out the snacks we brought, if anyone wants them," Kyra told Cam, handing him the basket containing fruit, cereal bars, and bags of chips they'd scavenged from the kitchen.

Wes pushed past them and headed to the hearth, where he stooped and threw a log on the fire with more force than necessary. Tarek's gaze shifted between Kyra and Chase.

"What happened?" he repeated.

Kyra stepped inside the Bride's Parlor and leaned against the wall. She let her eyes slide closed for a moment. It was at least ten degrees warmer in here than anywhere else in the house, and yet still chilly. The fire was in a constant fight against the damp and cold. She wondered if it was futile.

"I want to check on Ali first."

"Kyra, wait."

"Let her go, man."

"She's fine, Kay, just sleeping," Gerry said, when Kyra asked after her aunt. He was sitting in the chair beside Ali, sorting through Loriann's medication case. Asher was watching him, his miffed hawk expression firmly in place.

"What are you doing?" She gestured to the case.

"Ms. Oma needs her meds," Gerry explained, turning over one of the prescription bottles. "But she doesn't remember what she's taken today, and many of these have specific instructions when administering, or shouldn't be mixed. Aysha Skye must have had a schedule."

"It was on her phone," Asher said. "She kept everything on her scheduler." He shifted his weight. "Is Loriann in any danger?"

Gerry rifled through the containers until he selected one, holding it up. He gave it a shake. "This is the only one that she needs to take. If she takes her doses too close together, there won't be a significant issue. Her side effects may be more pronounced, but to miss a dose could be potentially harmful."

"How harmful?"

Gerry frowned. "It's safer for her to take a dose now. If Aysha didn't give her a dose at dinner, and Ms. Oma skips another, she could be in danger of stroke or seizure."

Asher's entire body went taut. "Give it to her."

Gerry's brow creased at Asher's commanding tone, and he frowned. He glanced at Kyra, who nodded, and then back at Asher. "I will," he said, his confusion written across his face.

Kyra excused herself and returned to Tarek and Chase. She took a steadying breath. Tarek's jaw tightened while they told him about Ben, the destroyed cables, the stolen cashbox. When she told him about the gun locker key, he visibly paled.

"And you didn't think to tell me immediately?" he growled through clenched teeth.

"I didn't want to cause a panic. If I'd gone running straight to you, everyone would have known something more had happened. We're barely holding onto control here. If they find out someone has access to an arsenal of firearms, it'll be a full panic." It was a half-truth. The other half, was that she hadn't been ready to say it out loud, to make it real.

Tarek grumbled, but he didn't argue. They were only safe if everyone remained calm.

She took the water bottle Chase handed her and leaned against the back of one of the room's many chintz armchairs.

"Does anyone know what's in the gun locker?" she asked.

"Camilla might," Chase said. "She seems to know the most. You know it is possible the killer just took the box for the cash. Or one of the staff found Ben and saw an opportunity."

Tarek ignored him. Kyra had to agree. They weren't that lucky.

"Do you want me to ask her?" Chase asked.

"No," Tarek said with a shake of his head.

His gaze had come to rest on Wes Silva, who was still fussing with the fire. Kyra could practically hear Tarek's thoughts: *The coincidences are too convenient. The killer knows Verinder House well. He knows about the passages, the basement, and laundry room. Ben's office. About the cash box and the gun locker.*

Tarek had suspected Wes of killing Elise and Assaf before, but with the discovery of Ben's body, and the missing gun storage key, he looked convinced. Wes had access and opportunity. It was no secret how much he resented the off islanders, or how much he hated Kyra. He would tick off all of Tarek's suspect boxes.

Wes must have felt them watching him, because he turned around and scowled. He stood up and stalked toward them, his hands clenched into fists. Kyra forced herself not to take a step back. He stopped a mere foot away and glowered at Tarek.

"What are you whispering about?"

"Nothing," Tarek said, uncrossing his arms.

Wes's watery eyes shifted left until they landed on Kyra. His mouth twisted. "If you have something you want to ask me, Collins, just ask it."

Tarek seemed to consider it. Then he asked, "Did you kill the property manager?"

If the question surprised him, Wes didn't let it show. "I did not," he bit out through clenched teeth.

"Tar," Kyra warned.

Chase reached out and gripped her forearm. He pulled her out from between the two men. "Don't," he whispered. She doubted they'd come to blows, especially if Tarek thought Wes was armed, but she didn't object.

"What about Assaf Maloof?"

"No." Wes's chest rose and fell.

"And Elise Elmer?"

Wes's jaw slackened, then his eyes narrowed to slits. "That was an accident. She fell."

Tarek cocked an eyebrow. "Did she? And what about Ms. Babcock? Was that an accident, too?"

Wes's jaw fell open.

"Lots of accidents, don't you think?"

Wes managed to close his mouth but didn't answer.

"Where is Aysha Skye, Silva?" Tarek took a step closer. Kyra felt Chase's hand on her arm tighten. "Where is she?"

"The fuck if I know, Collins." Wes's temper snapped, but he kept his voice low. "Why don't you ask him!" He pointed to Cam, who was sitting with Ali. "He's a murder expert. Just like you. What do you really know about him or any of these people? He's an off islander, same as the rest of 'em."

"Stop it," Kyra snapped, her voice sharp. She glanced around, but no one was paying them any attention. "Just, stop. Please. Ben's dead. Elise is dead. Assaf. Is. Dead. Someone, any one of us, could be next."

"Kay," Chase said.

"No. This is getting us nowhere." She shook him off.

Wes and Tarek sniping at each other wouldn't get them out of this hell. She needed to put distance between herself and them. Grabbing a quilt from one of the chair backs, she found a spot on the floor, far away from the others.

She kicked off her slippers and pulled her legs up, tucking the thick blanket around her.

Something about Tarek's accusations didn't sit right. Wes was smart. He hadn't had to tell them about the cashbox. None of them would have known. Maybe he'd told them to frighten them, to destroy the fragile control Tarek seemed to have over the situation. A panic would draw the attention away from Wes. It might even cause them to abandon the relative safety of the Bride's Parlor. If they were separated, they were easier targets.

But if that was his strategy, he just had the opportunity to set it all into motion. If he'd picked a fight with Tarek and alerted the room to the lost gun locker key, whatever control they were clinging to would be lost.

Kyra pulled the blanket tighter around her shoulders, trying to conserve her body heat. Her bum went numb from sitting on the hard, cold floor. Except Tarek, who'd taken a position at the door, everyone else was near the fireplace, but they were gathered in their social groups.

Cam was still sitting with Ali, but now Chase and Gerry were with them. Asher was watching over Loriann with an expression Kyra couldn't decipher. Hedge was in a chair close-by, his eyes closed, and his chest rising and lowering in a consistent cadence. How anyone could nap in this situation, Kyra couldn't fathom.

Wes had joined his family on the perimeter. They sat a little away from everyone else, like there was an invisible divide separating Verinder House's staff from its guests.

Kyra worried her lip. She was missing some critical piece of information that connected the victims. All the deaths happened in areas that were supposed to be off-limits to the guests. The year-round staff, and the temps all knew the building, but Asher did, too. She'd seen him use one of the servants' corridors. And, of course, Ali. What Ali didn't know about this house could fit in a thimble.

All the assaults happened in close proximity. The killer must have been someone the victims knew and were comfortable letting near them. *But Ali didn't see her assailant. Elise may not have either.*

The killer knew what he was doing. Knew exactly what to do. There was no question that Ben's and Assaf's deaths were intentional. The murder weapons were still protruding from their bodies. Kyra hadn't looked closely at Assaf, but Tarek had. She'd heard every word he recorded on his phone. Assaf had no defensive wounds. Ben had died while spinning a pen. These were precise strikes. Kyra shuddered. Her gaze jumped around the room.

Who here knows how to kill someone?

Wes hadn't been wrong. Her uncle knew a lot about husbandry. He'd grown up on a farm. Chase, too, with his farm and sea captain's training, might have that knowledge. And Gerry was a doctor. None of them would harm a soul, though. Her uncle set spiders free, for christ's sake.

Kyra drummed her fingers against the top of her knee.

Assaf and Elise were still unconvinced about the merger. Albeit for different reasons. Asher wouldn't say why Elise was the holdout. Assaf was hurt by his dismissal. Loriann, Hedge, and Asher would lose millions, if not billions, if the merger had stalled. No, that wasn't it.

Kyra rubbed her eyes. She didn't believe the killer cared about the merger. The deaths were too violent. They felt personal. This was about something else.

Tali made a soft sound that sounded like a sob. She sat stiff-backed in one of the overstuffed chairs. Camilla had moved a stool close to her cousin. Her head was propped on her arms, crossed atop the arm of Tali's chair. Tali ran her fingers through Camilla's hair. They were comforting each other. It was gentle and intimate.

Either woman had motive to harm Kyra. After all, she

was the catalyst for their family's financial trouble, but Camilla had sounded sincere upstairs and Tali had been nothing but professional, sweet, even. And no one have could have feigned Tali's panicked reaction to seeing Elise's body.

But what about Ben?

She couldn't make sense of his death, no matter which way she turned it. He was the outlier. Ali, Assaf, Aysha, Elise, Kyra ... they were all visitors, off islanders who'd come to Verinder House as guests. Was it possible that Ben was just collateral damage? The killer needed to access his office, to cut the cables and take down the phones and Wi-Fi, get the key to the gun locker? A crime of convenience. It was obvious Ben knew and was unafraid of his assailant, that's for sure. He'd trusted the killer, so much so he'd left his back exposed, unconcerned, while he jotted down notes.

Kyra swallowed. There was only one person she could think of who knew the house, had a history of violence and a short temper, hated the off islanders, *hated her*, and had known financial problems. Then Kyra remembered what Grace said at Thanksgiving. Wes had gone deer hunting, brought the meat to his mother. Her skin broke out in a cold sweat.

Chapter Forty-Four

*S*HIT. *S*HIT. *S*HIT. Kyra's hands gripped her blanket. Her nails bit into her palms through the fabric.

She observed Wes from the corner of her eye, careful not to get caught watching. He was sitting on the floor next to the patio doors, his forearms on his knees, his head against the wall. His eyes could have been closed, or he wanted it to look that way while he watched them and cut them off from an exit.

She took in his clothes. Unlike the rest of the Verinder House staff, Wes had never been in a uniform. He hadn't worn the Verinder House lavender, but she hadn't paid close attention to what he had been wearing. He could have changed a hundred times, or not once, and she wouldn't know.

Kyra needed to get Tarek's attention without causing suspicion. They had to get Wes away from everyone. She glanced at Wes again. She couldn't tell if he was armed under his bulky jacket. If he was… *No, I can't think like that.*

Tarek cleared his throat to gain the attention of the room. Loriann poked Hedge until he woke sputtering muffled obscenities. In careful measured words, Tarek told them what had happened to Ben. There was an audible gasp and Camilla's hands went to her mouth. Her face went white. Tali blinked over and over. Tarek didn't mention the gun locker or the missing key.

"Are you sure?" Asher asked and then he spun around until he found her. "Kyra?" She folded the blanket and set it aside before standing up.

"I saw it. So did Chase and Cam and ... and Mr. Silva. Ben's dead."

Asher dropped into his chair, like his knees had given out. He propped his elbows on his thighs and rubbed his temples. Loriann didn't give her nephew a sideways glance.

Tarek reiterated that for everyone's safety, they'd stay inside the room. No one argued this time. No one said much of anything.

Kyra checked her watch. They only had to make it a few more hours.

"What if the police don't come?" Camilla asked shakily. "What will we do?"

Tarek shared a look with Chase that made Kyra leery. He slid his hands into his pockets. "Edgartown PD isn't aware of Assaf or Ben's deaths, or that Aysha is missing. It's possible we're not the highest priority on their list. If by sunrise they haven't arrived, Chase and Kyra will go to the fire station. They have a radio."

"What?" Hedge bellowed, lumbering to his feet. "Why them?" He flung his hand in Chase's direction. "Because he's the son of that bitch and a crooked politician? And who the hell is *she*?" He pointed to Kyra. "She's a nobody." He turned his glare on Chase. "I should have seen you sent to prison; you degenerate little pissant." His fist hit his chest.

"I'm the one in danger. I should go."

Kyra couldn't argue. She was nobody. Her life meant no more than anyone else's in this room. This was Tarek. He'd want to get her out first, to keep her safe, but he had to be insane if he thought she'd leave Ali behind. She looked at Chase, but he wouldn't meet her gaze. Instead, his stony stare was locked on Hedge Elmer.

"Shut up, old man. You're in no more danger than anyone else here."

Hedge made a sputtering noise, but Chase cut him off, pointing to the door. "Feel free to walk. No one will stop you." Tarek turned a sharp eye on Chase and Chase raised a shoulder in a lazy shrug. "It's five miles, give or take. I'm sure you'd make it."

Hedge grunted and crossed his arms over his chest, but he kept quiet.

"Mr. Hawthorn's right," Asher said. "This ... whatever *this* is, it's not about the merger."

Without meaning to, Kyra's gaze drifted to Wes, but this time he was staring back. His features twisted in his trademark sneer. Kyra looked away.

"How can you say that, Asher?" Loriann demanded. "What else could it be?"

"What do you think it's about?" Tarek asked at the same time Talita said, "Could it be the missing woman?" Her voice caught on a hiccup. "Could she have killed all those people? Will she kill us?"

"Aysha didn't hurt anyone." Loriann's voice was firm. She waved her hand. "She certainly had no reason to kill the property manager or Elise. Assaf?" Loriann shrugged. "It'd be easier to ask who wouldn't want to kill him, if we're being honest about it."

"Loriann," Asher warned. "Perhaps now is not the time." He threw a glance at Tarek, his meaning clear: do not give him a reason to suspect you.

"Calm down, Asher." Loriann sat back and her lips hitched up, her smile once again cruel. Kyra swallowed. "You know as well as I do that Aysha didn't kill Assaf or anyone else here. There's no reason for her to. I've given her everything she wants."

Confusion creased Asher's brow. "What are you talking about?"

Loriann pretended to study her nails. "I was planning on telling you when we got back to London. However, seeing as the merger is all but official, thanks to Hedge, there's no reason to keep it a secret." Her smile turned vicious. "I've recognized Aysha as my heir, alongside you, of course."

Asher's mouth fell open. "You did what?" His voice was sandpaper.

Kyra had never seen Asher truly surprised, but right now, he was dumbstruck.

Loriann sighed like the bombshell she'd just dropped had already become tedious. "She was going to leave us, Asher. Leave *me*. She wanted to take a position somewhere else. It was all I could do to convince her to stay."

"You're serious." Asher stood.

"Of course, I'm serious. Aysha knows too much about me, about the family, the company to be allowed to leave. You know that. I was surprised you didn't have a contingency plan already in place for her, actually."

Understanding washed over Asher's features. "It was her." He stared at his aunt, aghast. "That's how you hid the sexual assault allegations against Elmer from me. Kyra said you did Global's human resources due diligence. That you insisted on handling it yourself, but I requested those documents. Aysha sent them to me. You had her falsify them." His voice had gone dangerously soft. "You knew what he'd done. And you hid it from me. After everything."

"Of course I did," she snapped. "You're so sensitive when it comes to that nonsense. We need Global's infrastructure. Hedge needs money. It's a win-win. Aysha knew that. Aysha saw what there was to gain, and when she demanded her share, truthfully, I was impressed."

Asher's jaw went tight. "So she blackmailed you? And you just gave her the company?"

"Of course not. I'm not a fool, Asher. Only a quarter." Loriann waved her hand. "She wanted half."

Asher shook his head slowly. He fisted his hands at his sides. A draft fluttered through the room, causing the fire to sputter. Kyra swore the room dropped ten degrees.

"You've gone too far, Loriann."

"You've no right to be upset," she snapped. "I shielded you. You have your ethics. Your *morals*. You refuse to get dirty, Asher. So, I had Aysha do it. I did it for you. That's what family does." Loriann's voice rose, shrill and piercing. "You may be my nephew's bastard, but you are my son. I have always protected you and what we've built. And I'll keep doing it for as long as I still have breath in me."

Asher pressed his lips together into a thin line before dipping his chin. "Right, then." Without another word, he turned on his heel and stormed out.

"Asher, wait!" Kyra scrambled, looking for her slippers, ready to go after him, when a loud mirthless guffaw made her pause.

"Family?" Hedge sputtered, glaring at Loriann. "He's your what? ... Your *nephew*? And you didn't think that conflict of interest warranted disclosure?"

"Calm yourself, Hedge. You're getting exactly what you asked for. No one else would have given you the deal I did, if they knew what I know. Would they?"

Hedge grumbled something indiscernible. Every inch of Kyra's skin crawled in disgust. *I worked for these people.* She promised herself that if she got out alive, never again.

"Someone, go find my dear grandnephew before he gets himself killed." Loriann slumped back in her seat.

"I'll go," Chase offered, slowly getting to his feet. He rolled his shoulders.

"Wait. Where did Silva go?" Tarek asked, spinning around.

Wes was no longer in his spot by the patio doors. *The draft.* He'd slipped outside. Kyra took a mental attendance. *And where is Julia?* Kyra couldn't remember the last time she saw the chef.

"Wesley?" Tali's voice cracked, and she stood up. "Wesley's gone?" She gasped and her hand went out. "Cami?" Camilla grabbed her cousin's hands.

Tarek cursed. "We need to go after Asher. He's not safe."

"What?" Tali's shriek was breathy.

"What about my cousin?" Camilla demanded.

"Chase?" Tarek's hand was already on the door.

"I'm with you. Let's go." Chase nodded. "Gerry, lock the door behind us. Don't answer it for anyone except us."

Gerry promised.

"No!" Hedge yelled. "The policeman stays. Send someone else."

No one reacted to Hedge's outburst. Tarek's eyes found Kyra's, and he conveyed a silent message. *Please be careful.*

"Tar, Chase, wait." But they'd already disappeared.

Gerry turned the lock. Cam grabbed the iron poker from the fireplace and took a defensive position at the French doors.

Tali's sobs turned raspy. She hiccupped, but it sounded more like a wheeze.

"Oh, no. Tali! Help. Doctor!" Camilla yelled.

Tali's shoulders bucked, but not with sobs. She was fighting for air. Her mouth opened and closed, and her eyes were wide. She clutched at her throat.

"Shit." Gerry crossed the room to grab his bag next to Ali. "What's happened?" he asked Camilla, yanking on his stethoscope.

"I need water!" Gerry called to anyone who would listen. Kyra hurried to the drinks cart, but Ali beat her.

"I got it." Ali pulled two bottles from the cooler and went to help Gerry.

"Tali," Gerry spoke, his voice both commanding and soothing. "You need to tell me. Have you taken anything today?"

It was Camilla who answered. "No, she doesn't do drugs. She has asthma. It's brought on by stress."

"Where's her inhaler?"

"She keeps it in her purse or her work apron." Tears streamed down Camilla's cheeks.

"And where is it?"

"Her room? The kitchen?" Camilla shook her head. "I don't know."

Talita's lips slowly drained of color and her gasps sounded more desperate. Kyra remembered Tali couldn't seem to catch her breath when they'd discovered Elise's body.

Gerry rummaged through his bag and pulled out something that looked like a thick marker.

"Tali, we need to open your air passages. Do you understand?" Tali nodded between wheezes.

Gerry pulled open Loriann's medicine case. He shuffled through the bottles and pulled one out, handing it to Camilla. "Take this. Crush three pills and dissolve them in water."

"Wait, that's mine. What are you doing?" Loriann was standing.

Ali put herself between them. "You'd best sit, Ms. Oma," she said in her Ali voice.

"Tali, look at me. Everything is going to be fine. Try and relax. I'm going to administer epinephrine. Your heart rate and blood pressure will spike. You may have a bout of dizziness. Don't panic. I'll be right here." He turned to Ali. "Help me get her lying down, will you?" Ali helped Gerry lay Tali down on the rug, propping her head up with a pillow. Her wheezes became less pronounced. "Hold her hand."

Gerry unscrewed the cap and plunged the component into her thigh. Tali's entire body spasmed. And she sucked in air. Her chest heaved as oxygen flowed back into her bloodstream.

Kyra watched from her corner behind the bar cart, just a few feet away from where she'd last seen Julia sitting on the bench. Julia. *Did Wes follow his mother out? Or did Julia follow him out?*

Kyra couldn't remember when she last saw Julia, but that she was missing now, at the same time as Wes, made her very nervous. She bit into her bottom lip and ran her palms down the front of her jeans. Chase and Tarek wouldn't be looking for Julia, and Asher left before they discovered Wes and Julia's absence. Kyra swallowed. Asher could be in danger. Chase and Tarek definitely were.

Tali's ragged breathing softened and subsided. Gerry and Ali eased her into a sitting position. They propped her against the loveseat, supported by pillows. Gerry held the stethoscope to her back. His fingers lingered on the pulse point at her wrist.

"Tali? Tali?" Camilla sobbed as she handed Ali a bottle of cloudy water.

Gerry slipped off his stethoscope and slung it around his neck. His voice was soft as he spoke.

But Kyra was no longer paying attention. Just beyond the bench, Kyra noticed the thin black line in the wall and beside it was a rectangular plastic panel painted to match the wallpaper. *The pocket door to the service hallway. Julia must have gone that way.*

She used her keycard. The lock disengaged, and the door slid open a sliver. Pressing her fingers into the crack, she pushed. The panel moved silently on the well-oiled rails and disappeared inside the wall.

Kyra peered into the dark beyond, but it was hard to see with the bright light behind her. She glanced back at the occupants of the parlor. No one was paying attention to her and before she could talk herself out of it, Kyra slipped into the service corridor. On the other side, she let go of the door and it slid closed with a soft *snap*, plunging her into darkness.

Chapter Forty-Five

KYRA GASPED AND reached out into the nothing in front of her. Her hands flailed, and she stumbled to the right, until her hands hit rough plaster. "Fucking hell," she mumbled, as she splayed her fingers and ran them along the wall, searching for the light switch.

Her fingers tripped over an old-fashioned knob and her breath hitched. She turned it. Dim light sputtered from the dust-covered sconces spaced too far apart to effectively illuminate the hallway, but it was better than nothing.

As usual, she'd rushed ahead without thinking, and she wasn't sure where to go from here. She could go back into the parlor and wait, or she could try to find Asher and Julia, get them to safety. Something about Julia's disappearance right after Asher stormed out, and they discovered Wes's absence gave her a feeling of trepidation.

Kyra rubbed her eyes. If Tarek found her wandering around the house, she wouldn't need to worry about Wes murdering her. Tarek would kill her himself, but she'd never forgive herself if Wes Silva harmed any of them because she chose to do nothing. She let out a steadying breath and crept down the hall, away from the Bride's Parlor.

Like the other service corridors at Verinder House, the

floor was covered in thick patterned carpet that muffled sound, and it had been narrowed to make room for storage. All along the left side were built-in shelves and cabinets that almost reached the high ceiling. Events' supplies, like extra service ware, glassware, and flatware, were stacked haphazardly. She noted bottles of alcohol and mixers for the bar cart, and stacks of table linens in muted colors. Further down, the shelves held glass vessels and vases of varying heights and widths. Decorations. For weddings or corporate events. The ugly plastic marble stands were clean and free of dust. Stacks of burgundy linens sat on the shelf above, next to a pile of cardstock. She pulled one from the top. The Omega Media and Global Media logos were at the top, followed by an agenda for a formal dinner. This was a staging area. It held all the rentals and décor for the originally planned Thanksgiving gala.

She replaced the dinner program. Kyra's eyes traveled the length of the hall. *This must connect to the ballroom.* She continued walking. The hallway felt too long. She swore that the Bride's Parlor was right next to the ballroom. But the darkness played tricks, messed with her depth perception. The hall was shorter than it looked, and it came to an abrupt end in front of a single door cast in shadow. She checked the wall for the keycard panel but didn't see one. Kyra pressed her hand to the door, gave it a tentative push. It swung forward an inch, then recoiled back. *A swinging door.* She inched it open, holding it with the tips of her fingers, and peeked inside.

It wasn't the ballroom.

It was the first-floor service stairwell. Where they'd found

Elise.

When they'd been exploring, she and Tarek had tried this door, but it'd been locked. Kyra stepped inside and let the door swing back and forth with a groaning *thwap, thwap, thwap.*

Kyra stared up the spiraling staircase and across the vestibule. *Which way would Julia have gone? Upstairs? To the cellar? The kitchen?* Kyra frowned. There was no reason for Julia to sneak out to go to the kitchen. If she needed something, Tarek would have arranged for her to go. No, Julia wanted something, or wanted to do something without the others' knowledge. Using the passages, she could travel around the house nearly undetected. Kyra craned her neck, looking up the narrow stairs. She put a slippered foot on the tread, and with her hand on the wall, she climbed.

Elise's blood was still caked into the thin crevices between the wooden slats. Kyra paused on the tread, and studied it, careful not to touch it. It was a ghastly reminder that they'd had missed their chance to escape.

Kyra hustled up the last few steps to the second floor, eager to get away from the scene of the first crime. Her foot slid out of her slipper, and she crashed forward, catching herself on the landing. The rough wood bit into her palms.

"Shit." She checked her hands. Just surface scratches. She wasn't even bleeding, but a tiny splinter poked out from the heel of her palm. She squinted at it and held her hand out, taking advantage of the light spilling into the stairwell from the north wing hallway.

Wait.

Kyra froze. All the halls at Verinder House were poorly

lit. *Where is the light coming from?* Kyra pulled the splinter out with her nails and dropped it on the floor. She crept forward. The light illuminating the stairwell was a beacon pulling her toward it.

Kyra inched into the hallway. She stepped into the pool of warm light streaming from the open door directly across from the service stairs. Her gasp was audible.

That's my room.

Chapter Forty-Six

"TAREK?" KYRA STEPPED closer to the open door. From her angle, she couldn't see inside. A shadow passed. Someone was in there.

"Tarek? Is that you?"

If he was inside their room and he found her wandering around alone, he would flip right the fuck out. Sucking in a deep breath. She stepped through the doorway.

And froze.

What the...

"Julia?"

Julia Silva was standing next to their bed. The room had been ransacked. The armoire doors had been thrown open. Her clothes, Tarek's clothes, their things were strewn about the room. And the safe. It was open.

"What are you doing?"

A sound, an all too familiar one. That *clack* of metal on metal. Kyra stopped breathing. Julia raised her arm.

A cold sweat broke out on Kyra's skin. She couldn't tear her eyes away from the scene in front of her, because there in Julia's hand, pointed right at Kyra's chest, was Tarek's gun.

Chapter Forty-Seven

"Julia? What are you doing?" Kyra asked, her mind reeling.

"Hands up." Julia motioned, bringing her left hand to cup the bottom of the magazine well, steadying her aim.

The motion struck Kyra as practiced. Kyra blinked.

"I won't tell you again, Ms. Gibson. Put your hands up where I can see them." Even while aiming Tarek's pistol at her, Julia's tone was formal, reserved, too detached to be courteous.

Kyra raised her hands to shoulder height.

"Please, turn around."

Kyra's heart thrashed against her ribs. "Julia? What are you doing?" she tried again.

Julia's thumb flipped the safety. Kyra had seen Tarek check the switch a dozen times. He'd even made her learn.

"Double-check, triple-check. It should always be engaged, Kyra."

"Turn around."

Kyra turned. With her back to Julia, she felt more vulnerable. The hard metal of the barrel bit into her shoulder blade.

"Upstairs. Now." Julia pushed her again, this time with

more force, urging her forward.

Kyra crossed the hall and stepped back into the servant's stairwell.

"Please. Julia. What's going on?"

"Quiet, Ms. Gibson. Upstairs."

Kyra climbed. She hugged the wall, keeping to the widest part of each tread. Julia's steps were steady and sure. Every time Kyra slowed, the barrel hit her shoulder blade, just hard enough to sting, urging her up, up, up.

Some part of her brain wondered how she was being held at gunpoint *again*. The irony that it was the one Tarek packed to be kept safe wasn't lost on her.

"How did you know about his gun?" Kyra asked.

Julia ignored the question. But of course, Julia would know about Tarek's firearm, would know he took it with him, that he was meticulous about it. Kyra had told Grace and Charlie about it over dinner at their house. Julia had been there. She was always there, with her homemade bread and pots of fresh butter fading into the background, lurking and listening. *Just like here.*

Kyra reached the third floor and stepped away from the landing and toward the hallway.

"No, you're still going up, Ms. Gibson." Julia's tone hardened, verging on disdain, the first hint of any emotion other than polite detachment.

"What?"

"Outside."

Kyra balked. She needed to get away from Julia or wrestle the gun from her. But Julia's assured actions, how she held the pistol, that she hadn't needed to look to disengage the safety, left little doubt in Kyra's mind that Julia was comfortable with guns. Even if Kyra was able to take it from her, she wouldn't know what to do with it.

The barrel of the gun prodded her forward toward the door to the widow's walk.

At the base of the stairs, Kyra halted. She turned around, lowering her arms.

"It's locked. I locked it."

Julia shook her head and motioned with the gun. "Open it, or I'll shoot you right here."

Kyra backed up the stairs, her hands on the railing. Her heel hit the base of the iron door. She reached for the door handle, pressed down on the latch. She felt the click of the mechanism releasing. Her eyes found Julia's and Julia's mouth stretched into a sneer so similar to her son's Kyra's heart skipped.

Keeping most of her weight held back, Kyra feigned pushing it open. "I can't. It's too heavy."

Julia's sneer deepened. Her arm holding the gun rose an inch, and the gun went off.

Kyra screamed and threw her hands over her head. She stumbled down two stairs. Her hand grasped the railing, and she pulled herself upright. She stared at the door.

Not more than six inches to the right of where she'd stood was a tiny perfect hole. Julia had shot between the ironwork filigree.

Kyra stared.

Julia shrugged, and her smile lost some of its cruelty. "I didn't miss, Miss Gibson. I lived on this property for years. Mr. Verinder taught me to shoot. Now, open the door."

Kyra pressed her body against the heavy door and pushed. It inched open. The wind blasted against it, and Kyra gritted her teeth and leaned. Suddenly, the wind caught it, and the door blew back with a *boom*. The momentum had Kyra stumbling through the doorway and out onto the widow's walk.

She fumbled and flailed, her hands seeking the railing. She gripped it. The rusty metal bit into her palms. Without letting go, she whirled around.

Julia was already in the doorway.

"Go to the end," Julia shouted over the wind. Kyra shook her head. *No.*

"You're jumping, or I'm shooting you." She cocked her head to the side and waved toward the far southern end of the widow's walk.

Icy wind blasted Kyra's back, cutting through her fleece. Her hair whipped against her skin, stinging her cheeks and neck. She shuffled backward, tripped over her borrowed slippers. She kicked them off. Under her feet, the wood planks felt damp and spongy with age and rot. Kyra back stepped, never taking her eyes off Julia. A gust of wind careened into her, throwing her off balance. Her hands, already numb with cold, tightened on the railing.

"Keep going." Julia motioned with the hand holding the gun. Kyra crouched. She half crawled backward along the widow's walk. The decking was no longer level and slanted toward the ground. She kept a firm grip on the rickety railing, praying it wouldn't give way.

She told herself not to look down, but it couldn't be helped. Her gaze was pulled to the slate roof tiles, the gutters beyond, all the way to the granite patio below.

Kyra bit her lip hard. She tasted blood. The sharp pain helped her focus, kept her from falling to pieces. She needed to get off the widow's walk, but the door was behind Julia. She'd never get past her.

Kyra raised her chin, eyeing the edge of the widow's walk. She could go over the side, but if she fell and hit the patio, she'd die. Behind her, she could jump. She'd have to clear the chimneys and the lawn to hit the pool. Kyra didn't know how far it was from the building. And if by some miracle she made it, she'd have to hope that she hit the deep end and win the fight against the pool cover. Too many *ifs*.

The balconies. Her heart skipped. She and Loriann's mirrored suites. Maybe she could slip straight down, just at the edge, and aim for Loriann's balcony below. It couldn't be more than twenty feet. She could survive that fall. Probably.

Loriann's balcony was her best option, but she couldn't see it from her vantage point. She knew it was at the end. Like her suite, Loriann's room would be the last one in the south hall. It would look straight out onto the back gardens and Cape Poge. She guessed it'd be below the southern-most end of the widow's walk behind her.

Kyra kept inching backward, with one eye on the roofline, the other on the woman who'd made her countless meals over the months, who was beloved by the islanders and her friends.

"Why? Why are you doing this?" Kyra asked, hoping to distract Julia and buy herself more time.

"You ruined my life." Julia's voice barely carried over the howling wind, and Kyra stilled. "You ruined my son's life.

My family. You ruined everything." Julia approached, one slow step at a time.

Her black apron, still slung around her neck, flapped in the wind. Kyra gulped and stared at it. *Julia's black apron.* She'd worn one of the lavender ones at dinner. Realization hit Kyra like a gust of wind, icing her blood in her veins. *Oh god.*

Julia was a chef. One who took great pride in her traditional, methodical approach to preparation. Anything she could do herself, she did. Of course, she knew how to incapacitate and slaughter.

Assaf. Ben. She'd butchered them. Kyra gagged. *Ohmygod.*

"But why Assaf? Elise?" Her voice shook. "You don't even know them."

"Off islanders," Julia spat. Her features twisting into something gruesome. "You need us and hate us. You work us to the bone." She held up her fist. "For what? For your *vacations.*" Her mouth wrapped around the word like it was vile. "Then you leave us to fend for ourselves for the long winter. With nothing but what we've scraped together!"

Kyra reached the end of the widow's walk. She pressed her back against the chimney.

"But Ben?" she asked, trying to keep Julia talking. "Ben is like you."

"No! He's worse than all of them. He's a parasite, living and working here season after season. Working for them! This isn't his home. He came here from the mainland. Lives in a house they gave him. Hires other mainlanders like him. Gives them the jobs the islanders are owed." Julia's shoulders rose and fell. Her body shook with rage. "He represents the worst people. These companies that buy up our property, take over our island. Bring in more mainlanders, who take what is ours. Selfish, greedy, outsiders! Like you!" Julia screamed.

Kyra recognized the fanatical gleam in Julia's eyes. She'd seen it before. A righteousness that had warped into madness.

"You tried to kill my aunt. Why?"

Something flickered in Julia's eyes, something that was almost like regret, but it just as quickly disappeared.

"I thought it was you." She shrugged. "But she doesn't belong here, either. None of you do."

Kyra scanned the patio, the lawn. Empty. She assessed the slope of the roof. Loriann's balcony should be below her, perhaps a bit off to the side. She'd have to hop the railing, and slide down the tiled roof, and hope she'd angled correctly, or splatter on the pavers below.

Her heart banged against her sternum. She could no longer feel the railing against her palms, could barely move her fingers.

"You mainlanders." Julia was mostly talking to herself now, her voice too high pitched, maniacal. "You come here and take and take. You suck us, suck *me*, dry! I have nothing left. *Nothing!*"

Something moved in the corner of Kyra's eye and her gaze shifted below to the patio. A shadow? A person?

It didn't matter. She had nothing to lose. She leaned as far as she could over the railing, and just as she felt it shift, she screamed, "Help me!"

Two figures shot out from the shadows. Male voices.

"They can't help you. Now, jump."

Kyra's eyes widened, and she sucked a breath in through her teeth. She pushed back against the chimney, getting as far away from the edge as possible without letting the railing go.

"I said jump, Miss Gibson."

Kyra hesitated. She met Julia's eyes.

"*Jump!*"

The gun fired.

Kyra shut her eyes and let the railing go. She threw herself out of the way of the bullet. There was an instant of free falling.

I've gone over. Kyra waited for the impact.

Too soon, her elbow hit wood. Then her hip. When her chest struck the decking of the widow's walk, her scream was cut off and all the air was forced from her lungs. She lay there, dazed. For one second. Two. Then her fingers clawed the old decking as she scrambled back, her heels sliding against the slimy wood, until her shoulders hit the chimney.

Julia stepped closer. Rage and mania glittered in her unblinking eyes. She leveled the gun at Kyra's face.

A figure appeared behind Julia. Kyra's heart beat out of control. Her spine seized. *No.*

"*Mãe.*"

Chapter Forty-Eight

WES SILVA EMERGED from the shadows as he stepped out onto the widow's walk.

"*Mãe*," he said again, his voice so soft Kyra had to strain to hear to him. "*Mãe*, stop this." He called his mother a third time, and Julia whipped around.

"Wesley." Her voice hitched. "Go back inside."

"*Mãe*, what are you doing?" He looked at Kyra pressed against the chimney. "This isn't you. You don't hurt people."

"They hurt us, Wesley. They hurt you. She, and those off islanders, they hurt you!" Julia spat and waved the gun at Kyra.

Kyra flinched.

"No, *Mãe*. I made a mistake. This." He waved between them. "The family's loss. Losing Dad's business? That is all because of what I did. I fucked up. And when I tried to cover it up, I made it worse."

"But she…" Julia pointed the gun at Kyra. "If *she* had never come here. You'd have found a way out. We'd still have your father's company. I wouldn't have to work. Tali would be with our family." Julia looked back at her son.

Making as little sound as possible, Kyra pulled her feet under her. She moved into a crouch. Wes's gaze darted to her, and she froze, but it flicked away, back to his mother, and Kyra rose to her feet, inch by inch.

"No," he shook his head. "It wasn't her fault." He raised his hands. "It's mine. And I am so sorry. But this? It won't solve anything." His hands dropped to his sides.

"They'll go away." Julia's voice was strained, and Kyra realized she was crying. "They will all go away. We'll be left alone. We can *live*. That is all Luis ever wanted for us. A good life."

"Dad wouldn't have wanted this." Wes stepped closer. "*Mãe*, give me the gun."

Julia didn't move. Wes stepped further out onto the widow's walk. Behind him, another figure appeared.

Tarek.

Relief flooded Kyra's system, and she sagged against the chimney. Tarek pressed a finger to his lips.

Wes spoke again, this time in Portuguese. His words were fast as he crept closer to his mother. The wood creaked under his weight. Then he was close enough to touch her.

He reached out his hand. "*Mãe*, please."

The gun shook in Julia's hand. Wes wrapped his larger one around hers and he gently pried the gun from her fingers. Without looking, he passed it behind him to Tarek.

Tarek reset the safety. He rushed past Wes to Kyra. His hands grasped her arms.

"Kyra." He scanned her face, her body, checking her for injuries.

"I'm not hurt."

"Fucking hell." He crushed her body against his in a bruising hug. "You're going to be the death of me."

Kyra turned her head enough to see Julia step away from her son. Dread pooled in her stomach. "Tarek," Kyra whispered.

Julia was speaking rapidly in Portuguese. Kyra didn't know what she was saying, but Wes had gone white.

Tarek let Kyra go. "Mrs. Silva?" Tarek raised his hands, conciliatory. He stepped closer. "Mrs. Silva, calm down. Everything will be okay."

But Julia's words were coming faster, dropping like stones between quick gasps for air. Wes was shaking his head.

"*Mãe*, no. We can fix this."

Julia shook her head. She stilled and gave him a mournful look, and then, Julia turned.

And jumped.

"*Mãe!*" Wes surged forward. His body hit the railing.

Tarek leaped toward him. The screeching sound of metal ripping tore through the night, so loud the wind went quiet. The railing gave way. It tumbled and clattered to the patio below with a crash.

"Tarek!" Kyra heard her own scream. Then another, whose, she wasn't sure.

"Kyra! Help!"

Kyra peeled her eyes open. Tarek was on his stomach. Wes was scrambling against the roof, his left hand in Tarek's. A tile came loose and shattered on the patio. Another.

The crack of slate on stone spurned Kyra into action, and she scrambled to Tarek's side.

She grabbed hold of his belt, planted her feet as best she could, and leaned back with all her weight. She felt them slip forward a fraction of an inch.

"Don't let go."

She didn't know who Tarek was talking to. Wes. Her. It didn't matter. Her grip tightened. Her shoulder burned.

She slipped forward.

Then Chase and Gerry were there. Gerry grabbed Tarek. Chase lay down beside him and reached for Wes. Then they were hauling him over the side, cursing and falling to the floor in a tangle of limbs.

"Get inside. Move!" someone ordered.

Someone grabbed her under her arms, yanked her out from under Tarek and Wes, and pushed her toward the door.

Kyra stumbled through and down the steps. She hit the wall and sank to the floor. Wes was right behind her. He collapsed to his hands and knees. His head hung low between his shoulders. Then he leaned further forward and buried his face in his hands.

"Wes?" He looked over at her.

For the first time, his features weren't twisted with hatred, but now only with despair. His cheeks were red and wet. He looked away, and Kyra knew.

Julia was dead.

Tarek and Chase wrestled the door closed.

"Where were you?" Tarek asked, sucking in deep breaths of air.

"She locked us in," Gerry said, bent over, his hands on his knees. "Chase broke through the patio doors. We had to run around to the front to get back inside."

"I heard the gunshot, and I broke through the glass."

It was then she noticed his sleeve was dark with blood. "Chase."

"Nothing Ger can't fix." He slid down beside her on the floor and pulled her close with his uninjured arm. "I'm beginning to think you have a death wish. Can you please stop getting shot at?"

Kyra huffed a laugh that sounded like a sob and was mostly adrenaline and relief.

She rested her head against Chase's chest. "I'll try."

Chapter Forty-Nine

TAREK HELPED KYRA down the stairs. His hand wrapped tightly around hers. They paused outside the now empty Bride's Parlor for Gerry to collect his bag, then they headed toward the foyer. Wes Silva plodded behind them, his work boots *clomping* with each footfall.

Everyone was sitting on the steps of the grand staircase, wrapped in coats and blankets. Ali stood when she heard them.

"Kyra!" She threw her arms around her niece.

"I'm okay, Ali." Still her aunt fussed, running her hands over Kyra's arms and shoulders, until Kyra grabbed her aunt's hands. "Seriously, I'm fine. I promise."

"What's happened?" Loriann asked, her voice shaky.

Kyra let Tarek explain in English, while Wes spoke to Tali and his cousin in hushed tones in Portuguese. Tali howled, a cracked, broken sound of raw grief. He sat next to his sister, and he and Camilla held her as she sobbed.

Chapter Fifty

SOFT TENDRILS OF gray light filtered through Verinder House's tall windows. Kyra stood and, pulling the blanket tighter around her shoulders, moved closer. She peered outside to see the long spindly shadows cast by the trees. Dawn was breaking. Finally.

She thought she heard a noise, a keening bleeping sound. She listened again. No. Nothing. Not even the sound of birds.

Tarek was instructing the group to get their things. That he, Gerry, or Asher would escort each of them. Kyra rested her forehead against the glass, let her shoulders sag under her exhaustion.

Then she heard the familiar crunch of tires on gravel. It got louder.

The blanket dropped from her shoulders, and Kyra sprinted for the front doors. She threw them open. Her socked feet hit the gravel just as an SUV rounded the copse of trees and rolled down the driveway.

"Kyra!" Tarek shouted.

The vehicle came to a halt under the porte cochere, and the passenger door sprung open. A dark-haired woman jumped out.

"Aysha?" Loriann appeared in the doorway. She gripped the doorframe with both hands. "Aysha, is that you?"

"The fuck have you been?" Asher demanded, holding onto Loriann, like he was supporting his aunt's weight.

The driver's side door opened and a man in his twenties exited the car. He ran his hand through his dark hair and gave them a sheepish smile. *The man from the road race?* "And who the fuck is that?"

"I'm Will."

"I'm so sorry." Aysha gushed, her words tumbling over each other. "I was only going to meet Will for a drink. I wasn't going to be gone long. Then I drove off the road, and I couldn't get the car unstuck and I walked across the bridge to his house. I didn't have any service. I used his phone, but I couldn't get through. And the tide," Aysha babbled and tears streamed down her face. "Please, Loriann, you have to believe me…" Her voice trailed off as she took in their faces.

Will, brow furrowed, came around to her side of the car.

Aysha stepped back closer to him, grabbed his arm. "Why are you all outside?"

Bleep! This time there was no mistaking the loud blare, and Kyra flinched.

Two more SUVs, ones with Edgartown Police Department tags, broke through the brush, followed by an ambulance. They came to a stop behind Will's car. Aysha blinked at the procession, then turned back and looked at Loriann, her brow creased in confusion. "What's happened?"

Chapter Fifty-One

TAREK WRAPPED HIS arm around Kyra's shoulders, pressed his lips to her temple. "We'll see them soon." Kyra nodded, watching her aunt and uncle push their luggage through the doors of the Vineyard's tiny airport. Cam turned and raised Iggy's hand in a final goodbye. Kyra wiped away a stray tear and let Tarek lead her back to her car.

The last twenty-four hours had been a whirlwind. The EMTs had taken Ali, Tali, Chase, and Gerry to the Martha's Vineyard Hospital where Chase's arm was stitched up, Tali's asthma was treated, and Ali underwent a slew of tests under Gerry's supervision. Kyra and Cam hadn't been allowed to go with them. She and everyone else were taken to the police station and questioned. For hours. And then they were re-questioned.

She and Tarek were finally released late last night and allowed to return home. As they were leaving, they'd run into Asher in the police station's reception area.

"Give me a minute?" Kyra asked, gesturing to Asher.

When she approached him, Asher slid his hands into his pockets and asked with a nod in Tarek's direction, "So, you're sticking to your decision, then?"

"I am."

"Well, can't say I'm not disappointed."

"What's going to happen now?"

"It's not really your concern anymore, is it?" He raised an eyebrow at her.

She shrugged. "I meant with Hedge."

Asher blew out a long breath. "If any of his victims come forward, they will have my full support and the support of the new Omega Global."

She'd expected nothing less. She turned away.

"Wait, Kyra?" She stopped, turned back. "I want you to know. I'm happy for you." He pressed his lips together in a wan smile.

"I'm sorry?" she asked.

"I always thought you were waiting for something in London. That your gig with your firm was a pit stop until you found something that suited you better. I thought maybe running the new company together, that would be it, but well, these things never go as planned, do they?"

"No, I suppose they don't."

"Perhaps one day you, your policeman, and I will look back at that dinner and have a laugh." Kyra gave him a look, and he chuckled, but it sounded sad. "No, you're right. Nothing funny about it." He reached out and gripped her shoulder. "You take care of yourself, Kyra, love. You're one of the good ones. The best one, if you ask me. Don't lose my number."

She watched him walk out to a town car that would take him straight to Logan Airport and on to London. She hadn't been disappointed in him when he'd gone straight back to his great aunt. It'd never been a question. Asher was loyal to a fault.

Loriann hadn't bothered with pleasantries or goodbyes, just an email with the name of the new law firm that would be handling her legal affairs, sent by Aysha.

The news covered the story, calling it the most horrific event on the island since something called the Playhouse Tragedy. There was to be a service for Julia in a few days' time, and Kyra had heard the island community had come together to support Tali and Wes. She'd see them again, and hoped that when she did, they'd meet, if not as friends, at least not as enemies.

Kyra snapped in her seatbelt and waited for Tarek to start the car. She rested her head against the seatback and watched as workers strung Christmas lights along the roof of the tiny Martha's Vineyard Airport.

"So, what's next?" he asked.

"Lunch?" she suggested, realizing she was hungry for a pub lunch at Gully's.

"I meant for you," Tarek said and leaned forward to start the car. "What will you do now?"

It was many questions in one. Would she find a new legal job? Would she stay on the island? Would she stay in the States? Should he stay? She smiled at him, happy he was asking.

"I'm not sure. We'll have to sort something, eventually."

"We'll have to sort something? Eventually?" Tarek paused, and turned to face her, his green eyes shining.

"I'm pretty good at people wanting to kill me," she said with a shrug, and Tarek laughed, a warm rumbling sound.

"But I'm not sure how to transition that into a career on the island." She smiled and entangled her fingers with his. "But we have plenty of time to figure it out." Her gaze met his, apprehensive. "Together?"

"Yeah," he said with a full, wide smile. "Together."

She gripped her partner's hand and sat back in her seat. She looked out the window, taking in the island, *their* island, as they drove home to Edgartown.

FIN.

Thank you for reading **Widow's Walk**. *I hope you enjoyed my homage to one of my favorite films,* Clue. *I'd love to hear what you thought, what you liked, loved, or even hated, what mysteries you'd like to see Kyra and Tarek solve next. You can write to me at raemi.ray@gmail.com and find me on my website at www.raemiray.com. Please consider leaving a review. Reviews positive and negative are how readers find writers. You have my deepest gratitude.*

Until the next ferry over ~ Raemi

Acknowledgments

Writing *Widow's Walk* was the most difficult thing I've done in a very long time. I've always wanted to write a locked room mystery. The intrigue, the lies, and machinations, the unveiling of shady characters, these are the building blocks of a great whodunnit. I knew *Widow's Walk* needed these elements. However, the story's short timeline, the number of characters, the plot lines, and the close third person POV presented challenge after challenge. The first draft was rough. The second, worse. It really didn't start coming together until the double digits. In the end, though, I'm very proud of this installment of the Martha's Vineyard Murders series.

As usual, this was not a free solo. I had help and support on all sides. I am indebted to you who gave up your precious time to console me, critique me, tell me the harsh truths, and less harsh, but no less easily received, compliments, to you who made me laugh when I wanted to cry. You made this book something I can be proud of.

Thank you to Joanna, Usha, and Jerry for your unwavering support and encouragement. To Amanda for talking to me every day, whether you had time or not. To Chris for watching dozens of murder mystery movies with me. To Monique, Mike, Georgia, Gemma, and Fletcher for letting me bogart their summer holiday and for touring Chappy with me. Maybe next time we'll see sharks. To Christine, for being my island partner in crime. Can't wait for dinner at Port Hunter and cocktails at Fishbones again next summer.

To the teams at AME and N.N. Lights for helping me get this series in front of readers. To my Tule family, Hannah, Heidi, Jaiden, Lee, Mia, and Monti for all your hard work on this book and its beautiful cover.

And of course I could not forget my intrepid editor, Sinclair Sawhney, who asks the right questions and, more importantly, demands the right answers. This book's existence is in no small part thanks to you. I love the doors we've opened in this installment and I'm excited for the story to continue.

You all have my most heartfelt thanks.

If you enjoyed *Widow's Walk*,
you'll love the other books in...

Martha's Vineyard Murders series

Book 1: *A Chain of Pearls*

Book 2: *The Wraith's Return*

Book 3: *Widow's Walk*

Available now at your favorite online retailer!

About the Author

Raemi A. Ray is the author of the Martha's Vineyard Murders series. Her travels to the island and around the world inspire her stories. She lives with her family in Boston.

Thank you for reading

Widow's Walk

If you enjoyed this book, you can find more from all our great authors at TulePublishing.com, or from your favorite online retailer.

Milton Keynes UK
Ingram Content Group UK Ltd.
UKHW031950281024
450365UK00008B/423